LiVE A LiTTLE

a RASTiS MELCHiOR iNVeStigatioN

Aaron Huggins is a high school student from Kinglake- a mountainous region north-east of Melbourne, Australia. He grew up in a family with a healthy appreciation for British humour, which has flavoured his writing with hints of Terry Pratchett, Douglas Adams, Doctor Who, and Roald Dahl. His favourite types of books are Science-Fiction, Fantasy, and Murder Mystery. Aaron hopes to make a career as a writer when he graduates. *LIVE A LITTLE* is Aaron's first novel, and he completed it at the ripe old age of fifteen.

LIVE A LITTLE

a RASTiS MELCHiOR iNVESTigATiON

AARON HUGGINS

 Up & Up MEDIA Published by Up & Up Media
Melbourne, Australia

Up & Up Media, Australia

Copyright © 2019 Aaron Huggins

The moral right of the author has been asserted.

Cover Design by Up & Up Media
Typeset and arranged by Up & Up Media

First published 2019 by Up & Up Media, Australia

Up & Up Media
Melbourne, Australia
www.upandupmedia.com.au

First Edition

ISBN 978-0-6484938-9-1

Printed Locally: Australia, USA, UK

LIVE A LITTLE

Chapter One

Eluxure, 2430

Rastis Melchior looked out the window of his temporary lodgings at the beautiful scenery of Eluxure; the emerald green hills, the brilliant blue sky locked in such an embrace with the distant horizon that it seemed it would take quite some coaxing to let go. The landscape, dotted with sunny glades and whatever took the planet's inhabitants' fancy, was said to be amongst the most stunning in the galaxy. Truly, the retirement planet lived up to its claim as the "ideal retirement" for all those who were loaded with enough cash to afford a retirement villa on the beautiful landscape.

That, thought Melchior, was the one undesirable thing

about it. Not the aforementioned beautiful landscape- nobody could have a qualm with that- but rather the retirees themselves. Hardly any of them had earned their extensive wealth, or indeed their pensioners' package, fairly. Some inherited it, yes, but the vast majority of the retirees had acquired their great wads of money through manipulation and dishonesty. They were no better than criminals, although nobody thought of them that way because they were rich, influential criminals.

It's funny, thought Melchior drily, *that the one thing separating common crooks from the residents of Eluxure is money.*

'So, when do you have to return to Sildrone?' asked Inspector Corwin Tirranar from his comfortable position on one of the hotel's luxurious armchairs, jolting Melchior out of his thoughts of crooked retirees. He glanced over at his old friend, thinking truthfully that he would not lament his departure from the planet.

'Tomorrow,' Melchior replied. 'But it's been good seeing you again, old friend.'

Corwin grimaced. 'You can leave out the old, Rastis. It still beats me how you seem to defy the talons of age.'

In truth, Corwin was an entire generation or two younger than most of the residents of Eluxure- the police force required younger, fitter members regardless of how little happened on Eluxure- and Rastis, with his eerie immunity to external age, was a generation or two older even than the retirees. He was not about to join them, however- those of his race had twice the lifespan of humans. By Reptid years, Melchior was in his forties, though it was difficult to place a digit on him, such was the timelessness of Reptids. He stood now at his full height (which was rather impressive compared to most bipeds), clad in a crimson robe that clashed magnificently with his turquoise colouring. His skin was strewn with scales, a cluster of which was scattered across his nose like freckles, and despite his reptilian appearance, his face was remarkably humanoid.

Compared to Melchior's exotic, colourful appearance, Corwin could be described as pleasantly dull. His face was unremarkable but the shape of his features and the way he carried himself told those who met him that he was undoubtedly an agreeable, moral person.

'Ah well,' he sighed now. 'I'd best get back to the police station before too long. Have we got time for another round of Silder Sau before I have to dash?'

Melchior smiled. 'You know I will only beat you again, but if you're willing to lose for the forty-eighth time...' he said without a hint of gloating in his voice. Corwin knew better.

He also knew that it was impossible to tell with Melchior, and that he'd probably be wasting his time if he tried to discern the teasing tone that was probably hidden somewhere within the Reptid's voice. Instead, he relented, agreeing that yes, Melchior probably would beat him again, and drained his glass of *piloto*. 'Forty-eight,' he mused. 'You have an evilly long memory, you old lizard.'

'Please refrain from calling me a lizard,' Melchior winced. 'I am a *Reptid,* as I have told you many times.'

'Lizard, I find, rolls easier from the tongue,' was Corwin's argument.

Melchior could not for the life of him think how. His race tended to avoid the letter *z*. Put delicately, the way their tongues were formed tripped over the consonant and mangled it into the shape of an *s*. As a result, Melchior disliked the word *lizard* even more, as when he said it, it came out as *lissard.* And *lissard,* as Corwin knew very well and in fact took great enjoyment in, meant 'lavatory' in Reptid.

Corwin stood, preparing to leave, and set the glass which had until recently held more than a substantial amount of *piloto* back on the table with some regret. It was then that he remembered something he'd been meaning to tell Melchior.

'I nearly forgot!' he said suddenly. 'The talons of age... I'm surprised I didn't tell you sooner.'

Rastis looked at him expectantly.

'Rastis, do you know of a certain Dunwall Tenzebah?' Corwin asked.

Melchior was surprised, curious as to why Corwin had decided to bring this particular individual up in conversation. 'The owner of Elixir, correct?'

Dunwall Tenzebah was indeed a famous name. He had already been rich when he had acquired Elixir, which was a substance like no other found anywhere in the galaxy. The so-called 'miracle drink' was said to make the drinker immortal. Tenzebah became both richer and, apparently, immune to all known diseases and ailments, and incapable of dying. Furthermore, old age had as much effect on him as it did on Melchior- no doubt what triggered Corwin to mention the billionaire. Nobody knew how Tenzebah had acquired Elixir, and few knew how it worked, but his name became famous overnight. Everyone always knew where Dunwall Tenzebah was, and he made no efforts to privatise his life.

'Yes, him,' Corwin replied. 'Well, I was meaning to tell you he's here on Eluxure.'

Melchior did not have eyebrows, but he raised his forehead as though he did. 'Now that is very interesting,' he said. 'Dunwall Tenzebah is the one figure you would least expect to retire.'

'That's what I thought, too,' agreed Corwin. 'It was all hushed up when he arrived, which isn't like him at all. It's as though he wanted to escape the press.'

This was something Melchior, as a well-known private detective, could relate to. But Dunwall Tenzebah was the sort of man who prefered to draw attention *to* himself rather than away.

'He lives not far from here,' Corwin went on. 'Not in the city, of course, that's where all the young people are. But he's got this mansion just outside Liesopolis, called Kenderye.'

Melchior frowned (or he would have, but for his aforementioned lack of eyebrows). *What,* he thought, *is a man who may well live for a thousand years doing on a retirement planet?* The last the Reptid had seen of him- on the news not too long ago- Tenzebah had seemed full of life he never thought he'd have, and even had a certain smugness about him that told everyone that yes, he could live for longer than them all, and that he basked in the fact.

Melchior voiced his as yet unspoken thought, but Corwin did not have a straight answer to give.

'I don't know why he's here, no,' he said. 'But he's certainly acting out of character. I caught a glimpse of him as he drove past on his way to Kenderye, and he seemed... worried.'

'Worried?'

'Yes,' Corwin said. 'I can think of only two reasons why he'd be on a retirement planet. One; money...'

Melchior nodded. 'There could be a will,' he said. 'That clearly specifies *on their retirement my heir shall inherit my fortune.*'

Corwin acknowledged this with a nod. 'Or two; he's scared.'

'He has little to fear,' Melchior said. 'How can you kill a man who can't die?'

Corwin nodded again. 'I agree. He can't possibly expect to sit out the rest of his immortal life fretting that someone will take it away from him.'

'He fears something different, then,' Melchior offered. 'My guess would be that he thinks someone will steal Elixir.'

'That certainly fits,' Corwin replied. 'Sure, nobody can kill him, but he doesn't exactly want to share, so somebody might have a crack at stealing Elixir.'

'If somebody does, and indeed if they succeed,' said Melchior, 'then that would be a robbery well worth solving. Tenzebah carries around Elixir wherever he goes, so I'm told. In a hip-flask, perhaps? Whatever the case, you'd have to render him unconscious before you could get at it. And realistically, who would have the opportunity?'

'He's probably just paranoid,' concluded Corwin cheerfully. 'A lot of billionaires are. Probably even immortal ones, too. Really, Dunwall Tenzebah has nothing to fear.'

It was then that the door to Melchior's hotel suite burst open quite suddenly by an agitated man in a police uniform, who looked as though he hadn't quite expected to find the Inspector playing Silder Sau with a giant lizard.

Urgency was greater than his bewilderment, however,

and he spoke immediately to Corwin.

'Sir, you're needed at Kenderye, urgently,' he panted.

Corwin looked equal parts concerned and surprised. 'Why? What's happened?'

The policeman swallowed as if he didn't quite believe his next words. 'It's Dunwall Tenzebah, sir. He's been murdered!'

ChapTeR Two

1.

Claine Soliss sighed and gazed out the window as the woman behind the reservation desk deactivated her guest code. It would be a shame to leave Eluxure behind, especially considering her stay had been far less productive than she had imagined. She had been a freelance journalist for some years now with her self-published newspaper, *The Galaxy Roamer,* but the trouble was that, despite her insistent pursuit of a story, she never seemed to get much in the way of material. However, Claine was a sophisticated, strong-minded young lady, and the pursuit was one she kept up, hitching a ride from one planet to another in the hope that an enticing story might pop up.

Her latest search had been on the retirement planet, but that too had proved disappointingly fruitless.

'So you're leaving Eluxure now, then?' Fenice, the hotel receptionist, asked her.

'Unfortunately,' Claine sighed again. 'And without my captivating story, either.'

Fenice handed her the digital receipt, a thumbnail-sized chip. 'I wouldn't worry, dear. Nothing much happens on Eluxure anyway,' she said. 'The clue's in the name.'

Claine smiled at her, still a little disappointed at her limited success on the Leisure Planet, and took the chip, pocketing it almost unconsciously as she contemplated her next step.

Hoisting her ever-present holo-camera (an ingenious device that was made to look like a retro Earth camera) Claine turned to leave the hotel but was stopped in her tracks by a low voice from the stairwell on the right side of the registration desk.

'...Dunwall Tenzebah...' said the voice.

With the reflexes of a Serva-Cof Warrior, Claine darted past the stairwell and hid herself behind one of the lavender-hued plants that lined the lobby, ears pricked for further snippets of conversation from whoever was coming down the stairs. The plant was in an excellent position, one from which Claine could eavesdrop effectively on even the most confidential conversations.

Fenice, meanwhile, stared at her from behind the desk,

one hand still outstretched from giving Claine her receipt. The journalist signalled for her to look away, trying to make her movements frantic enough that Fenice would get the message, but not so frantic as to attract unwanted attention from pretty much everyone else in the lobby.

The secretary, thankfully, *did* get the message, and turned her gaze to the papers on the desk before her, but she continued to watch Claine out the corner of her eye, probably wondering what on Eluxure or off it she was doing behind a pot plant.

Claine, of course, was eavesdropping, something all good reporters know how to do. The name, Dunwall Tenzebah, had caught the attention of her journalist brain. Everybody knew who *he* was, especially reporters, and maybe, just maybe, there'd be a story in this.

'How did this happen?' asked the voice.

'I don't know for sure, sir. Inspector Rodarth said he'd fill you in when you arrived at Kenderye,' replied a second, one that sounded as though it had just run a marathon, and that contained a hint of disbelief at something.

'I see,' said the first, clearly not happy with this arrangement.

'Liesopolis Police have two Inspectors, then?' inquired a third voice, one that had a strange, pleasant flow and emphasised unlikely syllables.

'Yes,' answered the first. 'But in Inspector Rodarth's eyes, he's my superior. He enjoys...beating me to it, I suppose.'

Claine frowned, wondering if she'd really get something juicy out of this. The next words she heard, however, erased her doubt completely.

'It's understandable that he would want to keep this quiet, though,' the third went on. 'It would not be wise to make public the fact that Tenzebah has been murdered.'

Claine clapped a hand over her mouth so they wouldn't hear her gasp. *What* did he just say? It couldn't be possible.

The three men entered the lobby, passing the lavender plant in which Claine sat, completely still, without so much as a second glance. Two, she saw, looked like policemen- one in uniform and one in the sort of coat worn by Inspectors of the Galmarora star system. The other was a different kettle of fish. Tall, with scales and turquoise skin. With a jolt, Claine recognised him as a Reptid. Reptids, in general, chose to isolate themselves from the rest of the universe. The fact that there was one on Eluxure could mean only one thing...

As soon as the policeman and the Reptid had exited the hotel, Claine let out the deep breath she'd been holding for several minutes now, and extricated herself from the ornamental bush before darting over to a thoroughly bewildered Fenice.

'What was all that in aid of?' the receptionist wanted to know.

Claine fished the digital receipt from her pocket and gave it back to Fenice, whose confused look grew all the more profound.

'Extend my reservation,' she told the receptionist, eyes shining with the thrill of a potential scoop. 'I think I've found a story well worth checking out.'

Claine pushed through the crowd, discreetly following the three men at a close enough distance to perhaps chance across more information. They were walking along Grandpath, the massive walkway that lead out of the city, towards the area where the Inspector's vehicle was probably parked, so she doubted she would hear too much- the men would have to be extremely stupid to talk openly about it in a crowded place. Then again, she conceded, they *are* men. But the Reptid would definitely have more sense- especially if he was who she thought he was.

Still, though, there was a chance she'd hear *something* else. Everyone else would only hear vague, out of context snippets, and those who didn't weren't listening hard enough to gather anything meaningful from their words. Claine, on the other hand, was following them closely with her ears more pricked and her attention more focused than the other pedestrians.

'I don't know anything more than you do,' the Inspector was saying. 'Rodarth is like a toddler- he doesn't want to share anything, even if it is details that I should know. But anything I know, I've told you; just that...*he* moved here a few months ago and it looks like he was para-'

'Shh, Corwin,' said the Reptid.

Corwin looked mystified. 'These people are hardly going to know who we're talking about.'

'Most of them don't, and most of them aren't listening,' the Reptid replied cryptically.

Claine's eyes widened, and she stopped elbowing pedestrians aside with her holo-camera, as though any movement might give her away. She was certain he had been talking about her, and if not her specifically, a generic eavesdropper. Which, in this case, *was* her. She was mystified as to how the Reptid might know of her existence. Unless, of course, the Reptid was who she was now pretty certain he was.

Corwin took a glance behind him and Claine looked down at the ground. Then he looked at Melchior again. 'You mean, someone's been spying on us?'

Feeling that there was not much point in remaining concealed, Claine pushed past an elderly couple with what looked like fish tanks over their heads and walked up to where the three men stood.

The other policeman looked at her with a small frown on his face as though he didn't quite make the connection between her and their mysterious listener.

The other two did, however. Corwin looked at her with mixed curiosity and disapproval and Melchior studied her with a small smile on his turquoise face.

'How long have you known I was following you?' she asked the Reptid.

'I saw you in that pot plant the other day,' Melchior revealed, surprising everyone. 'You can't see behind it from the stairwell, but you can from the exit. As we left the lobby I took a brief look to see if you were there again, but rest assured, I would not have known you were there had I not seen you previously.'

Claine looked impressed, and that's because she was. 'So you *are* him, then?'

Melchior put his head to one side.

'Rastis Melchior,' she said. 'You know, the detective? You *are* him, aren't you?'

'Indeed I am,' Melchior replied. 'But may I ask what you were doing in a pot plant on two separate occasions?'

Claine had the decency to look slightly embarrassed. 'Well, I was sort of...listening. I'm a journalist. Freelance, by the way. I couldn't stand working for a mainstream newspaper. You might have heard of my own publication, *The Galaxy Roamer.*'

Corwin's expression was transformed into one of exasperation. 'And how much did you hear?' he asked her, dreading the answer.

'Well,' said Claine carefully. 'I heard that,' (she glanced

behind her shoulder) '*you know who* is on Eluxure, or he was until he was murdered, and I also heard that he might have been 'para'. I assume 'para' was the beginning of 'paranoid'?'

Corwin sighed and rubbed his face, contemplating Rodarth's reaction to this. 'In other words,' he said, 'you heard everything.'

Claine tried to look guilty and failed spectacularly. 'If that's all there was to hear, then yes.'

The Inspector eyed her, wondering what to do with her. *Obviously,* he thought, *we can't let her go and tell everyone about it via a report that really shouldn't be allowed to exist.* On the other hand, there wasn't much he could do to stop her, and if she came with them it would only give her more material. He was still contemplating this predicament when Claine herself came up with a solution. 'What if I come with you to Kenderye,' (*good grief, she knows about that too,* thought Corwin) 'and then you leave me outside with a police officer so that I don't get inside the house and gather extra material.'

Corwin felt obliged to use a suggestion of his own, but a suggestion of his own was currently non-existent, so he had no choice but to use the reporter's.

'All right, you can come with us, then,' he told her grudgingly. 'But that's it.'

Claine smiled sweetly at him, which did nothing at all to reassure him. 'Good compromise, Inspector,' she said cheekily. Then, much more uncertainly; 'Uh, Claine Soliss, by the way.'

'Trust me,' said the Inspector drily. 'I don't plan on further acquainting myself with you.'

2.

'Vasail!'

Galion gave a start at his name and swore as he bashed his head on the underside of the Cullovinum 360 Shuttleship he was working on, but ignored the pain flaring through his cranium and slid out from beneath the spacecraft.

'Mr Termal?' he asked. The angry Kerra'lai stuck his crimson head out of the cockpit and glared down at Galion's grime-smeared one.

'You still haven't done the screw-fuses yet, have you, boy?' Termal yelled, much louder than was necessary, but then that was just his speaking voice.

Galion tried to omit any traces of argument from his own voice as he addressed his boss in the way he was supposed to. 'I couldn't, Mr Termal, sir. The electro-clamps were too tight and I had to wait for Shulls to fix the auxiliary-'

'Shut up and do what I asked you to do, kid!' Termal barked. 'You've been slack as it is. I can think of half a dozen things you haven't done yet that I told you to do.

You're lazy, and that don't get a good job done.'

Galion clenched his teeth. 'No, Mr Termal. I'm on it.'

'Good!' The Kerra'lai boomed, though judging by his expression he didn't give the impression he found anything 'good' at present.

As Termal retracted his angry crimson head back into the cockpit, Galion rose and dusted off his olive overalls before kicking the trolley he had been lying on back under the ship with such force it struck the open undercarriage with a resounding *CLANG!*

He turned to enter the main body of the ship, but before he could, Termal stuck his head back out of the cockpit and yelled, 'Oh, and Vasail? I'm gonna pay you for today's work, even though you did none, but don't bother coming in tomorrow. You don't work for me no more!'

Inside the cockpit went the vibrant head, leaving Galion in a worse mood than he was already.

The Charracopa was the most popular bar on Eluxure, although that was hardly anything to boast about considering it was probably the only one. None of the retirees ever entered a bar, although a fair percentage of them probably won their vast fortune in one. Instead, the Charracopa was a favourite hangout for anyone who came and went. Nobody, of course, stayed on Eluxure for long-there was nothing to do, and the city Leisopolis was only really used as a drop-in port if a spaceship pilot wanted a drink or needed to fuel up. Nevertheless, the Charracopa was always packed, as whenever anyone left the bar they were replaced by some other visitor. It was in this bar that Galion sat now, drinking a pitchon of the least potent beverage he could find and trying not to catch the attention of a group of Ackaracki whose main function was to drink several gallons of inciner-whisky and cheat random people of their *feristii.*

He looked up sharply as someone sat at his table, expecting to see one of the Ackeracki, then relaxed as he saw that it was Dendern Shulligan, Shulls for short and Galion's fellow mechanic.

'So old Termal fired you, eh?' Shulls asked.

'Yeah,' replied Galion gloomily. 'But it was bound to happen, wasn't it? He's been mad at me for weeks.'

Shulls lit a *cetrice* pipe and sat back with it clenched between his grinning teeth. 'When is he ever *not* mad?' he asked around his pipe.

Galion took another sip of his drink. It was weak, alcoholically speaking, but he pulled a face nonetheless, unused to the sort of beverage that had the potential to intoxicate its consumer. 'The thing is, though, Shullsey, I don't have anything to do now. I only came to this giant old folks' home because Redn Termal offered me a job. I'll have to hitch a ride off Eluxure and then what? Calmooth?'

'I hear you, Galion,' Shulls replied, taking a swig of

Odar's Brew from the other side of his mouth to where the *cetrice* was firmly clamped- something that can't have been an appetising *or* particularly healthy mix. 'Look,' he said after a minute of thinking. 'I'd say your best bet would be Fersilt Tenzebah.'

'Tenzebah?' Galion interrupted. 'As in, Dunwall Tenzebah?'

Shulls nodded. 'The immortal's his dad. Anyway, Fersilt is on Eluxure visiting his old man about something, and-'

Galion spluttered into his bubbling nectar. 'Dunwall Tenzebah is *here*? On Eluxure?'

'Jeez, lad, how can I speak if you keep interrupting? Yeah, Dunny's here. Don't ask me what an immortal's doing in an old folks' home, but there you go. Anyway, Fersilt's got his nose out of joint because he's been expecting to inherit the family fortune-'

Galion couldn't stop himself. 'But Dunwall can't die, so that pretty much dashes Fersilt's hopes of inheriting the goodies he's entitled to.'

'Exactly,' Shulls said, professionally ignoring the fact that Galion had done the opposite of what he'd just asked him. 'I think Fersilt's been trying to bargain with his dad so that he can access some of the stuff he should've got if Dunwall *could* die. But that's not important. What's important is that Fersilt is the owner Nebula Corporations- one of the big mechanics companies- and I reckon he wouldn't say no to some fresh blood.'

'You think he might employ me?'

Shulls shrugged. 'I dunno. But he's your best bet. If you give him a shot and he says no, then you'll be no worse off than you are now.'

Galion considered this, weighing up the options. There were only two- Calmooth or Fersilt Tenzebah. Then, his mind made up, he drained his glass and set it down on the table. 'Where can I find him?' he asked.

∞

Kenderye loomed over them like a monolith, covering an acre with its many verandahs, balconies and towers. This wasn't counting the elaborate gardens, which covered an acre of their own and were sculpted delicately into topiary and elegant hedges. Blooms of all varieties ringed the pathways in a way that was both elegant and quaint- saspilia, mondanythus, wilder bucklesythe...they lent the place a comfortable, pleasing look. In the very centre of the well-kept grounds was an enormous fountain shaped like Astelpine, the Adranozadi System's god of eternal life, holding aloft the infinity symbol, from which spewed crystalline water that pooled into the basin before being recycled through the statue and out the fountain again, in an endless loop. *Appropriate,* thought Melchior, considering who had until recently lived at Kenderye. *But quite possibly a little bit too much.* Then again, that was

Tenzebah. Always ready to announce to the world that he was immortal. *But,* Melchior frowned, reconsidering, *from what Corwin said, it seems as though Tenzebah* didn't *want to be noticed.* If this was the case, the fountain was most certainly too obvious for a man who was currently hiding...

As they continued towards the main house, its awe-inspiring size became all the more apparent. Melchior wondered how much it had cost, and whether everyone on Eluxure had a not-so-humble abode as large and expensive as this. *Probably,* thought Melchior, somewhat gloomily.

This was very obviously the house of a very rich man, albeit a very dead one. It had evidently been there for years before Tenzebah's sudden migration to retirement, and the Reptid wondered if the billionaire had made the purchase recently. No...he discarded the idea immediately. As soon as Dunwall Tenzebah made a purchase like this, everyone would know. More likely, Kenderye was a family estate, passed down from generation to generation to Dunwall. That way, Tenzebah could retreat in private without going through any paperwork.

There were three police vehicles outside the house when they pulled up beside it- the only sign that something had disrupted this seemingly idyllic retirement. The cars rested on the ground due to their lack of wheels, but Melchior knew that the technology on Eluxure, being considerably more expensive than that on most planets, enabled such vehicles to hover a metre above the ground. Other planets could manufacture cars like this, but most of their money went to space travel and planetary affairs rather than the pretty pointless creation of flying cars, which performed no better than normal ones but did give those who drove them a certain sense of superiority.

Around the cars stood several policemen, looking slightly confused as though they couldn't comprehend how this particular case could exist.

'Inspector Tirranar,' one greeted Corwin as he caught sight of him, the Reptid, Claine and Thaligger- the police officer who had alerted them of the murder.

Corwin nodded in response, then introduced Melchior and the reporter. 'This is Rastis Melchior, a detective and an old friend of mine...' The policeman nodded at Melchior without seeming to acknowledge his lizardidity, a fact the Reptid liked. '...And this here,' Corwin continued, indicating Claine, 'is Miss Claine Soliss. She is a journalist who *insisted*,' here he threw a glance at Claine, 'on accompanying us. I don't want her on the scene of the crime, so I'll leave her here under your watchful eye, Cadez.'

Constable Cadez nodded in response. 'Right you are, sir,' he replied, winking at Claine and not looking very disappointed about a pretty young woman being under his watchful eye. Claine smiled sweetly at him, and Melchior sighed inwardly, knowing that she'd probably try to exploit his willingness to "look after her" in order to get inside the house.

Corwin, on the other hand, didn't seem to notice. He was busy looking up at Kenderye's impressive bulk. 'Where would I find Inspector Rodarth?' he asked Cadez.

'He's in Tenzebah's chambers, sir. That's where the body is,' replied the policeman quickly and dutifully. Despite his apparent weakness for good-looking girls, Melchior noted, Cadez was quick and efficient in delivering information. But now was not the time to take note of the members of the police force. Now was the time to assess a murder scene and take note of the members of the household.

'The maid will show you to the scene of the crime. She's a N'choth'ni, by the way. You know what Rodarth thinks about them,' added Cadez with a roll of his eyes. *Apparently,* thought Melchior, *this Inspector Rodarth is not only unpopular with Corwin.*

'Thank you, Cadez,' said Corwin. 'Thaligger, you can leave now, it's well past the end of your shift.'

Thaligger thanked the Inspector and left at a pace much more suited to his portly frame.

Melchior followed Corwin to the majestic front door, still pondering several things; the obvious symbolism in the fountain; the very existence of Kenderye; and the fact that Cadez had met the maid even though he'd been posted outside...

The Reptid shook his head. The case had barely started and he already had many questions about its circumstances. Questions, he predicted, that would double on examining the crime scene...

Chapter Three

1.

Tenzebah's chambers were untouched but for the body, and, according to the maid, everything else was where it should be. The grand room suite, Melchior thought, was similar to that of ancient kings of planets like Regalder and Earth, in both size and splendour. A huge four-poster bed stood to one side of the room, its satin curtains, royal purple in colour, drawn so that they obscured the bedspread. To the other side of the chambers sat an armchair fit for Admuscay XVII of Regalder Major, in front of a magnificent fireplace coated with a salverice finish. Further away, towards the splendid outdoor balcony was a sebberwood desk. The desk, it seemed, was used for little, and a holomail desktop took up most of its space. Melchior pondered on the presence of the holomail. If nobody knew Dunwall Tenzebah was on Eluxure, he would not be receiving many messages.

It appeared just as one would expect an expensive bedroom chamber to appear, except for the fact that in the armchair sat a skeleton that probably used to belong to Tenzebah himself.

A thin man in a long coat looked up from where he squatted beside the armchair as Melchior and Corwin entered the room. His eyebrows were permanently raised over prominent eyes, which peered over a flat nose, the bridge of which was much higher than normal.

'Ah, Inspector Tirranar,' said the man, who Melchior knew immediately was Rodarth, as he rose to Corwin's level. Melchior's level was a difficult one to achieve, so Rodarth was eye level with his chin.

Corwin nodded, not taking his eyes off the skeleton. 'How the blazes did *this* happen?'

'Deprivation of Elixir, I should think,' Rodarth answered smugly. Melchior could tell that he enjoyed knowing something Corwin didn't. 'He was found by the maid, like this. Elixir has been stolen, too, and we are fairly sure that's what killed him.'

Corwin glanced at him, then returned his gaze to what used to be Tenzebah. 'What do you mean?'

Melchior cleared his throat. 'The deceased, then, had to

keep drinking Elixir in order to retain his immortality?'

Rodarth seemed to notice the Reptid for the first time, which was remarkable, as failing to notice a Reptid is no easy feat. He looked at him now with a certain distaste that Melchior knew and disliked, then turned to Corwin and said in an accusatory tone, 'Who's this, then?'

'Rastis Mel-' began Melchior, but the man managed to cut him off without directly addressing him.

'Tirranar?' asked Rodarth, slightly louder than Melchior, leaving no doubt as to his dislike of the Reptid, or more accurately, Reptids as a whole.

Corwin looked uncomfortable. 'He's an old friend of mine- a detective. I thought he might be able to help. You know, with the-'

'I thought I specified, Inspector Tirranar,' the man said, cutting him off, 'that we were to keep this particular case strictly confidential. Or did it slip my mind?'

'Look, Rodarth,' Corwin spoke now with reinforced authority. 'You're no more my superior than I am yours. We're both the Inspector of Liesopolis Police, and therefore you are not entitled to give me orders!'

Rodarth gave him a thin smile that made Corwin feel like punching his colleague in the face. 'You're perfectly right, Tirranar. However, I have more experience, and that is reason enough to instruct you to do something you never would have thought of yourself.'

'Perhaps I wouldn't have,' Corwin said, 'but I did do

something *you* never would have thought to do, and that's bring Rastis here. He's much more experienced than both of us in these matters and he's a very old friend of mine. Nothing ever happens on Eluxure, so we don't know what to do if something does. But Melchior *does* know what to do, so I believe it wise to let him in on the case!'

Rodarth had lost his thin, infuriating smile, which had been replaced by an infuriated glare. 'Be that as it may, I will not work with a Reptid!'

An ugly silence settled over the room. Rodarth's pallid complexion had developed a colourful tinge, while Corwin's was vibrant with indignation. Melchior's face, on the other hand, was scarily expressionless.

It was the latter who broke the silence, and when he did it was on an entirely different subject.

'The skeleton isn't fresh.'

Corwin turned to look at it once more, distracted, as did Rodarth, so taken aback by this random remark that he forgot his bias and studied the skeleton with closer scrutiny.

'What?' asked Corwin, frowning.

'If the effects of Elixir deprivation were instantaneous- for example, if they stripped the flesh from the bone to produce what we see here, then Tenzebah's remains would appear identical to either of your skeletons,' elaborated Melchior. He paused; 'not mine, though, considering I am *not* a *human,* but a *Reptid.* And *our* skeletons are much more *reptilian.*'

Rodarth's eye twitched in response to Melchior's none-too-subtle reassertion that he was not like the Inspector. This gave the Reptid a certain satisfaction, which had been his intention when he rammed home the fact that he was an alien.

Corwin arched his eyebrows at Melchior, feeling that perhaps it was a good thing that Rodarth refused to acknowledge his existence.

'This skeleton, however,' continued Melchior, 'has been what it is- a skeleton- for several years.'

Rodarth seemed to be struggling, as though he wanted to tell the Reptid he was being absurd but didn't really actually want to tell the Reptid anything, because he was a Reptid. Corwin, however, voiced what Rodarth was thinking, albeit in a much more civil tone than how Rodarth would have said it.

'But how is that even possible?' he asked.

Melchior thought. 'When did Dunwall acquire the Elixir?' he responded.

Corwin looked at Rodarth, who had no choice now but to answer. 'Fifty years ago.'

Melchior nodded.

Corwin chewed his lip as if wondering where Melchior was going with this.

'Imagine, then, if Dunwall Tenzebah had died then, like he would have, had he not discovered Elixir. How would he look now?'

All eyes drifted once again to the skeleton.

'Like that,' admitted Corwin.

Melchior inclined his head. 'So if Dunwall neglected to take Elixir, the result would not just be *death*. No, instead, he was returned to how he would be now *had he never owned the miracle drink.*'

'And how does this help us?' Rodarth asked sceptically.

'It helps us,' replied Melchior, 'because it means the culprit was someone who knew what would happen if they stole Elixir away from him. Or, at least, had a pretty good idea. And as far as we know, *nobody* knew what the effects would be.'

'But if Dunwall had to take Elixir on a regular basis, surely he knew that he was in danger of forgetting, or that his life depended on taking it?'

'My guess would be that Tenzebah had no idea,' Melchior replied. 'He knew, of course, that he had to keep drinking it in order to retain immortality, but he was ignorant of the fact that if he forgot, he would die. If he missed a dose, he wouldn't have worried, as he was of the impression that he could simply catch up whenever he chose.'

'Then you're saying it could have been an accident?' Corwin asked.

Melchior shook his head. 'It's unlikely, especially seeing as Elixir has been stolen.'

'But surely whoever stole it had no idea what would happen?' Corwin asked.

'Perhaps,' said Melchior. 'But our thief is clever enough to steal Elixir, which means he or she knows enough about it for this to be possible. Also, Tenzebah may well have died anyway without Elixir to sustain him. He was, after all, a very old man.'

Rodarth cleared his throat. 'Thank you, lizard. I'll take it from here.'

He referred to Melchior as a lizard not in a joking way like Corwin had done, but in a deliberately derogatory tone.

'So, who are our suspects?' Corwin asked Rodarth, evidently wanting to evade Rodarth's displeasure, as Melchior crossed to the bed and began examining the drapery. 'We've only met the maid so far.'

'Well, the maid is one, yes. Tenzebah probably employed the chitterer because she's so obedient,' said Rodarth. 'Can't fathom how they have a mind of their own sometimes.'

Over by the billionaire's magnificent four-poster, Melchior clenched his jaw. 'Chitterer' was a highly offensive word for a N'choth'ni- insectoid people from the Callose Star System. The racist term referred to their feelers and the 'chittering' sound they made when agitated or emotional. What Rodarth said was true- well, some of it. N'choth'ni *were* more obedient than other races- but

32

that didn't mean they weren't independent. Or that they had to like it.

'It's unlikely she did it,' Rodarth continued. 'Wouldn't have the brain capacity. All they're good for is cleaning, isn't it?'

Melchior stuck his head through the curtains, hiding his face from view. His calm composure was one of his signatures, but if there was one thing that disrupted it, it was someone as racist as Rodarth. The bedspread, he thought to himself, was actually quite nice. It matched the same royal purple as the curtains and was made of luxurious, expensive material.

'Who else is there?' Rodarth continued. 'Oh, Dunwall's wife, of course. Marsine Tenzebah. She used to be very devoted to him.'

"Used to be", wondered Melchior thoughtfully. *Used to be because he's now dead, or used to be because of...something else? Did Marsine Tenzebah have a falling out with her husband prior to his demise?*

'Then there's Miss Trissilan Glamure,' Rodarth went on as Melchior retracted his head from the bed curtains and wandered towards the desk as if he wasn't looking for clues.

'Who's she?' asked Corwin.

'Tenzebah's "assistant",' Rodarth replied in a tone that hinted at something more than "assistant". Again, Melchior mused on the significance of *"used to be"*.

'And finally, Dunwall's son, Fersilt,' said the thin Inspector. 'Head of Nebula Corporations, a mechanics company. He hasn't spoken to his dad in years, but nevertheless he was entitled to Dunwall's fortune on his death, as well as the last profits made from his business.'

'What business was Tenzebah in?' Corwin inquired. 'He'd hardly need to work.'

'He imported goods, mostly- chemicals, minerals, valuables...that kind of thing,' said Rodarth. 'Anyway, that'll all be Fersilt's now. He's here at the moment, on a business trip, even though he's been on rocky terms with his dad.'

I doubt Fersilt was too happy when he found out he wouldn't be inheriting the family fortune, thought Melchior. *Especially considering he probably would have died long before Dunwall...*

But before he could ponder further on this, the door to Tenzebah's chambers burst open and none other than Claine Soliss entered the room, clutching her holo-camera, which she used now with a quick *flash!* before anyone could stop her.

'Really sorry,' she said unconvincingly. 'Do you know where to find the toilet?'

Corwin frowned as if contemplating why anyone would take a camera into the bathroom, and in what way it might assist.

Rodarth, on the other hand, looked equal parts

surprised and furious. 'Who let her in?'

Cadez took this moment to appear behind Claine, looking vaguely embarrassed. 'I'm sorry, Inspector Tirranar, sir. She said she needed to go to the toilet.'

'I presume you knew this was a deception?' Rodarth asked.

Cadez looked uncomfortable, and made an awkward nodding sort of thing with his head.

'What did you tell her, then?'

'First door on the left.'

Rodarth glared at him. 'And then?'

'Well, seeing as I was already in the house, I thought it wouldn't hurt to take a peek upstairs...' Claine said.

'You have no authorisation to be here,' Rodarth told her. 'How did you know about this case anyway?'

This was when Corwin took a strange interest in the overhead light and Melchior examined the French doors that lead onto the balcony with more scrutiny than was necessary.

'And that,' said Claine suddenly, eyes widening, 'would be the body?'

'Step away from that, please,' warned Rodarth.

'What could possibly reduce someone to a state like that?' Claine wondered, staring at the skeleton much like Corwin had.

Rodarth, evidently seeing that she would not listen to him, turned instead to his colleague. 'Tirranar, what's the meaning of this?'

Corwin, again, looked uncomfortable, as he shifted from foot to foot. 'Well, she might have overheard us discussing the case, and-'

'She might have overheard you doing *what*?' burst Rodarth. 'I knew you were incompetent, but-'

'The case would have remained a secret,' Corwin interrupted, 'if Miss Soliss had not been lurking where she was. We were perfectly safe to discuss it.'

'And now we've got a reporter on our hands. We can't stop her from going public!' Rodarth countered.

'It's funny, you know.'

The Inspectors stopped arguing and looked at Claine, surprised. She was standing by the skeleton, clutching her holo-camera.

'What is?' asked Corwin, mystified.

'Well, when someone's being murdered, they tend to notice, don't they?' she said.

Rodarth scoffed. 'Well of course they do, girl!'

Melchior, on the other hand, was looking at her intently from his position near the balcony, a thoughtful frown on his face. 'Go on,' he said.

Claine glanced from face to face. Evidently, she hadn't expected her comment to arouse such interest. 'In that case, then, why didn't Tenzebah *do* something about it?' she asked. 'I mean, it doesn't look like he struggled, or tried to call out for help.'

Melchior saw a lot of logic in that statement. The crime certainly didn't fit how they thought Tenzebah had died as snugly as it should. The chambers were, as Claine had obviously noticed, untouched. The only thing out of place was Tenzebah's skeleton, just sitting there calmly as though he had just patiently waited while he decayed and shrivelled into a pile of bones. Judging by what Melchior had heard of Tenzebah, the billionaire had not been a man who would accept death so easily. Perhaps he didn't know he was dying? Melchior entertained the idea for no more than a moment, discarding it once he'd thought it through logically. No, he thought. That couldn't be it. It was inconceivable that a conscious person would be ignorant of their own death.

Corwin and Cadez looked as though they too saw the logic in Claine's observation, but Rodarth was not so open about his surprise, instead choosing to act as though he already knew this.

'Yes, thank you, Miss Soliss,' he said, evidently miffed that he had not noticed this possibly vital clue earlier. 'The police have taken note of that. It's all under control.'

Claine seemed to have developed as much liking for the Inspector as Melchior had - specifically, close to none. She raised a sceptical eyebrow in his direction. 'I didn't doubt it for a second, Inspector. Perhaps you would be interested in being interviewed about your progress in the case? I'm sure you're constantly on the ball.'

Melchior felt that Claine would probably like nothing more than to say something nasty about Rodarth in her digital newspaper, and Rodarth himself probably knew it.

'As far as I'm concerned, you won't be interviewing anybody about this case,' said the Inspector. 'Cadez, if you could show Miss Soliss out-'

He was cut off by the far door swinging open to admit a young man in a leather jacket and jeans. He stopped dead when he saw Melchior, Corwin, Rodarth, Claine and Cadez all staring at him.

'And who the devil are you?' asked Rodarth.

The newcomer took in the scene in an instant- the Inspectors, the skeleton and the chambers- and adopted the manner best suited to what he saw.

'Galion Vasail,' he said. 'I'm a journalist for the Eluxure Gazette.' Here, he glanced at the skeleton again.

'You don't look much like a reporter,' Claine observed, eyebrows raised as she took in his choice of clothing. Melchior had to agree with her there. In fact, he knew for certain that Galion Vasail was not a journalist at all- unless there were a lot of journalists who went around with tool belts around their waists and those digital bands around their wrists that employees had to wear in a workplace.

No, thought Melchior. *This young man is a mechanic. But what's he doing here?*

Galion stepped over to the armchair, where Claine still stood with her arms crossed. 'So, this is the body, I see?'

he said.

'Obviously,' replied Claine. 'But it is also my story, and I don't appreciate *newspapers* stealing a story I heard about first.'

'Too late,' Galion smiled, every inch the irritating reporter. 'I've heard about it now, too.'

Melchior marvelled silently at the mechanic's acting skills. If not for his giveaway clothing and lack of camera, even the Reptid would have been fooled.

Claine came face to face with him, her disdain for reporters who belonged to a mainstream newspaper evident on her face. 'Well, the Eluxure Gazette will have to wait its turn!' she growled dangerously.

Galion's brilliant facade wavered slightly in the face of the angry journalist, and Claine must have noticed it, for she allowed surprise to flicker over her face. If she was going to reveal him, however, she didn't get the chance, for Rodarth interrupted once again.

'I think you'll both find that this crime scene isn't the *Eluxure Gazette*'s *or* whatever you call your newspaper,' (he said that last bit to Claine with more malice than was necessary), 'but is in fact *my* case.' He turned to Corwin. 'Did *he* overhear you too?'

'Not that I know of,' Corwin replied truthfully. 'I have no idea how he found out.'

Rodarth exhaled sharply, closing his eyes in annoyance. 'Fantastic,' he said. 'Now the whole galaxy will know that

Dunwall Tenzebah's been murdered!'

Galion's facial expression transformed to one of genuine surprise as he looked away from Claine to stare at Rodarth.

'Dunwall Tenzebah?' he asked incredulously. '*He's* the one who's been murdered?'

A silence quavered in the air, the sort that occurs when someone has just let slip something they weren't supposed to. Then a delighted grin broke across Claine's face as she too looked at the Inspector, her expression transformed to one of satisfied glee. Rodarth's own face lost its colour as he realised what he'd just done.

'I thought you specified, Inspector Rodarth,' said Corwin innocently, completely straight-faced, 'that we were to keep this particular case strictly confidential?'

Rodarth shot him a brief but venomous glare before beckoning to Cadez, who looked as though he was trying not to laugh.

'Cadez, escort these journalists from the crime scene, and make sure they leave,' he said.

Claine started to protest, but Rodarth cut her off. 'Leave the crime scene *now,* Miss Soliss, unless you want to be fined for trespassing?'

The journalist shot him a loathsome look, but followed Cadez and an equally reluctant Galion out the door without further complaint. Rodarth, acting as though he hadn't just given the Eluxure Gazette confidential information before being discreetly roasted by his colleague, turned to Corwin.

'Tirranar- come with me. I intend to have interviewed everyone in the house by the time we leave.'

Corwin nodded, wisely pretending that he hadn't just said what he had, but couldn't help opening his mouth after a glance at his old friend, who had remained quiet since Galion burst in.

'Err, Inspector Rodarth...what about Melchior?'

Rodarth clenched his teeth, then, with what was evidently an effort, turned to face the Reptid. 'What about Melchior? Well, Reptid, consider yourself banned from the crime scene for the remainder of the investigation.'

Corwin looked shocked. 'On what grounds?'

Rodarth gave that thin little smile that seemed to yell 'punch me in the face!'. 'I think you'll find I don't *need* grounds,' he said. 'I'm an Inspector, and it is within my power to ban whoever I see fit to ban from the scene of the crime.'

Corwin glanced again at Melchior, but the Reptid looked like he had been expecting this.

'You know the way out,' Rodarth told Melchior cheerily, before descending the stairs with an indignant Corwin.

Melchior smiled, undaunted by Rodarth's announcement. *Yes,* he thought. *I know the way out. But I think I know a way back in, too.*

2.

Claine made a point of procrastinating as she followed Cadez out of the house. She took the stairs one at a time, pausing every now and then to admire a painting or wall ornament, then meandered down the hallway in a similar fashion, stopping to examine a nearby vase with excessive scrutiny when Corwin and Rodarth came down the stairs. The latter glared at her, and she smiled in return, claiming that she was just admiring the place, which nobody believed for a minute.

When she was finally outside, she scanned the gardens for who she was looking for. Cadez stood with a couple of other policemen, and she noticed another officer speaking to two men holding cameras and shaking her head. Reporters, from the *Eluxure Gazette,* probably. Wanting to get in on the scoop.

Finally, Claine spotted Galion beneath a drooping Anchora tree in the middle of the extensive gardens that surrounded the house, on the phone to someone- possibly a lift back to Leisopolis. Not intending to let him escape, she made a beeline for him and reached the Anchora just as he hung up.

'Oh, hi,' he said as he looked up and saw her.

'Who are you?' she asked, abruptly.

Galion tucked the phone- an old model, Claine noticed, possibly a 2420 design- into his jeans pocket and attempted to retain his 'journalist' act. 'I said, didn't I? I'm from the Eluxure Gazette. I heard about a murder, but-'

Claine cut him off. 'You aren't a reporter, though, are you?' She studied his clothes and tool belt. 'You're...a mechanic?'

Galion paused, then nodded. 'Yeah, okay. Well, I was. I got fired recently, so I'm looking for a job.'

'You're looking for a job at Kenderye?'

'Dunwall Tenzebah's son, Fersilt Tenzebah- he's in the mechanics industry. He owns a big organisation called Nebula Corporations, and I heard he was here.'

That made sense, but Claine was still a bit sceptical. 'Why the 'journalist' act, in that case?'

Galion looked mildly embarrassed. 'It was easier to get in that way, what with the police cars outside. I thought it made more sense. Turns out I didn't have to make my own way in, though.'

Claine knew what he meant. Cadez, who was posted on the front entrance, had been distracted by her sneaking upstairs.

'I couldn't find Fersilt, though, so I tried looking upstairs,' Galion continued. 'That's when I found the crime scene.'

And then he pretended to be a journalist to escape suspicion, thought Claine. She couldn't help being a little impressed at how he'd improvised. She nodded to the phone protruding from his pocket. 'Who were you calling, if it's not too personal?'

'Just a lift,' Galion replied. 'I'll need to get back to Leisopolis, try and see if I can leave on the first ship to Calmooth or something. I might find a job there.'

Calmooth was like a giant shuttle port, Claine knew. Crossed with a junkyard. 'Might' wasn't the right word- a mechanic would find no shortage of jobs there. But Calmooth was also famed for its extreme shabbiness and abundance of crooks and shady characters. No self-respecting person would visit the shuttle planet, however brief their stay was. And Galion came across as a self-respecting person.

He nodded to a point behind Claine, and she turned to see Rastis Melchior emerge from the house, his turquoise skin standing out against the red of his attire and the well-kept green hue of the surrounding garden.

'Do you know him?' Galion asked. He evidently didn't recognise Melchior, or perhaps even his species.

'That's Rastis Melchior,' she replied. 'He's a detective, the one who solved the Carvistine Mysteries.'

Galion gave her a blank look.

'The Gilworth Murder?' she prompted. 'The Lady Ernise affair?'

Galion shook his head. 'Sorry. The name's familiar, but I don't follow crime.'

It was probably a good thing, Claine decided, that Galion was only pretending to be a journalist. He didn't know the first thing about famous cases.

Melchior approached them along a path lined by brilliant crimson-leafed hedges, and greeted them in the traditional Reptid way.

'What happened?' Claine asked him immediately. 'After we left?'

'Well, for a start, Inspector Rodarth banned me from the crime scene,' Melchior answered.

Claine looked as outraged as Corwin had been. 'Can he do that?'

'I'm afraid he can,' said Melchior.

'They'll never solve it,' the journalist said. 'Not now that you can't help.'

Melchior smiled. He seemed pretty indifferent to the fact that he was unable to work on the case. 'I *can* help, though, Miss Soliss.'

Claine and Galion both looked at him, surprised. 'How?' Galion asked, stumped.

'A ban is a ban,' Melchior explained. 'So no, I can't investigate personally. But there's another way, if you two would be willing.'

His grey eyes, piercing and observant, didn't blink as he waited for a response. Claine, after a few seconds of waiting for him to finish, understood what he was asking. But in her mind, it was more of an offer than a favour. This was an opportunity to pen the article she'd been waiting for.

'We've only been asked to leave,' she said. 'But not banned. We can still come here to Kenderye and investigate on your behalf.'

Galion was surprised. 'Why would you want us to do that?'

'You both have the right skills to be detectives,' Melchior told him. 'Claine- you're observant. You spotted something I didn't about Tenzebah's skeleton. And as for you, Galion, that was better acting than Hoskitt Horne.'

Hoskitt Horne, Claine thought, was not a particularly good actor. It would have been more of a compliment if Melchior had chosen someone skilled to compare the mechanic to. It seemed, however, that Galion did not follow showbusiness any more than he followed crime, for he looked gratified.

'And what if Rodarth bans us as soon as he spots us in the house again?' he asked.

'I doubt he will,' Melchior replied. 'As long as he doesn't find out what you're doing there. He knows that you'd write an article on the case anyway, so he can't stop you doing that.'

'Well, I'm in,' said Claine. It was a win-win, really- annoy Rodarth *and* get a good scoop at the same time. 'I would have gone back anyway. Not a chance I'd miss a story like this.'

Galion, on the other hand, looked more doubtful. 'I should be leaving Eluxure soon,' he said.

'And go to Calmooth?' Claine asked, somewhat incredulously. 'You'd fit in as well there as Melchior would in the military. No offense, Melchior.'

'None taken,' replied the Reptid with a smile on his turquoise face. He turned to the mechanic. 'I presume you were here to pursue a job under Fersilt Tenzebah?'

Galion nodded, wondering how Melchior had worked this out.

'Well, in that case, you don't need to go to Calmooth. Fersilt is still here. And I can assure you, he's not going anywhere until this investigation is over. Then he will either be headed back to Nebula HQ, or prison, depending on the outcome. But until then, he's here in case you want to seek employment.'

Galion had considered this. But he'd still had doubts about it, until now. Melchior seemed to know what he was saying, and in any case this was a good excuse to return to Kenderye.

'I'll think about it,' he said. 'I'll take your advice and try Fersilt again tomorrow, at least.'

Melchior nodded. 'It's much better, I think, than falling prey to Calmooth.'

Personally, Claine agreed. She felt a little relieved that Galion had agreed to consider it. Melchior wasn't offering money, but he was offering Claine a top-notch story and Galion the chance to get another, better-paying job. Also, she couldn't help liking the strange Reptid. She never thought she'd get to meet someone as distinguished as Melchior, but she had now and she felt sort of compelled to help him find a way around Rodarth's unjust ban.

'I'll need to get back to Leisopolis,' Galion said. 'I'm staying at the Termal Mechanics lodgings, but I don't know how long that will last, seeing as I've been fired. I've phoned a lift back, if that's where you're going too?'

Melchior nodded. 'I believe you are staying at the Leisopolis Hotel, Miss Soliss? Considering that was where you decided to hide behind a pot plant?'

Claine grinned. 'Yes, that's where I'm staying. I was supposed to check out today, but...'

Melchior nodded. 'But then you eavesdropped on our conversation and learned of Mr Tenzebah's murder.'

Claine *did* have the dignity to look guilty, but she didn't use it and as a result looked as un-guilty as was possible. 'Yep,' she replied.

'In that case we would appreciate the lift, Mr Vasail,' Melchior said to Galion, who nodded.

'But...Mr Melchior...'

'Just Melchior is fine,' the Reptid smiled.

'So is Galion,' Galion replied. 'Mr Vasail was my dad.'

Melchior acknowledged this with a nod, then gestured for Galion to continue with what he had been about to say.

'Well, if me and Claine are going to be in Kenderye tomorrow, questioning suspects or whatever, what are you going to be doing?'

'Good question,' replied Melchior. He turned and surveyed the grand house once more, looming above them like a very expensive landmark. 'On a planet such as Eluxure,' he said thoughtfully, 'I can't imagine good fences make good neighbours. Especially in the case of Mr Tenzebah's fences...'

Chapter Four

1.

Melchior looked up from his breakfast as Claine sat down at his table, her holo-camera around her neck. She was wearing the same navy blue fur-lined jacket as she had been yesterday- her work clothes, perhaps- and an eager smile on her face. In her hands she clutched a creamy green drink that Melchior suspected was an avocado latte.

'Morning,' she said brightly. 'Made any advance on...' she lowered her voice. '*The case*?'

Melchior's non-existent eyebrows went up. 'Miss Soliss, *the case* has only just begun. I was not visited by a revelation overnight, if that's what you mean, nor did I get out of bed and interview Mrs Tenzebah by candlelight.'

'Sorry,' said Claine. 'But what *are* you doing today? Besides the whole fences and neighbours thing, which is a saying I never really understood anyway.'

Melchior swallowed a mouthful of acasatt before replying. 'The saying means that if you respect each other's property as neighbours, then you will get along well with each other.'

Claine tapped the pitcher of springwater in front of Melchior thoughtfully. 'Dunw- the deceased had some fairly...desirable property.'

Melchior nodded. 'Exactly. And if any of his neighbours wanted that property, they might be tempted to jump the fence.'

Claine grinned and sat back. 'Rodarth wouldn't have thought of that. This is why he's an idiot to ban you from the crime scene.'

Melchior finished his plate and mopped his mouth with a serviette. 'Maybe.'

'So you're going to question all of Tenze- all of the victim's neighbours, then?' Claine asked, and Melchior replied in the affirmative. 'And what do you want me to do?'

'Try to interview as many suspects as you can without Rodarth's knowing,' Melchior replied. 'It's best for him to think you're just snooping around of your own accord, which is a fair assumption, considering that's what you do best. Fersilt Tenzebah may not agree to being questioned by a journalist, however-'

'And that's where Galion comes in,' finished Claine. 'Provided he agrees to help.'

Melchior nodded. 'There's something else I want you to do, as well.'

Claine sat forward again, eagerly. 'And what's that?'

The Reptid nodded towards her camera. 'That is a holo-camera, is it not?'

'Yeah,' she replied. 'A model G887, retro design. Very good quality.'

Melchior nodded. 'Good. I want you to photograph as much of Kenderye as you can. Each room you visit, the garden, the outdoor swimming pool...everything you can.'

Claine looked doubtful for probably the first time in Melchior's brief acquaintance with the freelance reporter. 'That'll use a lot of storage.'

'It's important,' Melchior assured her. 'I need to see the crime scene closely without actually visiting Kenderye.'

Claine hesitated, then nodded. 'Anything else you want me to do?'

Melchior shook his head. 'That's it. You can put anything in your article-'

'I plan to.'

'-*as long as it isn't the finer details of the case.*' Melchior finished. 'Rodarth will definitely read your article. He'll want to see how much you know. If you say too much, he'll get wind of what you're up to. He might even ban you from the scene, like he did me.'

'Don't worry,' Claine replied, tapping her nose. 'Old Racist Pants won't suspect a thing.'

∞

Old Racist Pants was immediately suspicious when he saw Claine Soliss, complete with holo-camera and navy coat, walk up the garden path towards Kenderye.

'What the devil is she doing here?' he muttered to Corwin.

'She's a journalist,' Inspector Tirranar replied. 'You can't stop her from making a scoop if she wants to. Besides, she's already heard a fair bit about the case- so have the *Eluxure Gazette,* actually.'

Rodarth shot him a dark look, but had to admit that Corwin was right. Technically, there was no point in banning Miss Soliss from the scene of the crime.

'Let's not show her in,' he growled as she waved at them from over near the statue. He turned towards the house. 'I would prefer to question Mrs Tenzebah down at the police station, really, but she insisted on being interrogated here at Kenderye.'

Corwin nodded. 'She seems particularly attached to the house. It was where she and Dunwall were supposed to retire before her husband came across Elixir.'

'She would have been happy to come here now, then,'

Rodarth replied.

'I wouldn't say happy,' said Corwin. 'She and Dunwall had made plans to pass away together at Kenderye, but Dunwall could no longer pass away by the time they finally came to Eluxure.'

Rodarth nodded. This was all very interesting, and it was something he hadn't known prior to Corwin telling him. But he wouldn't have admitted it. 'I was being sarcastic, Tirranar,' he said.

'Of course,' Corwin replied. 'Sorry.'

'Good morning,' said Claine, who had by this time reached the two Inspectors.

Rodarth smiled at her, but it was the same thin smile that he had used on several occasions yesterday. 'No sign of the lizard man? Oh, wait, I banned him from the crime scene, didn't I?'

'I won't keep you,' said Claine, smiling sweetly as she walked abruptly into the house. With many mutterings and, 'wasn't even invited in's, Rodarth followed briskly, very much wanting an excuse to ban the journalist from Kenderye.

Claine did as Melchior requested as she meandered through the corridors of the Tenzebahs' not-so-humble abode, though she still did not understand why the Reptid wished to examine the house in so much detail. Maybe he wanted to look for clues- but he hardly needed to see every room in Kenderye to do that. She was so preoccupied in photographing the extensive corridors of the house that she collided with the maid, who was carrying a stack of bedsheets.

'Oh, I'm so sorry!' Claine exclaimed, bending down to help the N'choth'ni gather the scattered laundry.

'Thank you, Miss,' the maid said in the strange clicking manner of her race. Her accent was very well masked, barely noticeable, and her face was humanoid and intelligent despite its initially insectoid appearance. She showed how much Rodarth knew of her species if he thought they were primitive and weak-minded.

'You're that reporter, aren't you?' the N'choth'ni asked. 'You overheard the police talking about the murder.'

Claine nodded. 'It's terrible isn't it?' she asked, knowing that this was always a good entrance for a conversation regarding a murder case.

The maid hesitated, then nodded. 'Not so much as you would think, Miss.'

Claine remembered that N'choth'ni nodded when they meant no and shook their heads to say yes. That was the sort of thing Rodarth would dislike about them, but Claine just found it quaint and distinguishing.

'Why not?' she asked, surprised at the answer she'd received.

'Master Tenzebah was not...a *good* master,' the N'choth'ni said tentatively, as though she wasn't sure she should be divulging this information. 'He was like the Inspector. Not the nice one, the thin one.'

'Tenzebah was racist?' Claine prompted.

The maid shook her head vigorously. 'Yes. He thought I could do nothing but housekeep. Like I was not a person.'

This, Claine knew, would anger Melchior. Or rather he wouldn't like it. Claine found it difficult to picture Melchior angry. Another thing occurred to her, too- this revelation of the maid's would be a perfect excuse for Rodarth to put extra suspicion on her. Dunwall mistreated her, so she killed him.

But Claine found picturing the maid stealing Elixir as difficult as picturing Melchior angry- not for the reasons Rodarth might, that the N'choth'ni was too stupid. The maid was obviously an intelligent person, despite her way of speaking, which may have come across to some as stupidity but in actual fact was just her tongue unnaccustomed to making the sounds familiar to humans. But Claine didn't think the maid could steal Elixir because she didn't have the means or the nature. Even if there was someone the maid really disliked, she would not even think about murdering them.

'Maybe...don't tell the police that he mistreated you,' Claine said carefully, wondering if this was a wise move. 'Especially the thin one.'

'Why not?' asked the maid.

'Rodarth- that's the racist one- he might suspect you,'

Claine told her.

The maid shook her head. 'He already does.'

Claine frowned, thinking of several interesting ways of injuring the Inspector. 'Why? Did you tell him that Dunwall was horrible to you?'

'No,' said the maid. 'I have no...' she gestured vaguely, so she could have meant anything. *Tolerance? Guilt?*

Claine hazarded a guess. 'Alibi?'

The N'choth'ni shook her head again, which Claine remembered meant yes. 'The house is big, and I have to clean it all. So I was in the East wing when my Master was murdered. Nobody else was there.'

'Rodarth can't possibly think you had the means to *kill* Dunwall?' Claine said incredulously.

The maid nodded. 'He does not. But that does not matter. It is an...excuse to incriminate me.'

Claine resumed her mental list of things to do to Rodarth, but at the same time she found herself surprised that the maid knew the word *incriminate.* Then she corrected herself. Why *shouldn't* the maid know the word incriminate? N'choth'ni were easy to unwittingly judge. Their manner made assumptions easy, and Claine made a little mental note not to accidentally underestimate the maid.

'Sorry,' said the N'choth'ni now. She gestured her head towards the sheets in her arms. 'Bedding.'

She began to hurry up the stairwell to their left, but

Claine stopped her with a 'wait!'

The maid turned, surprised. 'Yes, Miss?'

'What's your name?' Claine found herself asking.

'T'chisa,' she replied, looking taken aback that someone might want to know her name.

Claine smiled at her. 'Pleased to meet you, T'chisa.'

T'chisa shook her head, still looking surprised. 'Yes, also,' she said, before hurrying the rest of the way up the stairs and out of sight.

2.

Marsine Tenzebah had craftily arranged the interrogation so that it seemed much more like morning tea. She poured some exotic blend into three cups and set out a tray of catrassi biscuits, and sat the Inspectors in comfortable armchairs. This behaviour may have been considered typical of an older lady, but Marsine eyed them throughout as though challenging them to accuse her.

'You and your husband had intended to retire to this house earlier, did you not?' asked the thin, pointy one-Inspector Rodarth.

'Yes, we did,' Marsine replied. 'I bought this house not long before Dunwall came across Elixir, from the real estate in Leisopolis. One of the more expensive homes, built by the previous owner.'

The other Inspector, Corwin, who was far more

proportionate, as well as far more agreeable, nodded. 'I understand you weren't entirely supportive of Dunwall's newfound immortality?'

Marsine took a sip of tea. 'True enough. I'm not going to pretend I wasn't disappointed. Dunwall and I had so many plans for our retirement together, but then he found Elixir and he didn't seem to care for our house on Eluxure any more.'

'Do you know what made Dunwall reconsider his decision not to retire?' Corwin asked.

Marsine set down her cup. 'Now, there I couldn't say. He was...scared, I think. Or perhaps worried is a better term. I don't know what about- he didn't confide in me. He just suddenly made plans to retire to Kenderye, and wouldn't tell me what had happened to influence his decision.'

There was a touch of bitterness in Marsine's voice that made Corwin think that she resented her husband's sudden distance from her- or she had, until he had been murdered.

Rodarth opened his mouth to say something, but he was interrupted by the door opening and Fersilt Tenzebah entering the room. He was of medium height, with a receding hairline, glasses and a business suit. He certainly didn't look like a mechanic, nor did he act like one. In fact, Fersilt never got his hands dirty, just managed his business from afar and took most of the profit Nebula

Corporations made from his employees' hard work. Corwin liked him about as much as he liked Rodarth, which wasn't very much at all.

'Are they giving you a hard time, Mother?' Fersilt asked, glaring daggers at the Inspectors.

'Nothing of the sort, Fersilt!' Marsine said. 'What reason do you have to think that?'

'For a start,' growled Fersilt, 'they seemed to insinuate, when they interrogated me, that you murdered Father.'

As if he really cares, thought Rodarth. All Fersilt worries about is himself and his business. He had been estranged from his father for a long while now, and there had apparently been no love lost between them. The only reason he had come to Kenderye in the first place was for his own benefit, not to make up with his father.

That Marsine had murdered Dunwall wasn't all Rodarth had insinuated. Fersilt was just as likely to have killed his father, if not more so. The whole reason for his being estranged in the first place was that Dunwall's inability to die stunted Fersilt's hopes of inheritance. If he knew a way to kill Tenzebah, he would've used it, just to get a bit of family fortune.

'It's my job to suspect everyone,' Rodarth interrupted Marsine's angry son. 'Including you, Mrs Tenzebah.'

'Suspect is an entirely different word to accuse,' spat Fersilt.

'I haven't accused anyone, yet!' Rodarth added the 'yet'

as an ominous touch, but it had no effect on the seething man.

Corwin realised, then, that Fersilt was indeed extremely devoted to his mother, balancing out the feud he had had with his father. He would defend his mother passionately, as he was demonstrating now.

'Could you please step outside?' Rodarth asked.

Fersilt glowered but did as he was told- something he wasn't used to. Marsine, meanwhile, remained mostly indifferent but maybe pleased that her son had been so willing to defend her against the police.

'What did you know of your husband's affair with Trissilan Glamure?' Rodarth asked.

Marsine's elegant eyebrows went up. 'His assistant? I'm afraid I don't know what you're talking about.'

'We understand that Dunwall Tenzebah was...carrying on with his assistant,' continued Rodarth.

Marsine began packing away the tea things. 'Like I said, if there was something between Dunwall and Miss Glamure, I knew nothing about it.' She stood. 'Now, do you know the way out or would you like me to escort you?'

The unspoken words were probably something along the lines of, *this interrogation is over now,* and there was nothing, really, that they could do except bid her goodbye and leave- it was more than clear that she had closed all further conversation.

Corwin wondered at that.

3.

Morfestire was every inch as impressive as Kenderye, in its own way. While Tenzebah's retirement mansion was in a vintage, classical style, with marble statues, greudstone pillars and saberwood furniture, the house of Sadrien Chasterleigh defined modern, with lots of revolving staircases and clever mechanisms hidden beneath a coating of bright white to give the whole house a fresh but slightly blinding appearance. This was a house that could just as easily entertain celebrities or a party.

So far, Melchior had had no luck with Tenzebah's neighbours. A Miss Lalait Malcoo was, in his opinion, a complete airhead who kept refilling her wine glass (at ten o'clock in the morning!), even though her glass was still a quarter full. She didn't offer Melchior any, as was the polite etiquette on most planets (except Plota, of course) but the Reptid would have refused anyway. His race didn't drink alcohol, and preferred water or gordnu. Lalait had known Dunwall was on Eluxure, but she claimed she didn't tell any off-worlders, seeing as she wasn't one to gossip. Then she proceeded to tell him all about how Marjune Pantheree was pregnant but her husband couldn't have kids, and how Cather Sterrid's stories of owalk hunting on the desert world of Mishtiik were all lies.

Melchior sat through all of this politely, which Lalait was probably incapable of doing, and, dutifully, did not tell her that Tenzebah was dead. Instead, he claimed that Elixir had been stolen, which was still the truth. There wasn't much harm in revealing the finer details of the crime, seeing as Claine would tell everybody in her next article, but to give Miss Malcoo gossip was like giving a child confectionary that contained more than 50% sugar. Seeing as it wasn't a good idea to give a child confectionary that contained more than 50% sugar, it probably wasn't a good idea to give Lalait gossip either.

Next he had visited Cather Sterrid himself, whoever he was. He had apparently convinced everyone in his neck of Eluxure that he was a retired big-game hunter who had braved the wilds of Scorpid and Mishtiik and slain the Alpha in a pack of sabril. If Miss Malcoo was to be believed, Sterrid had purchased the sabril Alpha's head that was mounted on the wall for a mere hundred asterti (plus his grandmother's cutlery) from a passing merchant.

Sterrid had also known about Tenzebah's presence on Eluxure, but he said he doubted anyone in Leisopolis save the police, or anyone off-world, knew he was here. He was mystified as to who could possibly have the ingenuity or the means to steal Elixir, which Tenzebah had kept on him at all times, except when showering or bathing. The skeleton had been found in an armchair, so unless Dunwall's chambers had a retractable shower-head above the hearth, the how was still a mystery.

But now, after a morning of going from one expensive house to another questioning deceptive, dishonest and pretty shallow retirees, Melchior was beginning to think his hunch- that a neighbour might know something useful that wasn't the details of Marjune Pantheree's domestic life- was leading nowhere.

Sadrien Chasterleigh was the last person Melchior would visit today, or else he felt he'd probably go mad. On Reptis, it was unbecoming of anyone to be in a state of psychosis, and Melchior wondered if that rule extended to a Reptid who was off-world at the time.

Sadrien's expensive modern house sprawled across the picturesque landcape like a bleached spider- not that it didn't have aesthetic value. Morfestire (a rather ugly name for a place of residence) was definitely nice to look at, but it was much less down-to-earth, more the sort of building that a glamorous young couple would buy. Sadrien might have bought it when he was part of one such glamorous young couple.

Mr Chasterleigh, if Mr was the correct form of address, was on the roof, standing by a brilliant turquoise pool that matched Melchior's skin tone, dressed in an expensive-looking paisley dressing gown. The pool, it seemed, was for ornamental purposes rather than practical, although it was perfectly usable. The water was untouched, not a ripple on its surface, and surprisingly clean. There were no specks of dirt or even algae, considering it was most likely never used. The job of cleaning it and filtering it was probably Sadrien's servants' job. Melchior wondered if Mr Chasterleigh employed N'choth'ni, and if they were treated as badly as Tenzebah's maid.

'Ah,' said Sadrien, as Melchior approached the pool. He'd aged well, that was for sure. His hair was grey but showed no signs of baldness and his face was so wrinkle-free that plastic surgery was almost certainly the culprit. He had obviously been very handsome in his youth, but now the combination of an old man's face and a plastic one just gave him an odd, timeless look. 'You must be the Detective chap. Mechonaut, isn't it?'

'Melchior,' Melchior corrected, though he suspected Sadrien mispronounced his name deliberately. "Melchior" was easy enough to remember, and Chasterleigh did not strike him as a man who forgot names that easily. In that case, the reason could only be that Sadrien was suspicious of Melchior's visit, and was trying to put him on the back foot.

'Would you mind telling me the purpose of your visit?' Sadrien asked, taking a sip of *chadris* from a wine flute.

'I'm here to inquire about one of your neighbours,' Melchior replied, taking the wine flute passed to him by Sadrien with little enthusiasm. That was rich people for you. Always drinking alcohol in the morning.

Sadrien's eyebrows arched in surprise. 'Oh?' he asked,

setting down his glass on a small, circular table and pouring himself some more from a jug. 'And which one would that be? Everyone here lives a fair way apart.'

'A certain Dunwall Tenzebah,' Melchior replied.

Clink! Sadrien's glass spilled over and poured into a puddle on the table. He swore, before apologising and calling for a servant to clean it up.

'You know him, then?' asked Melchior, intrigued by Sadrien's reaction.

'Doesn't everybody?' Sadrien answered. 'Being immortal's sure to make you famous, isn't it?'

'Did you know he was on Eluxure?' Melchior pressed.

Sadrien laughed. 'Of course I did. And if I didn't, I daresay Miss Malcoo would've told me. Complete mystery why he showed up on Eluxure, isn't it?'

Melchior nodded. 'Elixir has been stolen.'

Sadrien looked briefly surprised, then changed his expression to a thoughtful frown, moving his elbow from the table as a robot wiped the *chadris* vigorously. 'That's his immortality juice, isn't it? I bet Dun's off his nut.'

Melchior paused, contemplating this. 'You could say that, I suppose.'

'How did you think I could help you?'

'The residents of Eluxure have been in closer proximity to Tenzebah than anyone else recently. It's important that we find out all we can.'

Sadrien shrugged, pouring himself a fresh glass. 'If you

ask me, the thief is off-world by now. Probably took a shuttle to Glaminda first chance he got.'

There was a silence, Melchior thinking, as usual, Sadrien drinking *chadris* leisurely.

'It's a nice place you have here,' Melchior said eventually.

Sadrien nodded. 'It is, isn't it? I designed it to look exactly like my old house on Elapamp.'

So, thought Melchior. It *was* the sort of house a glamorous young couple would buy. Or at least, it looked exactly like one. The fact that Sadrien said *I* and *my* meant that the glamorous young couple in question were no longer a couple, for one reason or another, and it was probably best not to mention anything that might be conceived as 'prying'. Lalait probably knew exactly why Sadrien's husband or wife had left him, or vice versa, or why she or he had passed away...

'So, have you got all you need to know?' Sadrien asked now.

Melchior nodded. 'Yes, I believe so.'

Sadrien pressed a button on his wristband and spoke into it. 'Clurda, would you show Mr Melchior out, please? Now, thank you, not next year.'

Melchior took this very good opportunity, while Sadrien was distracted, to tip the contents of his *chadris* glass into Sadrien's pristine pool, which, he felt, was killing two birds with one very satisfying stone.

4.

Meanwhile, Galion Vasail was finding Fersilt Tenzebah exceedingly slippery to catch. The man strode about Kenderye like he was constantly in the middle of something important, but that was probably because he was more than used to being in the middle of something important, and was beginning to get very impatient with the police.

'I'm a very busy man,' Fersilt said to the police. 'I've got a dozen things I need to do, and I need to get to Glaminda as soon as possible. Nebula has hit a horrible service schedule snag, and they won't be able to sort it out without me!'

'You need to remain at Kenderye for the time being, sir,' said Cadez placatingly. 'Inspector Rodarth wishes all murder suspects to stay in the area until the culprit is found.'

'All murder suspects,' Fersilt scoffed. 'I don't know who it is, but it's certainly not me and it's certainly not Mother.'

'We only have your word for that, sir.'

'Is my word not enough?' Fersilt fumed. 'I'm a very important man, and my business is relying on me, now could you *please* arrange for me to be flown to Glaminda?'

When Cadez shook his head reluctantly, Fersilt stormed

off whilst looking as dignified as he could. Now, thought Galion, would not be a good time to approach him.

Instead, Galion went in the opposite direction, wondering if his journalist facade would get him anywhere. It was important not to speak to Fersilt or Rodarth when the other was present. One thought he was a reporter, and it was important the other knew he was a mechanic. If Rodarth found out he wasn't working for the *Eluxure Gazette*, he would probably be banned from Kenderye. And if Fersilt thought he wasn't a mechanic, his potential job would go down the drain and he would probably go to Calmooth. Although, he thought grimly, there wasn't much difference between Calmooth and a sewer.

Galion turned the corner and almost rammed into Inspector Rodarth and Corwin, who looked just as surprised.

'You're from the *Eluxure Gazette*, aren't you?' Rodarth said. The sentence, phrased like a question, was more a statement.

Galion quickly switched to reporter mode. 'Got it in one. I was on the crime scene yesterday, remember?'

Rodarth didn't want to remember, actually, but he did. Damn journalist had made him reveal top-secret information. Deceptive, that's what reporters were.

'I was just looking for you actually, Inspector,' Galion went on. 'I was wondering if you'd give the *Eluxure Gazette* an update on the case? Where we're at, you know?

Who you're suspecting? The readers love that sort of thing.'

'Get lost,' growled Rodarth. 'Don't bother me again. I'm sure the *Gazette* has enough confidential information to keep them going for a couple of pages.'

Galion couldn't resist letting out a short laugh at that. 'Too right. Thanks for the details yesterday, by the way.'

Rodarth glared at him- something the Inspector was good at. Then, having evidently decided not to punch Galion, since that wouldn't have looked very good, he continued down the hall. Corwin threw him a glance that said something like, *yes, good on you, but be more careful in future.* Galion wondered if Corwin knew he was a mechanic. Maybe Melchior had told him.

'That was pretty risky,' said a voice from behind him. Galion turned to see Claine leaning against the wall, her holo-camera raised and pointed at the ornate, decorative ceiling. She was grinning widely. 'But the look on Rodarth's face was absolutely priceless.'

'Hi,' said Galion. 'Found anything useful yet?'

Claine adopted a thoughtful expression. 'I don't know. Melchior wanted me to photograph as much of the house as I could. It's a challenge, but I'm getting there. And then there's that infernal reporter from the *Gazette* who's been snooping around.'

'What?' asked Galion.

'A real one,' Claine elaborated unnecessarily. 'You'd

better be careful. Rodarth might get suspicious if he finds two *Eluxure Gazette* journalists working independently from each other.'

Galion frowned. He hadn't thought of that possibility. He doubted they'd found out much, seeing as the police would be doing their best to keep Kenderye as reporter-free as possible. Hopefully Rodarth hadn't cottoned on to his act yet.

'What about you and Fersilt?' asked Claine. 'Any progress on that front?'

'He's as slippery as a fish, and also in a very bad mood,' Galion replied. 'I haven't talked to him yet. Did Melchior say what he was up to today?'

'Questioning the neighbours,' Claine told him. 'I don't know what he expects to find, but if he's on to something, that's great.'

Galion nodded. He couldn't help feeling intrigued about what the Reptid might find, or what the outcome might be, but he knew that his options were Fersilt, Calmooth, or bust. The latter two might have been pretty much the same. Still, he was surprised at his reluctance to leave the plot hanging. He'd taken a liking to Claine and Melchior, and sort of wanted to help solve the mystery. But again, he had other commitments, even if those commitments were either a bad-tempered man with an ego the size of Leisopolis or a planet of crooks and dodgy dealers.

Claine flicked through the photographs on her holo-camera. 'I've only been able to view them in 2D,' she said. 'I'll need a cobalt room to look at them properly.'

'And...you have one of those on Eluxure?'

Claine grinned. 'Not exactly. A cobalt room isn't really a *room*- it's a projector. But you have to be in a dark room for it to work. I've got my cobalt room set up in my hotel suite- fingers crossed the holo-photos turn out OK.'

Galion still wasn't sure he understood Claine's photographer talk, but he guessed he'd probably get it if he saw her cobalt room in action. 'What do you think Melchior hopes to find?'

Claine shrugged. 'Clues, I guess. But it would be much better if I could get a photo of Tenzebah's chambers.'

'Rodarth would ban you from the crime scene if he caught you in there,' Galion said. Claine nodded in agreement. 'And you can't really hide a camera that big, can you?'

Claine suddenly snapped her head up from the camera to look at him. 'Genius!'

'Excuse me?'

Claine turned her camera over and set it on a nearby ornamental stool, showing complete disregard for the fact that said stool had probably cost several million in any currency. 'This big old thing isn't my camera any more than my cobalt room is a room,' she said. 'Have you got a screwdriver?'

'Of course I do.' Galion produced a screwdriver from

his belt slightly bewilderedly and handed it to Claine, who began to unscrew the back of her camera. 'But I'm pretty sure that's a camera.'

'Holo-cameras are tiny,' Claine explained, prising the back off her device. 'All this,' she gestured towards what Galion had until recently thought was a camera, 'is just a housing. My holo's made to look like a retro Earth camera.'

'Which means...?' Galion prompted, none the wiser.

Claine removed a small device as big as her thumb from its casing. 'Which means *this* baby is my camera, and we can still get a photo of the crime scene!'

'How?' Galion asked, frowning. Then his expression cleared. 'Corwin?'

Claine grinned again, holding the "camera" aloft on her fingertip. 'Spot on.'

Chapter Five

Claine's room was not cobalt. It was, in fact, just like Melchior's, which made the Reptid question the architect's creativity. It had the same glass table, the same chairs, the same layout. Melchior was willing to bet it had the same gold-coloured toilet, too.

The table was taken up by a round metal disc with lots of flashing lights and intriguing science-y bits that fascinated Galion. Claine set the camera's memory card in the centre of the projector and fired it up. It made a clunking noise, which showed how much she needed a new one.

'This isn't very blue, either,' Galion remarked.

'Shut up, Vasail,' Claine told him, straightening. 'This isn't what makes it cobalt.'

'What do you want to find?' Galion asked Melchior. The Reptid was sitting in one of the chairs, probably the one he usually sat in in his own room.

'I'm not sure. Anything, I suppose. Hopefully something that leads somewhere.'

'Very helpful,' said Galion. 'Thanks.'

'Done,' said Claine. 'Galion, can you turn off the light?'

Galion complied, crossing to the door and pressing the switch on the wall beside it. Nothing happened, except the expected, which was the entire room going dark.

Then Claine pressed a button on her cobalt room and their surroundings changed so fast Galion felt a rush of vertigo that was gone as quickly as it had come. They were now in some sort of leisure room, with glass walls, doors, and roof. The only things that hadn't changed were them, standing in exactly the same position as they had in Claine's suite. Rather than sitting in an armchair, Melchior now sat in a wicker chair of some sort, and rather than holding the wall for support, Galion now grasped a succulent pot plant. He quickly retracted his hands before realising the spikes weren't hurting him. They were, however, tinged with a shade of blue- cobalt, he realised.

'What just happened?' he asked.

'Nothing,' Claine told him, smiling cheekily. 'We're still in the hotel. Why do you think I called this a holo-photo?'

Galion looked at the cobalt ceiling in awe. 'This...is a photograph?'

'Yep,' said Claine. 'Rodarth and Corwin have been using *this* place as an interrogation room for Marsine Tenzebah. She refuses to be interviewed at the police station, so they've just been questioning everybody here, just to be consistent.'

'Nothing of interest here, I'd say,' said Melchior. 'This room is empty except for a few chairs, a table, and a Maglothian Succuli.'

Claine pressed the button on her projector again and their surroundings changed once more. This time, however, Galion was prepared, and he noticed that the change in scene was very much like changing a slide in a slideshow. Except, of course, for the fact that they were *inside* the slideshow.

The next photograph was a hallway. Galion couldn't tell if he'd been in it or not- they all looked the same- until he looked at the ceiling and saw that it was the same as the one he'd seen Claine taking a photo of earlier, only cobalt. A few paintings hung on the wall, and Melchior examined them thoughtfully.

'See this painting here?' he asked. 'This is called Longevity, painted by Axl Mantis. It's very famous.'

'And it helps how?' asked Galion.

'It's about the Fountain of Youth,' explained Melchior. 'Which was supposed to make the drinker of its waters immortal.'

Galion still didn't see why this might be significant, but

Melchior didn't elaborate. Instead he requested that Claine change the slide.

This went on for quite some time, flicking from photograph to photograph. For the most part they discovered nothing of use, but occasionally Melchior would point something out, such as a stained-glass window depicting what he claimed was Miskitus the Purple drinking from the Goblet of Eternity. Kenderye seemed to be proudly showing off its owner's long life; paintings, mosaics, windows and statues were all relating to immortality in one way or another.

Galion tried sitting down once but when Claine changed the slide he found himself in the garden, and fell backwards onto his backside. He decided to stay standing after that.

Claine too was beginning to tire of incessant slide-changing, and after a few more photographs of absolutely nothing important asked Melchior if he wanted her to skip to the last slide.

This intrigued the Reptid, and he asked what the last slide depicted.

Claine grinned. 'You want to see it?'

When Melchior said neither yes nor no, she pressed a different button and the slide change sped up, giving Galion the sensation he was on a cobalt roller coaster. Eventually she reached the end of the slideshow and Melchior sat forward, a delighted smile spreading across his turquoise, reptilian face.

For they were standing in Dunwall Tenzebah's chambers, or at least an exact replica, save the cobalt hue and the fact that the fire was on pause, a frozen patch of flame caught mid-flicker in the lens of Claine's holo-camera.

'You genius, Claine!' said Melchior.

'It was Galion's idea,' muttered Claine modestly.

'Sort of,' muttered Galion truthfully.

Melchior stood and patrolled the room as he had done the day before, but this time examining its contents with much more scrutiny. Galion noticed that Tenzebah's skeleton had been removed from the armchair, probably taken to a morgue or something. It was unlikely Rodarth would gather any useful information from the immortal's remains.

'How did you get this photograph?' asked Melchior from the doorway that led to Dunwall's bathroom chambers.

'I asked Corwin to,' Claine explained. 'I told him it was for you, so he agreed to take a picture of Tenzebah's room.'

Melchior nodded, looking around. 'It really is very strange that the room is virtually untouched,' he said. 'Tenzebah was found in the armchair...yet there is no sign of a struggle. He kept Elixir on him constantly...yet it was stolen. Nothing adds up properly.'

'What's this?' Galion asked from Dunwall's desk. Melchior turned and looked at him expectantly.

'Photographs,' said Galion. 'Of Tenzebah, mostly, but-'

Melchior was at the desk in a flash. The photographs in question were in the old, inchery extract colour style, which hinted that they were of Tenzebah several years ago.

One showed him and Marsine Tenzebah, and Melchior suspected it was taken before Elixir, because they both looked happy and, more importantly, comfortable together. They looked around fifty, and they were standing outside Kenderye.

'This is when they had their idyllic plans for a retirement together,' Claine said quietly. 'Before Elixir became Dunwall's main obsession.'

Melchior nodded, moving to the next photograph. This one was even more interesting. It showed Dunwall as a young man, with one arm around another man. They were smiling wildly and standing in front of a shuttleship, obviously about to go on a big trip.

'What's this one about?' Claine asked, intrigued. She realised she knew little of the victim's past.

'Tenzebah used to be an adventurer,' Melchior explained. 'He and his friend used to travel all over the galaxy. I can't say I remember the name of the other man- and if somebody mentioned it I doubt I could place it.'

'When did they stop?' Galion asked. 'And why?'

'They went their own separate directions, I think,' said

Melchior. 'But they parted on good terms the first time.'

Claine raised her eyebrows as she scanned the other photographs. There were a couple of others depicting the pair. 'The first time?' she asked.

'They had one more expedition, later on,' explained the Reptid. 'Tenzebah had planned the whole thing out. He was very passionate about finding something. A particular, extremely desirable thing.'

Claine looked at the photographs again. One in particular showed Dunwall and his friend a fair bit older- fifty, if she understood what Melchior was getting at correctly. Tenzebah was holding something- a small knot of what looked like wood or plant matter.

'That's Elixir?' asked Galion, surprised.

'It would seem so,' Melchior replied. 'After all, if Elixir was just a drink, it would be finite. However, if *this* object is Elixir, it would last as long as the consumer- for example, if to make Elixir, Tenzebah put this...root in a container of water and infused it with its immortal properties.'

'What happened?' Claine asked, still looking at the photographs in fascination.

Melchior glanced at her. 'Tenzebah had a row with his friend. He wanted Elixir for himself. Desire will do that to a person. But his friend wanted it too. Neither wanted equal share, because that's not how Elixir works. It has to be owned by *one* person, and each man wanted to be that person.'

'Tenzebah won, then,' put in Galion.

'Cheated, more like,' corrected Melchior. 'I doubt he came into sole possession of the object fairly.'

Claine studied the second man in the photograph. 'I doubt his friend liked that very much.'

Melchior shook his head. 'Tenzebah became famous and rich, and his friend was forgotten, betrayed and cheated by his fellow adventurer.'

Elixir was starting to sound eerie and dangerous to Claine, as though it were something that influenced people's minds, turned them against each other. It certainly wasn't natural. But then, neither was immortality. She could understand why people like Tenzebah would be entranced by it, enough so as to turn on his oldest friend, but she couldn't fathom how anything could do that to an honest person. The way Melchior spoke of it, it was more than capable of changing the way a good man or woman might think and twist them into someone like...well, someone like Tenzebah.

She looked at one of the photographs of him and his friend as young men. Tenzebah was smiling, and Claine couldn't help wondering whether he had always been as bad as T'chisa had said he'd been recently. Maybe Tenzebah used to be a likeable person, but Elixir had somehow changed him into the person who had been murdered instead. Her gaze drifted to his friend. He was caught mid laugh, an arm around Tenzebah like they were brothers. It would've felt terrible to be betrayed by someone he thought was a good friend. Tenzebah had been old when he'd passed away. Maybe the unnamed friend was dead too.

'Why did Tenzebah keep these photographs?' asked Galion, jolting her out of her thoughts. 'If he betrayed his friend?'

'Nostalgia?' offered Claine.

'Possibly,' murmured Melchior. He too was looking at the other man in the photograph. 'He looks familiar...'

'Maybe you've seen other photographs?' Claine suggested.

Melchior opened his mouth to speak but before he could their surroundings disappeared in a flash as the cobalt was drained from the room and they were transported back to Claine's hotel room. Melchior looked behind him in surprise and saw Corwin standing in the doorway. A funnel of light streamed into the room from outside, cutting through the darkness and interrupting the slideshow.

'Sorry,' said Corwin. 'Am I interrupting anything?'

Melchior listened intently as Corwin filled him in on the investigations of the day. It seemed the police hadn't been getting anywhere, really, at least compared to the others. Marsine Tenzebah had been somewhat helpful, Corwin said. She had been the one who had bought Kenderye, and she had been bitter about Dunwall rejecting the retirement they had planned together. Nothing, really, that Melchior didn't already know. One interesting thing, though, was that Marsine denied knowing about an affair between Dunwall and his assistant, Trissilan Glamure, when said assistant claimed otherwise. Apparently, during her interview, Trissilan had said the relationship was 'no secret' and that Marsine had been a bit irked about it.

One of them was lying. Hiding something, whatever that might be. But unless the relationship was the motive behind the murder in some way, Melchior couldn't see why either woman would keep secrets regarding it. Overall, however, Corwin said that Marsine had appeared strong-minded for a 90 year old, and had met each of Rodarth's insensitive questions with elegance and dignity.

Fersilt, Corwin said with a sigh, had been exceedingly different. He remained adamant that neither he nor his mother had committed the crime. He was devoted to his mother, much more so than he had been to his father, and was certain that Marsine had not killed her husband. He had no facts nor alibis to support the claim, however, so they were both under suspicion still. Apparently he had been in Leisopolis at the time and his mother had been at Kenderye, so Fersilt had no reason to defend his mother so ferociously except for the already-existent devotion.

The poor maid had had a hard time from Rodarth, who

seemed to think she did it despite her lack of means or motive. Tenzebah had been cruel to T'chisa, but she wouldn't kill Rodarth, so she probably wouldn't kill Tenzebah either. T'chisa had no alibi, but she said she was at the other end of the house.

Trissilan had held herself elegantly and unemotionally, as though she wasn't affected by Tenzebah's death, although Corwin said he suspected she was. She had announced that she thought Marsine was the culprit, because Mrs Tenzebah was jealous, but was not as adamant about the suspicion as Rodarth was about T'chisa's guilt.

'So what have you been up to, then?' asked Corwin.

'I have been paying visits to Tenzebah's neighbours,' Melchior replied. 'Most of which were a waste of time.'

'Find anything useful?'

Melchior tilted his head to one side. 'Perhaps. The holo-photos taken by Claine Soliss were informative, and the one taken by you was *very* interesting.'

Corwin raised his eyebrows. 'Go on...'

'Ah, but isn't it a requirement for you to inform your colleague of anything you discover?' asked Melchior.

'Yes, unfortunately,' replied Corwin.

Melchior shrugged. 'Well, I daresay if Rodarth is as smart as he thinks he is, he'll find out for himself without my telling him.'

Corwin eyed him. 'You are slippery, Rastis, that's for

sure.' He paused. 'I could conveniently forget anything I discover, of course. So that I have nothing to inform Rodarth of.'

Melchior smiled. 'I found some very interesting photographs of Tenzebah with his friend. The one he found Elixir with, then cheated it from.'

'You found these in one of Claine's holo-photos?'

'The one you took, actually. If Rodarth hasn't discovered them yet he's hardly doing his job properly,' replied Melchior. 'I also couldn't help noticing that Kenderye features a fair amount of references to immortality. Especially the fountain out the front-Astelpine, the god of longevity.'

Corwin nodded. 'Immortality was a big part of Tenzebah's life.' He grinned at that.

Melchior nodded. 'It *was* his life. But he was hiding, wasn't he? He didn't want off-worlders to know he was here. So why decorate his house with statues of Astelpine and infinity symbols?'

Corwin didn't have an answer to that.

'But that's not all,' Melchior went on. 'Marsine Tenzebah said she bought Kenderye herself, before Dunwall even *thought* of going in search of Elixir.'

Corwin frowned, nodding. 'I think I see what you're getting at.'

'Indeed,' said Melchior. 'If this house was bought before Tenzebah's obsession with immortality...'

Corwin finished his sentence. '...then why did Marsine choose a house filled with references to immortality?'

Melchior nodded. 'Either Marsine has some amazing, hidden powers of prophecy...or there's something she hasn't told us yet...'

Chapter Six

'Have a look at that!'

Melchior looked up in surprise as the morning newspaper was thrown violently onto the table in front of him. Claine was seething about something, but Melchior had no idea what. He had spent the morning so far contemplating the case, and trying to recall the name of Dunwall's friend, in the unlikely event that the information should be of use. Claine's interruption was in fact a relief from all of this thinking, despite the fact that she was furious.

'Go on, read it!' she spat. 'They're a bunch of complete and utter-' here she used a very unladylike word to describe whoever she was raging at. Melchior looked down at the paper and examined it more closely. In a lavish, cursive font were the words *Eluxure Gazette*. And underneath, a front-page heading- *Is Immortality Overrated? The Impossible Murder of Dunwall Tenzebah*.

'They stole my scoop. The only good scoop I've had *ever*. The one time I manage to get something good, some primitive idiot from a mainstream magazine goes and pinches it!' Claine raged. 'It must have been that *mutricot* who was snooping around Kenderye the other day.'

'Like you were doing, you mean?' asked Melchior lightly.

Claine glared. 'That was different. I was snooping on your behalf. What beats me is how they managed to publish it so fast.'

Melchior scanned the page. The *Gazette* were extremely proud of 'their' scoop. The article was written in an irritatingly smug tone and the inferred massage was clearly *we know something you don't know*.

Dunwall Tenzebah, the famous owner of the miracle drink Elixir, and topic of many of our previous reports and articles, has been found dead in his retirement suite on Eluxure, under very suspicious circumstances. It seems more than impossible that an immortal man like Tenzebah could die in such a fashion, or indeed die at all, but it would appear that such an action was not outside his capabilities after all. This exclusive information, (said the paper, as the tone became gradually more arrogant), *was sourced from our infallible reporters, who were the first to know about the death, after the police, and who have gathered top secret information from the crime scene that other newspapers are yet to discover.*

'They don't know the details,' Melchior assured Claine. 'Whereas you do.'

Claine folded her arms and glared. 'Yes, but the buzz will have worn off a bit by the time I publish my own issue. There's nothing like being the *first*, Melchior. Being the second one to report a story just sounds like I'm jumping on the bandwagon.'

This was true. Newspapers had more ruthless competition than most contact sports. If one managed to beat another to a story they scored a point and were insufferable about it for ages. The *Gazette* had managed to score despite Claine being the better player, and she seemed determined to win the game.

Melchior continued to read the article. It covered the basics, but not the finer details, which of course didn't matter. The public only needed the basics to get worked up about something.

Police suspect murder, but a murderer has to know how to kill his victim, and until now, all thought him unkillable. The other residents of Kenderye, including Marsine Tenzebah, the wife of the victim, refused to tell our reporters anything, but we have managed to uncover information regarding Mr Tenzebah's reasons for retiring at such an old age. It seems that Dunwall was paranoid about something, or perhaps even scared, but experts say that Tenzebah had just grown increasingly senile in his old age.

'They've made half of it up anyway,' Claine fumed. 'Look at paragraph three, line four. They say they were "granted entry to the scene of the crime and gathered enticing information regarding the case." Tell me that isn't bull! The police wouldn't even *let* the reporter in, and I'll eat the next issue of the *Galaxy Roamer* if they know anything we don't!'

Melchior was secretly surprised that Claine had bothered memorising sentences from the article, probably for the sole reason of raging at it.

'Nobody cares whether the *Gazette* tells the complete truth or not,' Melchior pointed out. 'It's news, more specifically *big* news, and if it'll earn them wads of cash from newspaper sales, what's a few lies to them?'

'I'm tempted to find this Garro Tagg,' Claine fumed, essentially ignoring the Reptid, 'and knock his lights out.'

'Who might this Garro Tagg be? Not Galion, that's for sure.'

'Ha ha,' said Claine sarcastically and slightly menacingly. 'Tagg is the moron who wrote this junk.'

Melchior's eyes flicked to the bottom of the page. Sure enough, the author was credited as *Garro Tagg.* The Reptid looked at Claine shrewdly out the corner of his eye. 'He should be to easy find, if you want to...*knock his lights out.*'

Claine sat down heavily. 'Don't bother about it. I'm not going anywhere near the *Eluxure Gazette* head office, even if it is just to whack the *croddus* who wrote this junk. I bet it's the same idiot who was nosing about yesterday...what?'

For Melchior had looked up at her suddenly, a light in his eyes that told Claine that he had an idea. In this instance, she knew immediately what it was.

'Oh no,' she said. 'No, no, no.'

'I'm sure it isn't that hard an errand,' Melchior reminded her.

'Oh, come on, Melchior,' she said, 'You're already investigating *one* murder. You don't want to look into Garro Tagg's as well.'

'I'm trusting that you'll refrain from murdering Mr Tagg,' Melchior told her. 'Seeing as I need access to the *Eluxure Gazette's* archives.'

Claine pulled a face, doubting very much that she'd find anything in the archives except trash and lies. 'Well, what are you looking for? Last weeks Packerawl scores?'

'Anything regarding Tenzebah and preferably his friend as well,' replied the Reptid, ignoring her snipe. 'This edition here says that Tenzebah was the *"topic of many of our previous reports and articles".* The *Gazette* seems to be the planet's only newspaper, but since said planet is about as eventful as a cancelled concert, I'd say that's all they need. And if that's the case, they'll most certainly have an article *somewhere* about Elixir.'

Claine sighed and stood up once more. 'Fine. But if I hit someone, I'll tell them it was your fault.'

'Oh, before you go,' said Melchior, handing her what looked like some sort of memory stick. 'You'll need this.'

Claine frowned, taking it. 'What is it?'

'Illegal,' replied Melchior. 'But what are rules if you can't bend them?'

'Well, well, well, if it isn't that freelance journalist!'

Claine closed her eyes, trying very hard to retain a warm, friendly air, then turned and flashed a huge smile at who she presumed was Garro Tagg.

The *Gazette* reporter was all smiles, his gleaming white teeth contrasting with his purple-tinged skin. He wore sharp clothes, not generally the attire one would expect of a journalist, and walked with the barely concealed swagger of one who had just stolen a scoop and made a lot of money from it. He was indeed the reporter she had seen snooping around Kenderye on several occasions, except then his getup was not so obviously expensive, lest it attracted unwanted attention.

'I presume you read my article?' he asked her now.

Claine clenched her jaw, then remembered to smile. 'Yes, it was *very* interesting.' She took care not to mention the fact that she had purchased a paper copy rather than the more common digital edition because she couldn't quite afford it on top of her other costs.

'I noticed you at Kenderye,' Garro Tagg said. 'Trying to scrape a story, eh? Too bad I got there first.'

Claine had to force herself to do what Melchior had said and not resort to needless violence.

'Ah well,' Tagg continued. 'What brings you to the *Gazette* HQ?' Here he gestured grandly at the domed glass ceiling above them.

'I'd like access to the *Gazette*'s archives,' she announced, and admittedly found pleasure in Tagg's expression.

'Whatever for?' he asked, momentarily caught off guard. 'If you wish to gather information for your own article-'

'Not exactly,' she interrupted. 'I do wish to view your records of articles on Dunwall Tenzebah, but not for my scoop. I simply want to access your archives for the sole purpose of seeing what else you have to say on the immortal.'

Garro Tagg seemed to struggle for a moment. Then the toothy smile resurfaced and he spread his arms. 'Why not? I can't let you take anything from the archives, of course, but I have authorisation to allow you to view them.'

Claine smiled at him winningly.

'Follow me,' said Tagg, and began to walk towards a

flight of stairs with a door at the top which said, *STAFF ONLY. Please keep out or we will administer severe punishments.*

'Shame we can give the severe punishments a miss,' laughed Tagg. 'Seeing as you're with me.'

Claine couldn't help thinking that Tagg's mock-sinister tone was meant as a deterrent. He certainly didn't like the idea of a freelance reporter going through the *Gazette's* history, that much he made perfectly clear.

He opened his palm and held it against the door, which scanned it and made a mechanical buzzing noise.

'Authorised member recognised,' said a pleasant female voice smoothly. 'You may enter, Garro Tagg, reporter.'

The door swung open and Tagg entered, motioning for Claine to follow. She did so, and found herself in a room much more vast than she had anticipated. Rows upon rows of shelves upon shelves containing records upon records- or so she presumed. It was remarkable that the *Gazette* had been running for that long, and in fact that such a newspaper *needed* so much room for archives. Nothing much ever happened on Eluxure, that's what everyone kept telling her. The *Gazette* probably had to steal off-world stories as well as local. Either that or it was usually filled with trash like *Dame Dedgether Buys Yet Another New Evening Dress* and *A Big Welcome To Our New Retiree, Major Pritt.*

'The archives are arranged in columns and rows,' Tagg

explained. 'Columns are specific dates, rows are specific categories. Wherever there's an intersection, it signifies albums that are from both a specific category and a specific date.'

Claine found herself reluctantly impressed by the cataloguing. 'An ingenious system,' she said.

'Was there a specific date you wanted to examine?' Tagg asked her. 'Or should I just show you everything under *Tenzebah?*'

'He has a whole category dedicated to him?' Claine asked, surprised.

'His exploits before he located Elixir were widely read,' Tagg explained. 'His excursions to Malzyme and Tildive were all recorded by the *Gazette. We* were doing stories on Tenzebah *long* before he became famous.'

Interesting, thought Claine. An impressive claim to make, and one that demanded closer inspection. She was certain Melchior would be intrigued to learn more of the immortal's expeditions prior to his discovery of Elixir-whether it helped him with the case or not.

'I'd like to see all records of Tenzebah from 2380 and everything before it,' she said eventually. Garro Tagg's fine eyebrows went up. 'The year he found Elixir, is it not?'

'Yes,' replied Claine. 'I'm curious as to Tenzebah's pre-Elixir days, when he was a galactic adventurer. It must have been spectacular, travelling the stars...exploring exotic worlds...'

'Indeed it was,' Garro Tagg agreed, even though he himself had never been outside the Galmarora System. 'Such a shame his partnership with his fellow adventurer ended in such disagreement...'

Claine glanced at him, wondering if she'd get something interesting out of this reporter without having to consult the archives. 'Elixir, yeah? Both men wanted it, but Tenzebah managed to cheat it into his possession. I can't quite recall the name of his friend...'

Tagg shrugged. 'He was the sort of man who fades into history, merely because his partner, Tenzebah, achieved such fame. You'd be hard-pressed, I think, to find someone who knows his name off the top of their head. Ah- here we are.'

They had stopped at one of the intersections. A screen above them displayed the vibrant green lettering that formed the words *Dunwall Tenzebah & Immortality.* On the shelves below were rows of drawers, each marked with a time period. *2380-Present, 2362-2374,* and *2355-2359.*

Tagg crossed to the most recent date- "2380- Present" and pressed a button set in the middle to open it. He pulled out a small, circular, metal object made up of a disc inside a ring, and showed it to Claine.

'This is a digital record, I don't know if you've seen the likes of it before...' he explained, although Claine was well aware what it was. Tagg seemed to be hinting that she didn't have enough money to afford a digital newspaper, and Claine grudgingly admitted that he was spot on. That, however, did not mean she didn't recognise a digital record when she saw one.

'I've seen one before,' she told him, her voice a couple of degrees colder than before.

Tagg was mildly surprised. 'Of course,' he eventually said, outdoing her by going the opposite extreme and making his voice so warm it was obviously fake. He passed her the record. 'Be very careful with it,' he said. 'We wouldn't want the newspaper's records damaged in any way.'

Claine took the record and placed it in the palm of her hand before twisting the disc in the centre of the object and activating the file.

At once, a small hologram of a newspaper popped up above her palm, with the now-familiar *Eluxure Gazette* logo up the top of the page.

The article was titled *Dunwall Tenzebah Finds Elixir of Life,* and pictured a young Dunwall Tenzebah smiling and holding the strange root she had seen in the photograph in Tenzebah's chambers. The only thing was that his friend was absent from both the photo and the article.

'No mention of the other,' she remarked to Tagg.

'No, there wouldn't be,' Tagg said. 'Before Elixir, neither was more famous than the other. But when Tenzebah alone claimed rights to the miracle drink's discovery, nobody cared for the other half of the duo.'

Claine skimmed the rest of the article, but it told her nothing she didn't already know and nothing that helped her. The most it said about Tenzebah's adventuring partner was, *"Tenzebah discovered the Elixir when on an expedition to the remote dwarf planet of Kilmorim with a friend."*

To be remembered only as "a friend" while Tenzebah achieved fame and glory was unfair, Claine felt. But, on reflection, it could just as easily have been Tenzebah who was forgotten, and the other man renowned throughout the galaxy.

She deactivated the record and handed it back to the still-smiling Garro Tagg. 'Would it be possible for me to view the other files...?'

Tagg spread his arms. 'Go ahead.'

Claine crossed over to the alcove marked *2355-2359* and opened it while Tagg put away the other record. This one was visibly older, as the quality of the disc inside was not as good as the *2380-Present* volume. It still worked well enough, however, and when she activated the projection she was able to read the first article clearly.

Young Adventurers Set Off For Namaddas, was the title, and the accompanying photograph was, Claine realised, the same as one of the photos she'd seen in Tenzebah's chambers- Tenzebah himself and another young man, his as yet unnamed friend, standing in front of a spaceship, proud and excited smiles on their faces. Then she continued to read the article and her eyes widened as she finally came across what she was looking for- the name of the friend.

'Excuse me,' said Garro Tagg, jerking her out of her intense immersion in the article. 'Phone call.'

He fished a metallic, fish-shaped object from his pocket and placed it in his ear.

'Garro Tagg speaking. What?' he turned and walked around the corner, out of Claine's earshot, giving her the opportunity she'd been waiting for.

As soon as she was absolutely positive he couldn't see her, she swiftly deactivated the record and dropped it into her satchel, then closed its drawer as though it still contained the disc- just as Tagg came back around the corner. He looked disgruntled at something, which Claine found immensely satisfying.

'Sorry about that,' he said. 'I trust you've got all the information you need?'

Claine smiled at him, and this time it wasn't forced. *More than you'd think.*

'Just about,' she said.

Chapter Seven

1.

Marsine Tenzebah did not make any effort to avoid the question Corwin asked her.

'Yes,' she said. 'I lied. I didn't purchase Kenderye from the Leisopolis real estate.'

Corwin looked at her defiant, confident gaze, surprised by her forthrightness. He had not expected the impromptu interrogation to go so smoothly, and he suspected from the look of disdain with which Marsine always observed Rodarth that she would not have imparted this information had the other Inspector been there. Rodarth was inside the house at present, interrogating Miss Glamure again for some strange reason of his own.

'In that case,' said Inspector Tirranar, 'Where did you buy it?'

Marsine took a little longer to answer that one, choosing to gaze at the gardens for a few seconds before answering. 'I bought it from a man who wanted to be rid of it,' she said. 'I would have approached the real estate, but...this was before Dunwall was famous. We were rich, yes, but maybe not rich enough to afford a place on Eluxure. And so when this man offered me a deal, I couldn't refuse.'

'Was the transaction...entirely legal?' asked Corwin.

'Possibly not entirely. But if it was anyone who was doing the illegal part, it was most certainly him. I was just a buyer.'

Corwin wasn't sure this was entirely true. In most, if not all, dodgy dealings, the 'dodgy' part extended to both participants in the transaction.

'I wanted this retirement so much, you see,' Marsine continued. 'We'd planned it, we'd envisioned it as the perfect ending for us, and I wanted it to be exactly how we'd pictured it.'

Corwin found himself feeling sorry for Marsine. He could imagine what it might've been like to dream up the perfect retirement with your partner, then to have all that planning crushed like a bug. Yes, Marsine had bought their dream retirement, but it wasn't until now that she'd be able to live it...and now that partner was gone-murdered.

'Thank you,' he told her. 'You've been very helpful.'

Marsine Tenzebah shrugged. 'I'm glad. But I don't see what good knowing the details of the house will do.'

Corwin wasn't too sure himself. But Melchior was, and when Melchior was sure about something it was usually a good idea to just roll with it.

∞

'Oh, excuse me, Mr Tenzebah!' Galion said quickly as Fersilt strode imperiously past, and fell into step with him lest he escape. 'My name is Galion Vasail,' ('I'm delighted to meet you,' Fersilt commented drily) '...and I couldn't help overhearing before that you're a little short on employees...' he went on, unpertubed and possibly unaware that he might have just made a personal comment.

Indeed, if he had been intending to make Fersilt clam up, that certainly did the trick. The businessman stopped walking and glared at the younger man indignantly. This was good for Galion's legs, which were protesting from taking such long steps to keep up with Fersilt's practised stride, but it was not so good for Galion, who found himself under Tenzebah's scrutinizing gaze.

'The details of my business are nobody's concern,' he said. 'Especially not that of reporters. Now if you could leave me alone, I have some urgent matters to attend to.'

Galion knew he didn't. Fersilt never seemed to be actually busy, but pretended to be in order to hide his feeling of claustrophobia when stuck in Kenderye and unable to leave Eluxure. It was quite obvious he hated being cooped up while the police took their time to locate his father's killer.

'Wait, sir!' called Galion, nearly running to catch up with Mr Tenzebah Jr, who had already resumed his purposeful stride and was now halfway down the hall. 'I'm not a reporter! I'm a mechanic.'

Fersilt stopped again and eyed him critically, distracted from his "busy schedule" for a moment by Galion's sudden revelation.

'You do look much more like a mechanic than a reporter,' he said, looking at his clothes and tool belt. 'But I should like to know what exactly you're doing here, and why you have chosen to pester me so incessantly.'

'I got fired recently, sir,' explained Galion quickly, should Fersilt lose interest after a certain amount of listening to his plight. 'And I heard you were here, so-'

'So you're looking for a job,' finished Fersilt, unimpressed, in a tone that indicated that Galion was not the first person to approach him in such a manner, on such a topic. 'I see. Well, I'm afraid you're mistaken, Mister Vasail. I have no shortage of workers at this present time and I certainly have no need of more.'

With that he turned and began to ascend the staircase to

their right.

'But, wait, sir-'

'Not another word, please, Mr Vasail,' Tenzebah Jr cut him off loudly. 'I may consider you at a later time, if you have a resume and evidence to support why you think I should employ you, but for now, kindly do not press me!'

And then he was gone from view, leaving Galion standing at the bottom of the staircase somewhat dejectedly, unsure what to do or where to go.

Corwin found Inspector Rodarth in Trissilan Glamure's study, dedicated to Dunwall Tenzebah's messages, papers and files. He was not sure Rodarth actually had cause to interview the poor girl a second time, but generally that was the case- Rodarth rarely had reason to do half the things he did.

Miss Glamure, however, was still admirably composed, even though Corwin knew that Rodarth had probably been hammering her with unnecessary questions for the past half-hour. In fact, she wasn't even looking at the Inspector, but was thoroughly engrossed in typing something into a holo-computer in front of her.

'If you don't mind, Inspector,' said Trissilan, eyes on the projection, 'I'm in the middle of sorting out Mr Tenzebah's files. It's been a very taxing job and it is exceedingly hard to concentrate with you *breathing down my neck.*'

She looked up when Corwin entered and flashed her naturally disarming smile at him. The sun streaming in through the window caught her strawberry blonde hair in an oddly distracting way that Corwin guessed came in useful to her when seducing someone. For Trissilan was most definitely a seductive young woman, and it was quite obvious why Tenzebah had felt attracted to her despite their massive difference in age. This only reinforced Corwin's image of Tenzebah as a disgusting old man.

'Inspector Tirranar!' she gushed. 'I was beginning to wonder where you were. It's been *hell* sorting out these files, and Mr Rodarth here hasn't been helping.' She flashed Rodarth a glare, which he returned. Corwin did not fail to notice the fact that Miss Glamure very deliberately refrained from addressing Rodarth as Inspector.

'May I remind you, Miss Glamure,' said Rodarth, gritting his teeth, 'that this is a murder case, and the police expect nothing but your full co-operation!'

'I've given it!' Trissilan responded. 'I've given you all the information I know! I was here, in the study, sorting out Dunwall's bank details.'

Corwin frowned. Trissilan had told them *where* she was at the time of the murder, but he hadn't heard her say what she had been doing. 'What was it about Tenzebah's bank details that needed to be sorted out?'

Trissilan pouted. 'As I kept telling *him,'* she shot a look at Rodarth, 'Tenzebah had retired suddenly, out of the blue. There was hardly enough time to transfer *all* of his money to a retiree's account cleanly. And before you ask for the five thousandth time *today*,' (again this was aimed at Rodarth) 'I have no idea *why* he retired in the first place. I'm getting sick of answering the same old questions.'

A sudden thought occurred to Corwin. *Trissilan...Dunwall's personal files...why he retired in the first place...*

'Miss Glamure,' he asked slowly. 'You said you had access to Tenzebah's personal files.'

Trissilan frowned. 'Yeah. I'm the only one who does, now.'

'Well, in that case...' Corwin glanced at her holo-computer. 'Would you, by chance, give us access?'

Trissilan nodded. 'Well, I'd have to, wouldn't I, if you asked. The law and all that. What do you think you'll find?'

'I'm not entirely sure,' Corwin admitted. 'But if Tenzebah received a holo-message just before the date of his...impromptu retirement...then that message might contain a clue as to why.'

Trissilan's eyes widened. 'I'm an idiot. I should've checked that sooner. But Dunwall's files are a mess now he's dead. I didn't want to tackle them yet until I had to.'

'No,' Rodarth interrupted. 'You shouldn't've checked

that sooner. You should have given the police access to the victim's personal files sooner.'

'I didn't think they'd contain anything useful,' Miss Glamure replied insolently. Then she glanced at Corwin. 'If you think they'll help, I'll find it for you.'

She stood and began rummaging through a tray of electronic chips- datafiles, Corwin realised. Then she let out a triumphant 'a-ha!' and produced a small chip no bigger than a fingernail. Rodarth put out his hand but Trissilan made a point of ignoring it and instead placed the chip in Corwin's palm.

'This chip contains all of Dunwall's holo-messages between when he retired, a few months ago, to now,' she said. 'Good luck sorting through it all.'

'Thank you, Miss Glamure,' said Corwin, pocketing it. 'You've been very helpful.'

Trissilan smiled brilliantly at him, and Rodarth made a strange gutteral noise that sounded somewhere between a choke and a whimper, before sweeping out the room...

...and nearly collided with Galion for the second time in the past few days.

'Mr Vasail,' Rodarth said. 'Or should I say Garro Tagg? I saw the article in the *Eluxure Gazette*.'

Galion was plunged into improvisation, as he had no idea what Rodarth was talking about. He decided to roll with it, even though the slightest inconsistent remark could give him away completely. 'Garro Tagg is my pseudonym, Inspector.'

It was a fair guess. Rodarth had mentioned the newspaper that Galion was pretending he worked for, and it was clear that Garro Tagg was the author of an article on the Tenzebah murder.

Thankfully, Rodarth nodded. 'I also noticed, Mr Vasail, that you claim to know a great deal about the case?'

Galion adopted what he hoped was a self-important expression that in his eyes befitted a reporter who had just made a successful scoop- for he was fairly sure the scoop would have been very successful indeed. 'That's right,' he said with a bit of a swagger.

Rodarth nodded again, still looking at Galion with an unnerving intensity, his signature thin smile on his lips. 'Well, let me tell you now, "Tagg", you don't. And don't try claiming that you do, because I know for a fact that most of what you've written were complete lies.'

Galion continued to look at him self-importantly, and threw an irritating grin into the mix as well. 'You know what we journalists say. "What the public don't know won't hurt 'em".'

Rodarth ignored him and pushed past none too gently before crackling down the hallway like a brewing thunderstorm.

Galion looked at Corwin, eyebrows raised questioningly. *What's his problem?*

'Tell the lizard I've got Dunny's files,' Corwin said out

the corner of his mouth instead of a reply, as he too brushed past him.

Galion was left standing in the hallway contemplating the coded message. The lizard was obviously Melchior, and Dunny was Tenzebah- that was the nickname workers in Leisopolis gave to the until-recently immortal. And his files...could probably only mean literally his files.

'Come on, don't be shy,' Miss Glamure said, making him jump. She flashed him a seductive grin as he took a tentative step inside the study.

'You're a journalist, yeah?' she asked, looking him up and down with one eyebrow raised. 'Don't look much like one.'

'I get that a lot,' said Galion, not untruthfully.

Trissilan laughed. 'You aren't half bad, though. Bet you get that a lot, too.'

'Err...' Galion found himself distracted by her iridescent eyes, her golden-red hair, the shape of her vibrant crimson lips...'not really, no.'

He frowned, shaking his head. Trissilan was using vast amounts of charm, and he found it doing a fairly good job on his brain. But helping Melchior out was priority, and that included questioning suspects on his behalf.

It wouldn't hurt to let myself be seduced, he thought, *I'm sure that would make it much easier to get information.*

But he refrained. It occurred to him that Trissilan might

109

be part Pristilian. He'd heard about the women of Pristile seducing off-worlders by altering their brain patterns ever so slightly. He did not want his brain patterns altered, however slightly, but Miss Glamure seemed to be turning the old Pristilian charm on full-blast.

'What are you after?' she asked him, batting her eyelashes. 'I know you're already *very* well informed. I read your article.'

There was that article again. Galion made a mental note to read it before continuing his masquerade as a journalist. The real *Gazette* could very easily throw his entire impersonation out the window, especially if everyone on Eluxure had read the latest issue.

'I'm hoping to do a follow-up article,' he said. 'You know, to kind of give the readers updates on the case until it's solved.'

'I like it,' Miss Glamure said. 'But I do hope it's solved soon. I want Dunwall's killer caught.'

There was something in her voice then that wasn't a Pristilian spell. It occurred to Galion that Trissilan's affair with Dunwall had been much more than just a fling, and that the details of their romantic involvement had not been fully explained- by Marsine, who still refused to acknowledge that it had existed, or by Trissilan herself, who had more than reason enough to keep the whole thing as secret as possible.

'I think Rodarth suspects *I* did it,' she went on. 'But he

has no evidence. *You* don't think I did it, do you, Garro?'

Galion blinked, aware that she had called him by his supposed 'pseudonym', which was most likely some honest-to-goodness *Gazette* reporter's actual name. 'Uh, no, I can't imagine you murdering someone.'

That wasn't entirely true. He wasn't completely certain about anything with Trissilan- except for that the likelihood of her killing Tenzebah was fairly low. That aside, however, Galion was not convinced that she was completely incapable of killing *someone.* But that was probably not Rodarth's train of thought.

The Inspector seemed to have done a lot of *insinuating* in his investigations. His method seemed to be to accuse everyone of murder and see if anyone confessed. It was only a matter of time before someone cracked and confessed even if they were innocent. The maid, namely. What had Claine called her? T'chisa.

But Galion found it hard to picture Trissilan cracking.

'Sorry I can't help you more,' she said. 'I gave the police Dunwall's personal files...they wanted to check his messages, but I don't suppose you'll manage to get a hold of them.'

That, thought Galion, *might be easier than you think.*

'No, that's perfectly fine,' he said aloud. Trissilan had been of much more help than she thought- the conversation had not been a waste of time at all. Neither had Miss Glamure, for that matter...

But that was the Pristilian charm working on his brain patterns, wasn't it?

'It's been nice talking to you,' he found himself saying.

'And you,' she replied, a playful smile on her lips. She rose to leave the room, and stopped facing Galion in the narrow doorway, altogether too close for comfort. He could smell her intoxicating narristery-scented perfume.

'I'd better leave the *Gazette's* next article in your *very* capable hands,' she said. 'I look forward to it.'

Then she let go of his collar (when had she been holding it?) and swept from the room, leaving him standing in the study doorway with a freshly Pristilian-beguiled brain.

2.

Melchior was thinking. In fact, he had been for some time-it was a skill all Reptids possessed. Most humans, and indeed most intelligent life, would not be able to sit still, quietly, and just *think* for such extended periods of time. But as for Reptids, well, as a rule, Reptids had infinite patience and have produced some of the galaxy's best thinkers and philosophers.

Melchior was not a philosopher- nor would he have been welcomed as a Reptid should he return to his home world. But he *was* a detective, and such a role required patience and thought. He thought about Kenderye, and kept coming back to Marsine Tenzebah, who had bought a house decorated with coincidentally relevant references to eternity, *before* her husband had discovered Elixir. Ornaments such as the wallpiece depicting Ouroboros, the endless snake, and paintings of the Fountain of Youth could easily have been added to the decor after the mansion's purchase, but the statues of Astelpine, the inbuilt mosaics of Miskitus the Purple and the Goblet of Life...those things had come with Kenderye, as part of the package.

And then there were the other suspects. Fersilt Tenzebah persisted in imitating a constant rush of business, yet there was nothing business related he could possibly be doing from afar. His company may well be in disarray, as he constantly kept telling everyone, but it was unclear which of his sentences were true and which were conjured up to protect his reputation.

As for the other two, the maid and the assistant, Melchior had no idea. The maid, T'chisa, seemed increasingly timid, and whilst Claine was certain she was impressively strong, mentally, for a N'choth'ni, it didn't mean she wasn't fragile. And Trissilan Glamure... well, Melchior had not heard much from Corwin regarding her, except that she masked her true feelings well under thick layerings of charm.

And the skeleton, too, still puzzled the Reptid, though he knew all of this pondering was futile- it would get him nowhere until the others returned- perhaps with something useful.

Elixir had been stolen when Tenzebah was in his armchair, yet there were not the signs of a struggle one would expect from a direct burglary of something the victim kept on them at all times. It was also unlikely that Tenzebah had been drugged. Even if someone had managed to slip something into his last batch of Elixir, no available drug would put someone in a deep enough sleep for Elixir deprivation to take effect.

There was a sudden knocking at his door, followed by Corwin's voice: 'Hoy, Rastis!'

'Enter,' called Melchior, and the door opened to admit the Inspector, who helped himself to a gaffleut from the wooden bowl in the centre of the room before sitting down opposite Melchior with it.

'Do you want to know what I found?' he asked mysteriously, peeling the skin from the gaffleut, revealing the bright magenta flesh inside.

Melchior eyed him drily. 'No, I don't. I want to remain in ignorance until I find out myself.'

Corwin grinned easily and removed the centre of the gaffleut, discarding the inedible, caviar-like outer layer. 'Well, I won't tell you, then.'

Melchior fixed him with a piercing gaze, forcing Corwin Tirranar himself, stirrer extraordinaire, to relent.

'Okay, okay,' said the Inspector quickly, taking a bite of

the gaffleut. 'I've managed to access Dunwall Tenzebah's personal files.'

Melchior sat forward, pleasantly surprised at his old friend's resourcefulness. 'And have you found anything in them yet?'

'That's what I came to tell you about,' said the Inspector brightly. 'I believe we've found something very important indeed.'

'Which is?' asked Melchior. 'I know full well that you are deliberately procrastinating in order to prolong my discomfort. Trust me, I intend to ensure that you get as little enjoyment out of said discomfort as possible.'

'Well, I think we've got the reason for Tenzebah's retirement,' said Corwin, a faint smile on his face (for despite Melchior's vow, he was still enjoying "said discomfort" immensely.) 'I've put Constable Cadez on examining Dunwall's more recent holomail messages-should distract him from Trissilan Glamure, and-'

'Why does Cadez need distracting from Miss Glamure?' Melchior interrupted, momentarily distracted from the promised discovery.

Corwin rolled his eyes. 'Cadez has a certain weakness for pretty girls,' he said. 'So you can see why he might be attracted by Miss Glamure. Seems to have got it into his head that they've got a thing.'

'A thing.'

'Yes,' said Corwin. 'A relationship. But Miss Glamure, I

think, would not launch so easily into another affair so soon after her most recent lover's death.'

Very interesting, thought Melchior, and he wasn't sure who he found so- Cadez or Trissilan. He recalled Cadez, at the very start of the investigation, claiming he knew T'chisa, when he couldn't possibly have. Maybe his story of a fling with Miss Glamure was not a complete lie after all. If that was the case, it would add a new dimension to the whole affair, and possibly introduce another suspect into play...

'Go on,' Melchior said aloud.

Corwin opened his mouth to speak, but was interrupted by the door bursting open and Galion entering.

'No luck with Fersilt,' said Galion. 'He knows I'm a mechanic, but hopefully he won't mention it to anyone, like Rodarth. But besides that, he said he *might,* emphasis on *might,* "consider me" at a "later date". But for now, apparently, he's "very busy" and has "no need" of workers at the moment.'

Melchior frowned. Fersilt kept insisting that his company was in disarray in his absence, and according to Corwin, one of the things he had been complaining about was insufficient staffing.

'That said,' Galion continued, 'Today wasn't a complete waste of time.'

'Oh?' asked Melchior, intrigued but at the same time torn between Corwin's discovery and Galion's. His indecision was saved by Claine, however, who chose that precise moment to burst in with a triumphant smile on her face and a small metal disc in her hand.

'You won't *believe* what I've just found,' she said.

'Jump in the queue,' sighed Corwin.

Claine lowered her hand, but she didn't look put out. On the contrary, she looked prepared to wait, which was an admirable skill for a reporter to have.

'Go on, Galion,' said Corwin. 'What was it you were saying?'

'Well, I had a *very* productive talk with Miss Glamure-'

Claine's eyebrows shot up, proving that journalists can't stay completely motionless and completely silent simultaneously. '*Did* you, now?'

Galion went slightly red. 'No, I mean...I didn't- she didn't...' He stopped, and corrected himself. 'Well, it wasn't *my* fault that she tried to seduce me. She's part Pristilian!'

Melchior, who had been sitting with his fingers steepled in front of him, suddenly turned and looked round at him. 'You're certain.'

'Well, not *positive,* but I'm fairly sure she is,' amended Galion. 'From what I remember, Pristilian women seduce men by altering their brains, telepathically, yeah? It's like a love charm or something.'

Claine's eyebrows hadn't been lowered. She was still looking at Galion inquisitively, and there was a touch of humour at his expense in the tone of her voice and the line of her mouth. Galion suspected she might have been trying not to laugh. 'Go on,' she said.

'Well, Trissilan,' Galion went on, looking distinctly more uncomfortable than before, 'she was using Pristilian charm on me, full-blast, I'm sure of it. I was *almost* seduced.'

'Almost,' Claine repeated. 'So you weren't...even a little bit?'

'What makes you so sure that Miss Glamure's charm was not natural?' Melchior broke in, saving Galion from having to reply to Claine's comment- he had certainly gone a deeper shade of red than before.

'Well, when she'd left, and after it had worn off a bit, I sort of realised...' Galion glanced nervously around the room. Claine was still looking at him with a mix of curiosity and humour. 'I don't actually feel attracted to her. You know, normally.'

Corwin nodded. 'It certainly fits. Miss Glamure has a certain...distracting quality about her, but I doubt she's been using as much of a severe amount of Pristilian charm on Rodarth and myself as she has on Galion here.'

Melchior nodded. 'And it most definitely explains Constable Cadez's...obsession with her.'

Claine had a sudden thought, and she voiced it now. 'Do you think Trissilan may have been using her Pristilian...abilities to seduce Tenzebah? Maybe their "affair" was nothing more than her charming her way into a little bit more fame and wealth?'

'It's a possibility,' Melchior said, acknowledging the suggestion with a gracious nod. 'I hadn't considered such an...arrangement. But surely murdering Dunwall Tenzebah would hardly help there...'

'Unless,' murmured Corwin, 'there was the prospect of immortality involved...'

That, they all thought, was very possible. It gave Miss Glamure a deeper motive for murder- if indeed it had been she who had murdered Tenzebah.

'Corwin,' said Melchior. 'What is it *you* were about to say before Galion entered the room?'

'Ah,' said Inspector Tirranar, as the familiar grin resurfaced. 'You'd better be proud of me, Rastis. I took over sorting through Tenzebah's files from Cadez when his shift ended, but it was clear that we wouldn't be getting anywhere in the near future. The files were all jumbled, see- all the dates were out of order. Can't think how Tenzebah let his account get so untidy. Anyway, since the dates were out of whack, I thought, *what if I changed the category search*?'

'And...?' pressed Melchior.

'I changed the files to *by contact* rather than *by date,*' grinned Corwin, clearly loving this, 'and right up the top, I found one Unknown contact with a very interesting message.'

'Which was?' asked Claine slowly, a quizzical expression on her face.

'Well, I couldn't *bring* the files, of course, seeing as they're in police custody and I'm technically not allowed, but I wrote the message down somewhere, wait a mo...' he fished a scrap of paper from his pocket and cleared his throat, then glanced up and grinned cheekily. 'Shall I read it?'

'Yes!' said Melchior, Claine and Galion, both forcefully and simultaneously.

'Okay,' replied Corwin, 'It went like this:

Hello again, old friend. I'm sorry I haven't kept in touch, but the reason for me contacting you now is that I am going to reclaim what was mine- I think you know what I mean. And I think you know that I have the means to take it. I'm warning you, Dunwall, but you know it won't do you any good. I will *have Elixir.*
-S.C

There was a silence following the readout of the mysterious holo-mail. Then Melchior said, 'And that is why Dunwall Tenzebah retired.'

Corwin nodded. 'This S.C is obviously someone Tenzebah feared. They'd have to have been, if they managed to scare him enough that he'd go to Kenderye, the one place he thought he'd be safe- and which turned out to be his place of death.'

'I wonder if S.C knew he could kill Tenzebah just by taking Elixir?' asked Galion. 'And if Tenzebah himself did?'

'And more importantly,' added Corwin, '*Who* is S.C?'

Claine cleared her throat, immediately capturing the attention of the three men. Or rather, two men and a reptile.

'I think I can help there,' she said.

Galion raised his eyebrows in a perfect imitation of Claine earlier. '*Do* you now?'

'Ha ha, very funny,' she said. 'I made a trip to the *Eluxure Gazette* today-'

'Oh,' interrupted Galion suddenly, 'did you read-?'

'Don't ask,' was the flat reply. 'A bunch of cretins. And the *real* Garro Tagg was completely insufferable.'

Galion grinned. 'Unlike me.'

Claine shot him a look. 'Don't bet on it. Anyway, my *point* is that I managed to access the *Eluxure Gazette's* entire collection of records on Tenzebah articles of the past. *And,* I managed to steal some.'

She seemed to realise then that she had just confessed to theft in front of a legal officer. 'Err, if you could unhear that, Inspector Tirranar, that would be great.'

He waved a dismissive hand, though on his face rested an exasperated expression. 'Unhear what?'

Claine smiled at him, then held the metal disc aloft once

more. '*This,*' she announced, 'is the complete archival records of *Gazette* articles about Tenzebah from 2355 to 2359.'

'And,' Melchior put in, beginning to catch on to what Claine may have discovered, 'do they involve Tenzebah's still unnamed friend, by any chance?'

'They do,' said Claine. She set the record down on the table and twisted the middle ring. At once, a holographic projection sprung out of the disc- a newspaper article, titled *Young Adventurers Set Off for Namaddas.*

The picture accompanying the article was recognised by the others, like Claine too had recognised, as one of the photographs from Tenzebah's chambers.

'Read the article, if you will,' said Claine dramatically, 'and within it you will find mention of the same man who wrote our mysterious holomail message.'

Melchior did as requested, but did not have to read far into the article to see exactly what Claine meant.

"The 24th Century is a time for innovation and daring, and today's world praises and honours such adventurers as these two young men (pictured), who are about to set off for the abandoned world of Namaddas in search of artefacts, riches and fame. Dunwall Tenzebah, aged 25, is an avid researcher of worlds such as Namaddas, and is thrilled to be given the chance to travel there in the spaceship Crusade, *an expensive model of shuttle designed*

by Tenzebah's own father, Aikenald Tenzebah. The other half of the crew is an equally as daring young man by the name of..."

Here Melchior stopped reading, and his eyes darted back to the photograph, studying it with more intense scrutiny than he had before. Now that he knew who it was, he could easily see the resemblance. The young man pictured was very good-looking, and had blonde hair instead of grey, but despite the vast difference in his age then and his age now, Melchior could now see the until-recently-mysterious adventurer for the rich, arrogant retiree he was today.

'S.C,' he said, and he saw Claine smile triumphantly at the look of sudden comprehension on his face. 'Sadrien Chasterleigh.'

Chapter Eight

1.

Rodarth sighed as he saw Rastis Melchior through the window, approaching the interrogation room with a certain purpose that, for some inexplicable reason, the Inspector found ominous.

'What's he doing here?' he asked Corwin, sweeping an accusing glare on his colleague, whose own expression answered Rodarth's with a weary look.

'You banned Rastis from the crime scene, not the police station,' Corwin replied. 'And before you *do* ban him from here as well, I might remind you that technically you can't. If Rastis were reporting an offense he witnessed, for example-'

'He would probably investigate it himself without calling the police,' muttered Rodarth.

'OR,' continued Corwin, a little louder, 'if he were to confess to a crime, or to make a citizen's arrest or *anything* that required him to be at the police station, you could not prevent him from doing so.'

'I am aware,' sneered Rodarth, 'that I am unable to ban the lizard from the station, Inspector Tirranar. However, it *is* within my power to prohibit him from sitting in on an interrogation.'

'Unless I asked him to,' Corwin replied, and received a surprised look from Rodarth.

Before the Inspector could say anything, however, Melchior entered the room, inclining his head to both men before sitting down on their side of the table.

'So Inspector Tirranar asked you to...assist with this particular interview, eh?' Rodarth asked him.

Melchior met his gaze levelly. 'Inspector Tirranar thought it best, especially considering that I played a part in discovering Mr Chasterleigh's history.'

'Not much of a part,' smirked Rodarth. 'I seem to recall it was the police who discovered the holomail message in the first place.'

Corwin cleared his throat, looking pointedly at the two of them. He hadn't failed to notice the fact that in saying "the police", Rodarth was subtly including himself, despite the fact that it was mostly, if not entirely, Corwin who had found the mysterious holomail signed S.C.

'Should I call in the suspect?' he asked.

Rodarth grunted, which Corwin decided to take as a 'yes'.

'Constable!' he called, and Cadez responded almost immediately, sticking his head inside the door.

'Sir?'

'Please bring in Sadrien Chasterleigh,' Corwin instructed him. Cadez gave a nod and retracted his head once more.

A moment later, the door to the interrogation room opened again and in came Sadrien Chasterleigh, wearing a suit as white as his gleaming mansion and looking thoroughly disgruntled at being called into the police station as a murder suspect.

'What's all this about?' he asked.

'Take a seat, Mr Chasterleigh,' Rodarth said. Sadrien, seeing no other visible option, sat down facing the two inspectors (and Melchior).

'Do you recognise this holomail, Mr Chasterleigh?' asked Corwin, activating a hologram in the middle of the table. An image of the message sprung up, complete with the initials that matched those of the man in front of them.

Sadrien clenched his jaw as he read, but managed to answer the question both calmly and indirectly. 'S.C...that could be literally anyone.'

Melchior sat forward. 'Except it isn't. Is it, Mr

Chasterleigh?'

Sadrien looked at him defiantly, and Melchior pressed on. 'It's very convenient for you that history neglected to remember you- it means that you can still use your real name without anyone connecting it to that of Dunwall Tenzebah.'

Sadrien Chasterleigh's jaw tightened even further, but he still refrained from saying anything.

'We examined the newspaper, the *Eluxure Gazette's* historical archives,' Corwin put in, picking up from where Melchior left off. 'And we found your name, Mr Chasterleigh.'

Sadrien drummed his fingers on the table, silent for five long counts. Then he sighed and sat back in his chair. 'Fine. You've got me. Yeah, I was Dunwall's friend, not that it means much any more.'

He looked up at the inspectors, and Rodarth said, 'Go on.'

'Our fathers were both rich,' Sadrien continued. 'That's how we knew each other. Tenzebah was twenty-five, I was about nineteen, but we both had a passion for adventure, and so we made plans to launch a private expedition to Namaddas.'

'And you became famous as a result,' Corwin said.

'Semi-famous,' Sadrien corrected, somewhat ruefully. 'After Namaddas, we set off on another expedition, to Malzyme, about two years after. Brought back a few shiny trophies. Sure, everyone knew us, but that was pretty short-lived. Eventually we parted, went our own ways- Dunwall married Marsine, I married my Larillan. Everything was fine, and we still kept in touch with each other.'

Sadrien glanced up again as if to see whether they wanted him to keep talking, and saw that they did. He sighed again. 'About ten years later I became...obsessed with the fabled Elixir. Everybody thought it was a myth, but I was determined to prove them wrong. I spent hours every day researching Elixir, and finally I found something. A lead- that I might find Elixir on Kilmorim. And so I contacted Dunwall, and we patched up his father's ship, the one we used to go adventuring in- the *Crusade.* It was *my* expedition,' he said with a touch of bitterness.

'Well, what happened?' asked Rodarth, somewhat impatiently.

'We found Elixir, all right. It looked pretty disappointing, but it just *felt* like it was really... *"that which grants the owner eternal life"-* The Encyclopaedia Immortale, page 65.' replied Sadrien.

Melchior put his head to one side, interested. 'And why do you say that?'

Sadrien looked slightly surprised, as though he hadn't really thought of it very much. 'Well...it was strange. As soon as we found it, we were... *enchanted* by it. Like it wanted to be found. We'd planned to share ownership of

Elixir, but that wasn't how Elixir worked. It...made us *want* it for ourselves. Both of us desired eternal life, though I had never desired such immortality before. I set out for fame, not Elixir's power, but as soon as I found what I was looking for, I realised I wanted both. And Dunwall did as well. On the way back to Palpoutha- that was where we set off- we had an argument over Elixir. It got pretty heated, and eventually he stranded me on Kelxaragg and flew off with *my* artefact. Elixir *should* have been mine. Dunwall's fame should have been mine. But when he alone got back, he claimed I'd died on Kilmorim.'

There was a silence after Sadrien's story. He looked at the others. 'Happy? That's what happened on our last expedition together. He betrayed me, and stole my fame.'

'So you had every reason to kill him,' Rodarth summarised.

'Sure, I did,' Sadrien said. 'But that doesn't mean I did it.'

'You had every opportunity,' persisted Rodarth. 'You were on Eluxure at the time of his death. You had the motive, and what's more you *threatened* to reclaim Elixir from him.'

'I didn't kill Dunwall Tenzebah!' replied Sadrien, his voice several notches louder than Rodarth's. 'It doesn't matter what *you* think, Inspector, but I'm not the murderer. But believe me, I wish I was.'

'He fits all of the evidence,' insisted Rodarth.

After Sadrien had left, the Inspector had been adamant of his guilt, despite Melchior's probably better-judged opinion that things still didn't add up.

'Sadrien Chasterleigh is the only one who *could* have done it. He wanted revenge on Tenzebah for stealing his fame and his glory, and he wanted to reclaim what he thought was rightfully his- Elixir, just like he said in the holomail message.'

Melchior opened his mouth to say something here, but Rodarth did not leave him an opening in which to interject.

'He threatened Tenzebah into retiring, and in doing so brought him right into his clutches,' said Rodarth. 'And he knew just as much about Elixir as Tenzebah himself, if not more.'

'However,' interrupted Melchior, finally finding the opportunity to get a word in edgewise. 'However, two facts remain.'

Rodarth turned a sneering look on him. 'Oh? And what are they?'

'One; he refused to confess to the crime, even though everything points towards his guilt,' said the Reptid. 'Surely, if he had committed the crime, he would have felt that he had no choice but to admit to the murder.'

Corwin nodded. 'That's true.'

'Two,' continued Melchior. 'The other thing he did not

confess to was the holomail.'

Rodarth scoffed and turned away.

'If my previous observation was accurate,' said the Reptid, 'Then he would have admitted to having sent the threatening message if he had indeed committed the crime, as he would have felt there was no way out of the situation but confession. But since Sadrien did *not* confess to the sending of the holomail, it may mean that he did not send it. Which would mean that he is not as guilty as you think him, Inspector Rodarth.'

'That's hardly anything to go by, Rastis,' Corwin admitted grudgingly, which prompted a 'ha!' from Rodarth.

'It is not,' agreed Melchior. 'But in my experience, "hardly anything" is usually enough.'

2.

Melchior shielded his eyes from the glaring Eluxure sunlight as he stepped out of the police station and into the open. Leisopolis was in peak hour, but that hardly meant anything on the retirement planet. The busiest it got would be considered mild back on Sildrone, and he was forced to recall that he was in fact *not* on Sildrone, with its strangely shaped buildings and its many levels of airborne traffic racing past, and a long way down should an aircar lose power. Instead, Melchior was on lazy

Eluxure, with its slow-moving 'traffic' (which wasn't at all bad) and its constant, mind-numbing glare, (which was), to which he was unaccustomed, and to which he had no desire to *become* accustomed. Each to his own, he thought. If this was considered the 'ideal' retirement, Melchior decided that he would retire somewhere that was not considered ideal. Like Fiskerbab, or (heaven forbid) Morborgue. Anywhere except this ridiculously sunny planet with its rich, dishonest old people and its glorious landscape.

He would be exceptionally glad when this case was over. He had no idea who to suspect, and who was the more likely suspect, and to top it off he had to solve it on a planet such as Eluxure, with an incompetent, racist, *idiotic* Inspector.

'Leisopolis Shipyards,' said a voice nearby, tinged with impatience and infused with the brisk tone of someone who was late for something. There was a certain familiar, arrogant quality to the speaker's voice that made Melchior turn and look, then quickly turn back again, hoping he hadn't been recognised. The chances of this were quite low, seeing as he was both close to seven standard galactic feet and vivid turquoise.

Miraculously, however, the Reptid went unnoticed amongst the scatterings of what couldn't really be classified as a crowd, for Fersilt Tenzebah didn't give him a second look as he stepped into the robot-driven hover-car with a somewhat ruffled air.

Fersilt, of course, was confined to the area, like all suspects, and whilst he was perfectly allowed to venture into the city, the shipyards seemed an odd, and in fact suspicious, place to visit.

Melchior stepped forward as the hover-car took off down the street, and as the next one passed it scanned him holographically, recognised his posture as that used galaxy-wide by people who wished to hail such a vehicle, and screeched to a stop.

'Please select a destination,' asked the robotic system built into the vehicle, in a flat, completely computer-generated voice that made Melchior miss the intelligent Hovelocity driver robots back on Sildrone.

'Leisopolis Shipyards,' Melchior told it.

'Request computed,' said the robot. 'Please select a speed at which you would prefer to travel.'

Melchior had to think about that one. He wanted to get there quickly without beating Fersilt. Then it occurred to him that Fersilt was also in a hurry for whatever reason, and therefore would select the fastest speed available.

'Full speed, please,' he instructed, getting into the car.

'Request computed. Please enter the hover-car.'

Melchior did as he was told.

'Passenger status- inside vehicle,' said the pre-recorded voice, and a smiley face appeared on the screen in the front of the vehicle. 'Repeat request- Leisopolis Shipyards at full speed.'

The hover-car took off with a lurch. There was no noticeable acceleration- the vehicle went from stationary to full speed in less than a second, but Melchior's trust in modern technology, whilst little, was enough to assure himself that the robot knew what it was doing.

Gravity stabilisers detracted from the feeling that the he was in a rollercoaster, and in fact the sensation, once the lurch of sudden speed had passed, was as though they were still stationary.

Nothing but the best tech here on Eluxure, he thought.

As the scenery of Leisopolis sped past, Melchior kept his eyes on the hover-car in front of them- the one carrying Fersilt. Not that it would do much good- the expensive, Eluxure-made hover-cars would get them to the right place at the right speed just as they requested. Robot-driven vehicles showed no aversion to traffic or any of the other problems an "organic" driver would otherwise encounter, and always carried out the requests of passengers efficiently and exactly as they had been given.

That said, Melchior found the use of a Hovelocity vehicle, or whatever the equivalent was on Eluxure, exceedingly dull, as the driver had not the personality or the intelligence to make for any sort of conversation. In order to communicate with them, you first had to ask them a question, which they could only answer if it was within their programming or expertise.

Soon, the Shipyards came into view- they were, essentially, the city centre, seeing as Leisopolis' sole purpose seemed to be for tourists and for retirees flying in from their respective planets. A few spaceships and aircraft hovered in the air above it or, in the case of the larger, classic rockets, stood surrounded by scaffolding or security pylons. The smaller ships, used for cargo or personal reasons, rather than passenger-carting or touring, were in the huge hangars that stood in the centre of the Shipyards, unless they had just arrived or were preparing to takeoff. Melchior saw Fersilt's vehicle come to a sudden stop, going from full-speed to stationary again without so much as a jolt. Fersilt got out and looked around in a paranoid sort of way, as if somebody might be watching.

Well, Mr Tenzebah, thought Melchior, *I'm afraid somebody is watching.*

Fersilt approached the main hangar, and, after looking around him again, entered just as Melchior's car came to a similar, abrupt stop.

'You have reached your destination. Please pay directly.'

Melchior sat, not entirely patiently, while the car scanned his face, accessed his account and deposited the cost of the trip from his account to that of the hover-taxi business.

'Please get out of the vehicle,' said the robotic voice. 'Your payment has been processed. Get out of the vehicle.'

'Yes, yes,' muttered Melchior, swinging his legs out of

his seat and getting out of the vehicle.

As soon as he was out, the door closed and the vehicle sped off again.

That, thought Melchior, would be the last time he called a hover-taxi while he was on Eluxure, if, of course, he didn't have to in order to get back to his hotel.

Melchior opened the side door to the hangar as quietly as he could, hoping the creak it made didn't reach the ears of Fersilt. He crept along the side of a Venturer XC model shuttle-ship, with the words *Maskxav Malloki* emblazoned on the side, then stopped as he heard voices from just around the other side of the ship.

'I'm sorry, Mr Tenzebah, but we've had to make other arrangements. You know how it is-'

'Yes, I know how it is,' hissed Fersilt's voice impatiently. 'But I don't like it. I'm a very busy man, and I want this done quickly, efficiently and without leaving a trace.'

'You know I can't do that, sir. I don't care if your business is about to go down the toilet, but this is a very time-consuming operation, and-'

'To hell with your operation, man! This doesn't have to be as complicated as you think it will be. I'm offering a substantial amount of money and I refuse to be caught up with anything illegal in which you happen to already be involved.'

'We can't just change our entire schedule like that, Mr

Tenzebah, sir...'

The second, unknown speaker, who appeared to be a Shipyards worker, moved closer to the Venturer XC, and Melchior realised he would have to move, lest he be discovered. Scanning the floor, his eyes alit on a small metal tool of some sort- a spanner, maybe? Galion would certainly know, but the specifics of the tool were irrelevant- as long as it was heavy, that was all that mattered. Melchior closed his fingers around the object, counted to three, and tossed it across the hangar. It hit a small PodDule ship with a clang, making Fersilt and the other man look towards the place it hit with a sudden, surprised jolt. Using this momentary distraction to his benefit, Melchior darted across the gap between the Venturer and the next ship, a cargo holder by the name of *Shinderinnian,* perfectly aware that if Fersilt or the other man turned around, they would see him immediately.

But no, he made it to the *Shinderinnian* just in time, letting out a deep breath as Fersilt turned away from the place where the spanner had fallen.

'Do you have raspins in here?' he asked the other man with something that might have been disgust.

The other man, who Melchior saw now was clad in overalls and a cap, shrugged. 'We had an infestation last year- kept sneaking aboard the ships, nearly got sued by Prince Ackshthachra as a result- but we thought we got them all. Could be a couple left.'

Fersilt looked around the place with newfound contempt, as though it were still infested with the marsupials. Then he returned his attention to the yardsman.

'Now, look here, Smillis, this is very important...'

'So's this other gig,' grumbled Smillis. 'I tell you, we can't alter the schedule.'

'Fine,' said Fersilt through clenched teeth, clearly using all his willpower not to hit Smillis. 'I'll double the payment.'

Smillis' eyebrows went up so far his cap lifted higher on his head. 'What, with your business in financial struggles and all?'

'It's a small price compared to the one I'll pay if Nebula Co. goes broke, I assure you,' said Fersilt. '6 draudr and you'll do it?'

'6 draudr? That's 300 astertii! Done, mate, though I can't say I completely understand,' said Smillis, shaking Fersilt's hand bewilderedly.

'And you won't breathe a word of this to anyone?' Tenzebah Jr. prompted.

'Not a word, not a soul,' replied Smillis dutifully. 'That's my motto.'

'Yes, well,' said Fersilt nasally, still with the disgusted look he'd been wearing for quite some time now. 'Some of us have much more admirable mottos...'

'Come now, Mr Tenzebah,' grinned Smillis. 'You're

doin' business with me. Doesn't that make you a hippopotamus?'

Fersilt blinked. 'Do you, by any chance, mean a hypocrite?'

'That's the one, sir, that's the one.'

'Now, could I see the ship you'll be using for this, ah, operation?' Fersilt asked.

'Indeed you could,' replied Smillis. 'I've already got some o' the lads to load it up with your cargo, sir. It's that ol' girl there- the *Shinderinnian*.'

Melchior gave a start and glanced at the ship beside him, straight at the gold lettering that read *Shinderinnian.*

'Ah,' he said softly.

The two men's footsteps approached the ship, and the Reptid heard Fersilt's voice, much too close to where Melchior was hiding, say; 'She's a fine ship.'

'That she is, Mr Tenzebah,' said Smillis. 'She isn't used nowadays, but she used to be a cargo ship, so she'll 'ave no problem doin' a bit more of what she's good at.'

'And you're sure she can get past air control?'

'On Eluxure? Yes, sir. On Glaminda? Probably. Don't quote me on it, but.'

Fersilt glared at him. 'I won't pay unless you're absolutely sure this will go unnoticed.'

'Err...90% sure, Mr Tenzebah. Isn't that good enough?'

Fersilt exhaled sharply, and began to walk around the *Shinderinnian,* pretending to examine it when really he was just weighing up the odds, the risks, the chances...

He made a complete lap of the ship and came round to Smillis again. 'Very well,' he said. 'I'll pay what I promised.'

'Very good, sir.'

And as the two men began to exit the hangar, Melchior remained clinging to the underside of the *Shinderinnian,* hoping that they didn't notice the splash of turquoise on the otherwise uniform silver of the cargo ship.

He waited until he was absolutely sure that the two men were gone, then dropped to the ground with a somewhat painful *thud.*

Then he got to his feet and, checking to see that nobody else was in the hangar or about to enter it, he crept around to the very back of the ship, where two huge sliding doors concealed its contents from view. They were, however, unlocked, by an almost absurd stroke of luck, and Melchior managed to prise them open with little effort, revealing several rows of metal boxes inside. He jumped up into the cargo hold and looked around it in search of a lever of some sort. He spotted one hanging at the far end of the hold- a cratebreaker, evidently used for the very purpose he was about to apply it to- opening the boxes.

He gently ran the cratebreaker along the length of the box, then began to prise the lid from the rest of the container. It took some coaxing, but eventually it popped off with an uncomfortably loud banging noise that made him flinch, despite the hangar being empty.

He peered inside the freshly-opened container and was intrigued to find it filled with several bottles of a dark purple, cloudy liquid.

'Besterium nitrate,' Melchior murmured. 'Used in the manufacture of shuttle fuel...'

It was a very valuable substance, and he wondered how Fersilt had come into possession of it. Frowning, the Reptid picked up the lever once more and moved on to the next metal crate.

Inside this one were rows of more metal casings. Melchior took one out and gently clicked it open, revealing a cluster of jagged topaz-hued crystals.

'And orgite,' he whispered. 'What is Fersilt doing with all these chemicals and minerals?'

His own phrasing recalled to his mind something Rodarth had said when they were first investigating the crime. What had he said? Something to do with Dunwall.

"He imported goods, mostly" the Inspector had said, regarding the late Mr Tenzebah. *"Chemicals, minerals, valuables...that sort of thing."*

Melchior straightened, thinking at 100bvq an hour. These goods, the very goods that Fersilt had to make a shady deal for in order to get them to Glaminda, Nebula Co.'s HQ, consisted of chemicals and minerals, and Melchior was fairly certain that there were valuables in some of the crates as well.

In fact, Melchior was almost 100% certain that these goods had been redirected from Dunwall Tenzebah's transportation business...and into his son's possession.

And if that wasn't as good a lead as any, if not better, than he had no idea what was.

Chapter Nine

'Where the hell were you?' asked Claine.

Melchior looked at her in annoyance. He had evidently been up to *something,* for he looked noticeably ruffled as he entered the hotel lobby with the dignity of someone who was finding it very hard to be dignified, for whatever reason.

'Corwin dropped by, but you weren't here,' Claine told him. 'He told us all about the interrogation before Galion had to go, but he said you should've been here by now. We were all thinking you'd got yourself mugged or something.'

'Mugged?' asked Melchior incredulously. 'On Eluxure?'

Claine glared at him. 'As you deliberately refrained from telling me where the hell you were, I'd better ask again, hadn't I?'

'It's...somewhat complicated, I'm afraid,' interrupted Melchior. 'And a fairly long story, as well.'

'I'm patient,' said the reporter. 'I can wait.'

Melchior sighed. It was more than clear Claine was not going to give up. He could hardly understand her obsessive relentlessness- but then again, she *was* a journalist.

'I was sidetracked,' he said. 'I noticed Fersilt Tenzebah headed for the Leisopolis Shipyards, so I followed him there and got caught up in a very interesting matter-'

Fenice, the receptionist, suddenly cleared her throat from over at the administration desk, causing the Reptid to pause in his gripping tale and look at her in surprise.

'Excuse me, Mr Melchior,' she said. 'But there's someone to see you.'

Melchior's surprise became greater, as did his curiosity. Someone was here, at his hotel, at eight thirty pm, to see him? Who on Eluxure would do that? Not Corwin. He wouldn't bother notifying Fenice. Neither, for that matter, would Galion.

'And who might that be?' Melchior asked in answer to the receptionist's announcement.

Fenice nodded with her head to a point behind him, and he turned and looked, to see Marsine Tenzebah herself seated comfortably in one of the comfortable hotel lobby armchairs. She saw him looking at her with a fair amount of surprise and rose from her seat, smiling at him.

'Mr Melchior,' she said, 'I'm so sorry to be bothering you at this hour, but I had to come.'

'What is the problem?' asked Melchior. 'Surely nothing else has happened?'

'Not as such, no,' replied Marsine. 'But there *is* a matter I would like to discuss with you.'

Melchior gestured towards the stairs. 'Please, I'm sure you'll find it much more comfortable discussing it in my hotel suite, especially since I can provide refreshments for you free of charge.'

Marsine gestured with her hand to indicate declining his offer.

'Oh, no,' she assured him hurriedly. 'I don't want to keep you. It is not a matter which requires such extensive discussion. No, I merely want to officially hire you to work on the case.'

'Excuse me, Mrs Tenzebah?' Melchior asked, caught unawares by her abrupt explanation of the reason for her unexpected visit.

'I am well aware that you are already working on the case from afar, Mr Melchior,' Marsine said, 'and I am also aware that that dreadful Inspector has banned you from the crime scene, but if I hire you, officially, then that would be sufficient enough to override Mr Rodarth's ban, I think.'

'In what way?' asked Claine, a small frown on her face.

Marsine looked at her as though noticing her there for the first time. 'In order to claim that his ban overrides my actions, he will be forced to reveal the nature of said ban, and give a reason that will satisfy the law. Seeing as Rodarth's only reasoning was that Melchior is a Reptid, he will not be very anxious to reveal the nature of the ban. Therefore, he will have no other option but to accept my hiring of Mr Melchior.'

Realisation dawned on Claine's face as she heard this, seeing how Marsine's action might work to override that of the Inspector.

Melchior was nodding, having listened to all of this intently. This was evidently something Marsine had spent a while contemplating, and it sounded entirely logical to the analytically-minded Reptid.

'In that case,' he said, after a sufficient pause, 'I accept.'

'And I will be glad of your help on the case,' replied Marsine clearly relieved. 'Inspector Rodarth, I fear, is incapable of solving it efficiently, and I am thoroughly convinced that you are not. You will bring my husband's killer to justice. I am sure of it.'

∞

'So Fersilt has been redirecting his father's cargo ships?' Claine asked, somewhat astounded. 'Why on Earth would he be doing that?'

Melchior shrugged. 'I'm not completely sure. I mean, he can surely profit from such an operation- the cargo transported by Dunwall Tenzebah is expensive and valuable. But as to *how* he has managed to redirect them, well, that is slightly more foggy.'

Claine nodded, contemplating what Melchior had just told her. Then she grinned suddenly, mostly to herself, prompting the Reptid to probe her regarding its origin.

'Nothing,' was her automatic answer. Then, with complete disregard for consistency, she said, 'it's just that I didn't have you down as a sneaking kind of person.'

'Sorry to disappoint you, Claine,' he said, somewhat drily, 'but I am *not* a sneaking kind of person, and you will never have me down as one.'

'Uh,' she said, 'What, exactly, were you just doing, then?'

Melchior fixed her with a level stare that nevertheless betrayed just a hint of indignation. 'That was entirely different. The circumstances whilst working on a case are usually somewhat...independent of the circumstances in which one usually finds himself.'

'So basically,' Claine summarised, 'You *are* a sneaking kind of person, but only when you're working on a case.'

'I prefer to phrase it thus; I am *not* a sneaking kind of person when I am not working on a case,' Melchior corrected.

'When are you *not* working on a case?' asked Claine.

'I've read all the news articles on you, and you seem to have your hands pretty full.'

Melchior gave her a sulky look, causing her to laugh and amend herself- to an extent- by apologising and asking him if he had any suspicions, to which he replied, 'I have...theories, yes.'

'Share them, then,' replied Claine. 'I'd like to hear them.'

But Melchior shook his head, glancing at the timekeeper in the corner of his hotel suite. It claimed it was ten o'clock, late by any standard, (unless you counted that of the Night People of Noctival).

' *"This darkly hour latens, thus 'tis earlier no more,"* ' he said with regret appropriate to the rendition. 'Iltrotho, 2070. From his tremendous stage production *New Shakespeare.* If I remember correctly, that particular quote is from his modernised take on *Romeo and Juliet.*'

Claine just stared at him blankly. 'Excuse me?'

Melchior sighed, lamenting the lack of focus on history of human literature in the schools of today. 'I mean, Miss Soliss, that it is late, and therefore we have no time to discuss my wild theories, most of which, I admit, are unfounded anyway.'

Claine grinned at him, but got up out of her seat and made for the door. Just as she was opening it, however, she stopped and turned back.

'One more thing, Melchior,' she said, ignoring his

previous request for her to refer to him by his first name, Rastis.

'Yes?' asked the reptilian detective.

'What do you think about Marsine Tenzebah...hiring you?' she asked. 'Do you think this...clears her?'

Melchior shook his head helplessly. 'At this point, nothing that any suspect can possibly do at present will "clear them"- unless it involves a different suspect confessing, of course.'

Claine nodded. 'So you still think she could have done it?'

Melchior shrugged. 'I don't know. But I'm hoping tomorrow will shed some light on the subject...'

Chapter Ten

1.

Inspector Rodarth was having a bad morning, and it looked to him as though said morning would get no better. He had insisted on visiting Kenderye again, as there was nothing to be gained from the city or the police station. However, it seemed as though there was nothing to be gained from the crime scene itself at present, despite his best efforts. He had examined Tenzebah's chambers again, found nothing, examined the grounds, found nothing, and examined anything else that he had already examined prior to today, which was nearly everything. And found nothing.

Inspector Tirranar was seemingly making a point of refraining from helping his colleague in his examinations, and instead followed him about with an almost bored air, clearly seeing no benefit to this procedure. Rodarth, though he didn't want to admit it, was beginning to feel the same, but was nevertheless determined to make an enlightening discovery of some sort before the day was over.

As a result of all this effort to no avail, Rodarth had become increasingly more disagreeable even than before, but it was the final straw when he emerged from the house only to see Rastis Melchior strolling purposefully towards him through the gardens.

'I thought I banned that stupid lizard,' he spat. 'What's he doing here?'

'I would imagine,' said Corwin calmly, his eyebrows raised to let Melchior know that he too was unsure of the reasoning behind his presence, 'that he is here to investigate the murder of Mr Tenzebah.'

Rodarth glared daggers at him, not for the first time that day. 'One more snide remark from you, Tirranar-'

'And what, Rodarth?' asked Corwin. 'You are *not* my superior, as you well know.'

Rodarth looked as though he wished to say something, but Melchior was now in the vicinity, and all he had time for was a hurried, 'I'll talk to you later.'

Melchior smiled at Rodarth pleasantly as he reached where the two Inspectors stood.

'It is...a nice day, is it not, Inspector Rodarth, for

investigating? But, of course, I'm not here to discuss such trivial matters as meteorology.'

'What the hell do you think you're doing here?' snapped Rodarth. 'You're banned, remember? Or do Reptids have a more limited memory span than I thought?'

'I think I will let that racist comment pass, seeing as I generally refrain from severely injuring servants of the law, such as yourself- if, indeed, you *are* a committed servant, who does not occasionally stray from their master,' Melchior replied, coolly, calmly and without batting an eyelid.

Rodarth's dark look darkened further, and he moved forward until he was only a couple of centimetres away from the Reptid, eyes glaring furiously at Melchior's calm ones.

'What are you suggesting, lizard?'

'Reptid, I think you'll find, is the name of my species, not lizard.'

Rodarth gritted his teeth. 'Listen here, you shedskin,' he hissed, and Melchior's gaze wavered momentarily at the term, which was as offensive to a Reptid as "chitterer" was to a N'choth'ni. 'I am indeed a servant of the law, and an abiding one at that, despite what you might be insinuating. And as such a servant, I am fully entitled to officially ban you from the scene of the crime. I expect you to follow my ban by staying clear of Kenderye and keeping your scaly nose out of this case.'

'That is ENOUGH!' Corwin shouted, so suddenly that Rodarth took several steps back from the Reptid and looked at his colleague in surprise. Corwin was purple in the face and furious.

'I don't care, Mangery Rodarth, if you're an experienced Inspector or the King of Palloupai, it doesn't change the fact that you, sir, are a thick-skulled, cowardly, racist *pig.*'

Rodarth's face went red. He looked more furious than Melchior had so far seen him.

'*What* did you call me?' the Inspector whispered.

'Oh, I think you heard well enough,' said Corwin. 'Rastis Melchior is my friend, and a very old friend at that, and I will *not* have you flinging racism at him as though he's an under-evolved ape.'

'Well, in that case,' fired Rodarth. '*I* don't care if he's your *grandmother*, he is of a lesser species, and I shall treat him as one, Inspector Tirranar. As for you, I will not stand for you speaking like that to me again, you hear me? Despite our similarity of rank, I *am* more experienced than you, and will be treated with the proper respect that I deserve.'

'Excuse me,' said an elderly, cultured female voice from behind them, causing both to turn and look.

There, in the grand entrance to Kenderye Mansion, stood Marsine Tenzebah, clad in an elegant dress and viewing the two Inspectors- no, Melchior noticed, Rodarth- with mild contempt.

'Am I interrupting anything?' she asked.

'No, madam,' said Rodarth in an attempt at a calm tone, after a count of three. 'No, you are not.'

'Well, I wish to explain the presence of the good Mr Melchior here, if I may?' she continued, still excellently composed.

'Do,' replied Rodarth, shooting a glance at the Reptid.

'Well,' said Marsine, 'Melchior is here because I asked him to be. I hired him, as a matter of fact, to officially work on this case.'

Rodarth looked from her to Melchior, doing such a commendable goldfish impersonation he could have performed it on stage.

'You can't do that,' he managed to mutter between gaping and staring incredulously.

'I think you'll find that I can,' Marsine told him tartly. 'See, if you wished to prove that I cannot, then you would have to produce evidence as to why you banned him in the first place. And, if you don't mind my saying so, Inspector Rodarth, I very much doubt that you can produce such evidence.'

Rodarth seemed to fume for a few long counts, then grunted irritably before continuing to fume. Eventually he muttered something that was either 'fine, then. As you wish,' or 'fine them! And the fish!'

As it was unlikely that it was the latter, everyone took it to mean the former, and Marsine smiled sweetly at the fuming Inspector.

'Thank you, Inspector. You know how much it means to me to find my husband's killer.'

Rodarth muttered something else unintelligible, then signalled to Corwin.

'Inspector Tirrinar, if I may have a...professional word.'

Corwin's mouth tightened, and Melchior was surprised to see a look that may have been worry on his face.

'Of course, Inspector Rodarth.'

Rodarth's thin smile was back as he led Corwin around the corner of the house. Melchior frowned, sure that he had missed something- an exchange, perhaps- and wondered how much he had missed, or for how long he had missed it.

'Thank you for enabling me to work closer on the case,' he told Marsine. 'Though I do hope you understand that you are still a suspect, and I will have to question you as evenly as the others.'

Marsine nodded. 'I...understand completely, Mr Melchior. However, I do not like it.'

'You do not have to, madam,' Melchior assured her. 'But if you know anything that may help catch Dunwall's killer, I will need to know it.'

Marsine nodded again before disappearing back inside the house.

As soon as she was gone, Melchior crept with surprising stealth for someone so tall down the side of the house in the direction the Inspectors had gone. He peeked around the corner, fully aware that he was sneaking despite assuring Claine that he was not a sneaking sort of person, and saw Rodarth talking to Corwin in low tones. Corwin had the same strange worried look that Melchior had seen just before and had found odd. He found it no less unusual now.

Rodarth had his back to Melchior, so he couldn't see his expression, but his tone was angry.

'I've warned you, Tirranar. I've told you before not to question me, haven't I?'

'Yes,' was Corwin's short response.

'Yes, what?'

'Yes, sir,' said Corwin obediently. Melchior's eyes widened. He had not imagined that he would hear his old friend address someone of the same rank as he as 'sir', least of all Rodarth. Everything that they were saying suggested strongly that Rodarth was Corwin's superior, even though Melchior knew for a fact that he was not. Even someone with more experience should not be addressed by an equal as their superior.

'You understand that if you do anything like this again...'

'Sir,' protested Corwin, 'Melchior *is* my friend.'

'Be that as it may...' interrupted Rodarth, and left that phrase hanging.

'Yes, sir,' said Corwin, again with that alien obedience.

'Good,' said Rodarth. 'I'm glad you understand.'

Then Melchior was hurrying back towards the doorway, his mind racing.

2.

'Hoy, Melchior!' called Galion as he spotted the Reptid down the end of the hallway.

Melchior saw him and walked to him, nodding his head at him in greeting.

'What are you doing here?' he asked in surprise. 'Rodarth banned you!'

Melchior nodded. 'He did. But I have been hired by Marsine Tenzebah to work on the case, so here I am.'

Galion grinned. 'Good on her, then. I bet Thinlip wasn't too happy.'

'He was not,' agreed Melchior. 'In fact, I have just heard a very interesting exchange between him and Corwin...'

'Never mind that,' said Galion, which just proved how much he cared about such things. 'What were you doing last night?'

Melchior sighed. 'Not this again. As I was telling Claine, I saw Fersilt Tenzebah headed to the Shipyards, so I followed him by hover-taxi and saw him enter the main hangar.'

'Why would he go to the Shipyards?' asked Galion, confused.

Melchior gave him an exasperated look. 'If I could but focus your attention on the story rather than certain parts of it, I daresay I will tell you.'

'Sorry,' replied Galion, not looking very sorry at all- a sure-fire sign he was catching Claine-osis. 'But why *would* he?'

'Well,' continued the Reptid, 'I followed him- Fersilt-inside the hangar and hid behind a Venturer XC, listening in to a conversation between Fersilt and another man- a yards worker. They were talking about some deal that they had, which involved a mystery cargo and the problems caused by another, even shadier dealing that the yardsman's contacts were currently operating. They nearly caught me, in fact, and would have if I hadn't distracted them by throwing a spanner across the hangar.' ('You what?' spluttered Galion, a comment ignored by Melchior). 'I managed to sneak over to another ship, the *Shinderinnian,* but it turned out to be the very ship they were intending to use for this...manoeuvre. So Fersilt decided to examine the ship, and I was nearly discovered again, but I managed to cling onto the underside of the vessel. I heard them mention that the ship's cargo was bound for Glaminda- Fersilt's HQ- and it was clear that whatever they were doing was illegal.'

'What next?' asked Galion.

'Well,' said Melchior, enjoying himself despite himself. 'They left, and I managed to open the cargo hold of the

Shinderinnian, inside which I found several metal crates filled with expensive minerals and chemicals.'

Galion frowned. 'Why minerals and chemicals?'

'Do you remember what Tenzebah's line of business used to be?'

Galion cocked his head to one side, trying to recall the answer to the Reptid's question, but if it was present in his mind, he was unable to locate it. 'No, sorry.'

'He transported cargo,' said Melchior. 'Specifically, chemicals and minerals.'

Galion's expression changed to one of sudden comprehension. 'So...Fersilt has been redirecting his old man's deliveries...to his own business?'

'Spot on,' smiled Melchior.

'I'm not sure I want to seek employment with a crook,' said Galion.

'You worked for Redn Termal until recently,' Melchior reminded him. 'So if you feel you have to do better than him next time, I assure you that finding such an employer will not be very difficult at all.'

Galion smiled at him, his faith restored just a sliver.

Then Melchior nodded again and continued down the hallway.

'Where are you off to?' he asked the Reptid.

'Well, I should confront Fersilt Tenzebah at some point,' Melchior replied. Then he frowned slightly and said, 'If he is arrested, for one crime or another, whether it be the murder of his father or the redirection of his father's business...well, I'm afraid my previous comment may not be entirely truthful. But wherever you end up employed, I assure you it will not be Calmooth.'

Galion found this, too, slightly heartening. 'Oh, and Melchior... what do you want me to do now that you're here to investigate personally?'

Melchior smiled again. 'Oh, I still have use for you, Galion.'

'Yeah? What's that?'

'Well, I have a hunch that there may still be information to be found in the archive that Claine...obtained. If you could look through the albums?'

Galion sighed. 'Yeah, OK. I'm sure I'll find the whole process...exhilarating.'

Another smile from Melchior- a grin, this time. Then he disappeared around the corner.

Melchior was not long around said corner when he saw Claine in the next corridor, she saw him and she made a beeline towards the Reptid.

'Hi,' she said. 'Rodarth give you any grief?'

'The usual racist remarks,' he said lightly, though they had been much worse than usual, and he was indeed slightly affected by the use of the term "shedskin". It was highly racist and highly offensive, and it had taken his entire cultivated air of calmness to defy the instinctive urge to lash out at the Inspector.

'But he let you on the crime scene?'

'He had no choice,' replied Melchior. 'But I *did* overhear him talking to Corwin just before, after he defended me from a vicious tirade of insults. The conversation was most peculiar, in fact.'

'In what way?' asked Claine.

'Well, Rodarth was acting as though he was Corwin's superior- that isn't extraordinary in itself. But what made it so unusual was that Corwin *treated* Rodarth like he was his superior. And Corwin is not one to treat an equal like someone of higher rank.'

'That's odd,' Claine agreed. 'Any ideas why?'

'I don't know. But Rodarth seemed to be hinting that he could administer severe punishment if Corwin was not compliant.'

'*Punishment?*'

'I doubt the punishment would be physical,' Melchior assured her. 'But I was thinking more along the lines of blackmail of some sort.'

'Why would Rodarth need to blackmail Corwin?' asked Claine incredulously.

Melchior shook his turquoise head, at a loss. 'I know not. It could be nothing to do with the crime at hand. In fact, I very much doubt it. Most likely it is an internal police affair...'

Which meant, of course, that it was none of his

business...unless, Melchior thought, what was going on between Corwin and his "colleague" was a little bit more than just an internal police affair.

'Have you seen Galion?' asked Claine, interrupting his thoughts.

'Yes, I have,' replied Melchior. 'In fact, I have just subjected him to the tedious task of sorting through the rest of those records you...ahem, managed to appropriate.'

Claine grinned widely. 'I bet he doesn't like that.'

'He doesn't, rest assured,' Melchior informed her with a little smile. 'But I still think there can be information gained from the archives.'

Claine nodded. 'True. I think the same. But it's *what* that I'm a bit less certain about. Surely we know enough about Tenzebah, now we've discovered who his friend was...?'

'Perhaps,' offered the Reptid, 'Galion will find something that does not relate to Tenzebah directly...'

Claine shrugged. 'You're the deep thinker here. I have no clue, personally, but I'm sure you're several steps ahead.'

Melchior was not. Like it or not, he too was stumped. Or maybe that was not the ideal word- the opposite was more accurate. Everyone had suddenly become twice as suspicious as they had originally been, and it was impossible to know who to suspect, even as more developments on the case were made. Fersilt, of course,

had unknowingly produced potential evidence to murder-
if not that, then evidence to something illegal, at any rate.
Marsine may have thought she had been cleared, since she
had enlisted his help personally, but there was still every
reason to suspect her, especially since she still refused to
acknowledge her late husband's affair with Trissilan
Glamure.

'Possibly,' Melchior said in reply to Claine's question,
skillfully avoiding answering it with a simple "yes" or "no".

Claine seemed satisfied, however, and grinned at him
again- What was it with her continuous grinning?

'Ah, you'll solve it, Melchior,' she said, showing
remarkable faith in his crime-solving prowess. 'I'd bet
money on it.'

And Melchior, who would probably not, found himself
determined to ensure she won her bet- however
hypothetical it was.

Chapter Eleven

Knock-knock-knock!

'Enter!' came the impatient voice from within the room. 'If you have something worthwhile to say, that is.'

It was noted by the visitor, as he opened the door with a creak, how the room's occupant acted as though he were everyone's better, as though somehow his rank in the business industry automatically qualified him to speak to others like he was addressing an employee, or perhaps even a peasant.

'Oh,' said Fersilt Tenzebah, looking up from a piece of paper (which was obviously produced hurriedly on the announcement of a visitor, and was probably a restaurant receipt or something), as Rastis Melchior entered his temporary accommodations. 'It's you, Mr Melchior.'

'Indeed,' said Melchior, thinking that his identity was rather obvious now that he was in the room.

'How can I help you?' Fersilt asked in a tone that implied that he'd love to be of assistance, really, but he was very busy at the moment so could Melchior please leave? The piece of paper in front of him, which he was treating like a concerning letter of some description, *was* in fact a restaurant receipt, Melchior noticed, and therefore could be taken about as seriously as the man who was looking at it gravely.

'Oh, no specific matter, Mr Tenzebah,' said Melchior. 'As you're probably aware, your mother has hired me to personally investigate the case,' (here, he noticed, Fersilt's face softened slightly at the mention of his mother) 'and, as I have not had the opportunity to interrogate all suspects personally, I have taken it upon myself to do so now.'

'I see,' replied Fersilt. 'I have already been interviewed twice by that preposterous fool, Rodarth, and I would strongly object to a third interrogation under normal circumstances, as I am-'

'A very busy man,' finished Melchior. 'Yes, I am aware of that, Mr Tenzebah-'

'However,' continued Fersilt, 'if mother wishes it, which, I admit, is perfectly understandable, then I may as well entertain you, Mr Melchior.'

Melchior nodded to him in acknowledgement, once

again noting his attachment to his mother in contrast with the spite he'd had for his father.

'I'll begin by confirming that I was not on the best of terms with my father,' Fersilt said. 'We had an argument several years prior to his death- I'm sure you know what about. Inheritance. Our bloodline's inheritance, plus an added bonus from Dad himself, I'm sure. But he wasn't letting me have any of it, specifically claiming that as he was not yet dead, I would not receive even a small amount of the fortune.' He sneered slightly. 'Old fool. He couldn't die and he knew it.'

'Yet,' Melchior interjected softly, 'he did.'

Fersilt nodded, looking down at his restaurant receipt emblazoned with the words Teffilngon Eatery, with an odd expression on his face. 'Yes,' he said. 'He did.'

'Can you tell me, Mr Tenzebah, what were the exact "added bonuses" you mentioned?' Melchior asked him. 'You were referring to Dunwall's will, yes?'

'I was, yes,' agreed Fersilt. 'I wasn't referring to anything specific, however.'

'No? Not...his own line of business, perhaps?'

Fersilt looked up at him sharply- too sharply to be passed of as unsuspicious. 'What's it to you?'

'Everything, Mr Tenzebah, is useful to me when I am investigating a murder.'

Fersilt sighed. 'Well, in that case, yes, I did take over my father's business on his death. But it's not as though I benefited much from it. I can't *do* anything with it- sell it, even make minor changes. All profits made from it go to the family trust, rather than directly to me. A figurehead of my father's trade, that's all I am. I'm much more dedicated to my own business.'

Melchior nodded, beginning to see. 'So Dunwall's transportation business is useless to you. It's a shame, isn't it, Mr Tenzebah, that you cannot use the profits made from it to cover the costs of your own enterprise...'

His level gaze was trained unwaveringly on Fersilt's by this stage, penetrating his own levelness and causing his own gaze to break from the Reptid's.

'It seems to me, Mr Melchior,' said Fersilt softly, 'that you are hinting at my dishonesty?'

'I hint at nothing,' Melchior replied. 'I merely point out that you may benefit greatly from using your father's line of trade to help your own business...not that you are putting such a manoeuvre into operation, of course.'

'Of course,' repeated Fersilt. '...I understand how you may have come to that conclusion, sir. It would indeed put me in a very good financial position...but I can assure you, I have continued to run my father's business as he would have wanted me to run it- honestly and dutifully.'

Melchior smiled and nodded. 'Thank you, Mr Tenzebah. I will not take up any more of your time.'

He stood up to his full height, which was really very tall indeed and paused before he headed out the door.

'You are, after all,' he said, 'a *very* busy man.'

∞

T'chisa jumped violently when Melchior entered the grand kitchen area, spilling water on the bench in a massive puddle. When she saw who it was, she apologised and hastily began mopping it up, her sudden shock gone but her nerves still on edge.

Melchior immediately knew something was wrong. The N'choth'ni was acting extremely jittery, as though she had had some kind of a shock *before* the Reptid had accidentally caught her unawares. Or perhaps the word "jittery" was not accurate, but whatever the case, she seemed as though she was very close to succumbing to some sort of emotion, be it fear, sadness or anger.

'I'm sorry,' said Melchior. 'I should have announced my presence.'

'No, it is fine, sir,' said the N'choth'ni, nodding somewhat shakily, and the Reptid was not entirely surprised by the slight quaver in her voice. It was clear she'd been having a hard time. 'You just startled me...that is all.'

'Is there something bothering you, T'chisa?'

T'chisa looked up when he said her name. 'You are the detective,' she said. A statement, not a question. Then; 'A friend of the nice girl? Claine?'

'Yes, I am,' said Melchior.

T'chisa nodded, returning her attention to cleaning up the spillage. 'She is the first person who has been nice to me in...a long time.'

Melchior frowned. 'Why is that, T'chisa?'

T'chisa looked uncertain, as though she wasn't sure she should be telling this to a stranger. 'Master Tenzebah was...cruel to me. I have told Claine this. Also, his son and his assistant treat me with not much more respect. I cannot expect much of it, as a simple maid, but-'

'Of course you deserve respect,' Melchior told her. 'Everyone does...except for people who don't show it to others.'

T'chisa smiled at him, her antennae waving slightly. 'Thank you, sir. You are kind. Not like the nasty man. The Inspector. He is not kind.'

Melchior breathed out through his nose, thinking of various insults for Rodarth. 'He,' he told T'chisa, 'is not someone who deserves much in the way of respect. What has he been saying now?'

'He has been accusing me,' said T'chisa. 'Trying to force me to confess. He calls me names- chitterer, insect. And he shouts at me. I have nearly confessed, even though I did not commit the murder. I could not. I do not know how.'

'T'chisa, listen to me,' Melchior told her. 'Do not confess. I know that you didn't kill Tenzebah, but Rodarth wants an excuse to arrest you. Do you want to give him that excuse?'

T'chisa looked at him. Then she glanced down again and nodded her head slowly.

'Good,' said Melchior, satisfied. 'I will catch the real murderer. Then Rodarth will leave you alone. But, T'chisa- if you want my advice...quit this job. Get another, under a master who gives you the respect you deserve.'

Then he took his leave from the kitchen, leaving T'chisa to herself, hopefully more heartened, less frail, than when he had accidentally surprised her.

He had been meaning to question her, the way he had questioned Fersilt. But he suspected that T'chisa might crack if she were interrogated again.

And that would give Rodarth a pleasure Melchior didn't want him to have.

From there, Melchior's investigations grew increasingly useless, and he was beginning to think that he could have solved the case just as easily, if not more effectively, had he remained under a police ban. In fact, his presence at Kenderye had so far been to little or no avail, except, of course, for his overhearing of Rodarth and Corwin's conversation, and perhaps for his success in unnerving Fersilt Tenzebah. He was now fairly certain of what Fersilt was up to, but he was yet to discover whether or not it linked directly to the solving of Dunwall's murder.

And now, on interrogating Trissilan Glamure, he gained

yet more *nothing*, except to observe her closely as she went on about how she'd already told the police everything she knew. He noted the distracting strawberry blonde hair with the sunlight shining through its many waves, as Galion had described it, and noted that the young mechanic's suspicions that she was part Pristilian, made complete sense. There was no fact to support the theory, however, and her lineage was in fact her own business, and nobody else's. With an inward sigh, Melchior realised that her possible Pristilian blood had absolutely nothing to do with the case at all.

'I hope you've been making progress?' asked Marsine Tenzebah as he entered her favourite sitting room, with the glass ceiling and elegant tea tables.

Melchior paused in the door, wondering how to answer honestly and tactfully at the same time. He decided this was not possible, and decided to go with tact.

'Indeed I have, madam,' he informed her.

'Good, good,' she smiled, and he saw that she was in good humour. The Reptid wondered if she would indeed continue to be so after his next words.

'I...hope you realise, madam, that I must question *everybody*?'

'Of course,' said Marsine, taking a delicate sip of wullemberry and afferleaf tea and setting it down again on a strangely shaped saucer, deciding that it was too hot. The saucer made a clicking noise and a plume of steam rose from the cup and she took another sip, pleased now at the temperature.

'That includes you, madam.'

Marsine looked up at him stiffly and regarded him that way for several seconds. Then she said, in a voice that was equally as stiff, 'Of course, Mr Melchior. I am still a suspect, after all.'

The unspoken words seemed to be: *even though I am the one who hired you.*

Yet Melchior knew that she was quite aware that hiring a detective did not entirely rule her out as a suspect to murder.

'Well,' she said, taking another sip of tea, 'You'd better question me, then, if this case is to be resolved. I may give you something of use, at any rate.'

Melchior nodded to her and took a seat opposite her. 'Now...Mrs Tenzebah, may I begin with something of a...personal question?'

'That,' she replied, 'would rather depend on the question.'

Melchior went on, unperturbed by her answer. 'You have said before that you were unaware of an...affair between your husband and his assistant?'

'That is correct,' replied Marsine adamantly.

'In that case, Mrs Tenzebah, I'm afraid I must tell you that I believe you were not telling the truth.'

'And why not?' Marsine asked.

'Well,' said Melchior, carefully phrasing his words so as not to make the indignant elderly woman any angrier. 'It appears to me that Miss Glamure's affair with Mr Tenzebah was no secret.'

He glanced again at Marsine, who surprisingly said nothing, so he continued. 'According to Miss Glamure herself, everyone within the household was aware of it. And that, madam, includes you.'

Marsine remained silent for several more counts. Then she said, 'You are correct, Mr Melchior. Indeed, I was all too aware of it. My husband and I were as in love as can be- before he and his reckless friend discovered that evil drink.'

Melchior sat forward, intrigued by this sudden development in the conversation.

'After Dunwall started taking Elixir,' Marsine went on, 'he had no time for me any more. In his mind, he was but a young man, just beginning his long, immortal life. And to him, I was the opposite- an ageing woman, perhaps nearing the end of hers. Then along came Miss Glamure, that absurd young woman who thinks she's a noble or something. But Dunwall couldn't resist her wiles, her charm. She's younger than me, and indeed prettier. Who can blame him?' she said the last, rhetorical comment with undisguised bitterness.

Melchior regarded her, surprised at her sudden revelation. This, he found, gave her depth and, regrettably, a greater motive to accompany it. 'Forgive me if I misjudge, madam,' he said, 'but it seems as though *you* can.'

'You're right, again,' Marsine sighed. 'I was jealous, yes. And I hated him for carrying on with his assistant. But if you think I murdered my husband, you have indeed misjudged me. If I were to murder someone in an act of revenge, it would have been Trissilan Glamure.'

Melchior nodded, absorbing this. 'And, again, forgive me for asking this, madam, but why did you choose to deny your knowledge of your husband's infidelity?'

Marsine shrugged, but it was not a casual dismissal of Melchior's question; on the contrary, it was an answer. 'I don't know...I thought I'd be arrested for murder. If I admitted to feeling jealous and spiteful, I feared that I would be the obvious suspect.'

'Your motives, indeed, have strong basis, and, yes, they do incriminate you, Mrs Tenzebah. However, each of our suspects are equally suspicious, with their own motives. Don't worry, madam. You will only be arrested if we find proof that you were the culprit.'

Marsine smiled at him, obviously reassured. 'Thank you, Melchior. That, at least, is some consolation.'

'And, madam-' said Melchior, 'may I also ask you...from whom did you buy Kenderye?'

Marsine regarded him with some surprise. 'I'm afraid I can't say. I didn't deal with the original owner, you see-just one of his associates.'

Melchior stood up, disappointed at the anticlimax to the interrogation. 'Thank you, Mrs Tenzebah. You've been very helpful.'

'I'm glad, Mr Melchior,' she replied. 'I do hope you solve this horrible crime.'

'Even if the culprit was you, madam?'

'Well, if that is indeed the case,' said Marsine, 'then I think you would be a very commendable detective indeed.'

Chapter Twelve

1.

The workers all looked up as Claine strolled in, trying her best not to get noticed. Alas, she was easily noticed as the least grubby person in the garage, and winced as every single worker stopped what they were doing and stared at her. Eventually a guy with a face slathered with machine oil cleared his throat and got up from his position underneath the skeleton of a hover car, flexing none-too subtly.

'Uh, hi. Can I help you?' he asked.

'No, you can't, Mascal,' barked a female voice. Claine looked to see a short, stocky woman with her sleeves rolled up, exposing arms more muscular than Mascal's, and a cap fixed tightly on her head.

'Sorry about Mascal,' she told Claine. 'He thinks he can help any pretty young lady who comes along. Trust me, it's more like helping himself.'

She began cleaning her hands on a grubby rag, which looked as though it was only serving to make them dirtier. 'I'm Hellin, by the way. What's the problem? Need a car checked?'

'No, actually,' replied Claine. 'I'm a friend of Galion's. Is he here?'

Hellin's face adopted a surprised expression, and Mascal made a scoffing sort of noise from over by the deconstructed car, accompanied by a low, 'friend, huh?'

Hellin shot him a look, and Claine noticed that she was senior here. She also noticed that the rest of the workers, whilst pretending to be absorbed in their jobs, were all listening intently. An alien Claine couldn't identify had one eyestalk trained on the machinery he was fixing, but the other was pointed in their direction. Another man with a completely-tattooed face made a show of continuously polishing the one knob even though it was spotless. Claine was surprised that her wanting to see Galion had aroused such interest.

'Well, he doesn't work here anymore,' Hellin said. 'Old Termal fired him with no good reason, but he's still staying on the workplace premises. No doubt Redn knows, but it can't be long before he kicks him out. Poor guy's got nowhere else to stay until he's carted off to that hell-hole, Calmooth.'

'He won't have to go to Calmooth,' Claine said with more force than she'd intended. Hellin raised here eyebrows, and she added, 'Sorry. But I'm hoping it doesn't come to that.'

''Course you are,' Hellin replied. 'Nobody should have to wind up on Calmooth...unless they deserve it.'

'I heard Fersilt Tenzebah is on Eluxure,' piped up a man with an enormous lavender beard. 'You know, head honcho at Nebula.'

'Just rumours, Balfoota,' said a young woman with several small nubs like the horns of a baby dithrote across her forehead. 'They probs ain't true.'

Hellin glared at them, and their attentions snapped back to their work swiftly. 'Balfoota, Durith, shut up and work.'

She turned her own attention back to Claine. 'Sorry. Well, anyway, you'll find Vasail just down that way- I'll get Shullsey to show you the way.'

A round-faced man nodded obediently and gestured for Claine to follow him. She smiled in return and did as he requested, thanking Hellin and exiting the main garage after Shullsey.

'How do you know Galion, if you don't mind my asking, miss?' he asked her as he led her up a flight of rickety-looking stairs.

'Oh, uh...' that was a difficult one, actually. 'I haven't

known him long. We met here on Eluxure. I'm a reporter, you see- freelance, I self publish the *Galaxy Roamer,* you may have heard of it...'

'Sorry, miss, but that'd just be me, I'm sure. I'm not a reader of newspapers.'

Feeling a familiar twinge of annoyance at having her magazine unknown by everyone she met, Claine ploughed on. 'Anyway, I met Galion doing a story here a few days ago, actually.'

Shulls nodded. 'It's a shame that he doesn't have enough money to afford anything but a one-way ticket to Calmooth,' he said. 'Flights there are surprisingly cheap considering that nobody actually wants to go there. The space pilots prefer not to dock, actually. Calmooth has to send one of their own to pick up new arrivals.'

'Do you have any idea why...Redn Termal gave him the sack?'

Shulls shrugged. 'He's always had it in for the kid. No clue why, but it's like Galion couldn't do anything right. Eventually Termal just went ptilic- if you'll pardon the Geaux-Erraut,' he added hastily to cover his slip of a common tradie's swear word. Claine waved it off. 'Anyway,' Shulls continued, 'It's OK to talk about the boss, coz he's not here on Tuesdays. So I got nothing to fear. It's this one.'

He nodded at a door, on which hung a sign saying EMPLOYEE USE ONLY. Seeing as Galion was no longer an employee, Claine wondered what Termal thought about him staying in the worker's quarters.

'I'd better get back to work,' Shulls told her. 'Hellin'll bite my head off. When you're on her good side, she's an abs'lute legend. But if she thinks you're slacking off, she'll bite your 'ead off. See ya, miss.'

With a cheery nod, he walked back down the rickety stairs, yelling, 'keep yer pants on, 'Ellin! I'm coming!'

Claine knocked on Galion's door a couple of times, and she heard his voice saying, 'Come in, unless you're Mascal, in which case-' here he gave a colourful suggestion as to what Mascal should do if it were he wishing to enter.

She opened the door with raised eyebrows, and Galion, who was lounging on a small sofa watching a Packerawl match on holoTV, jumped to his feet quickly.

'Claine!' he said, and she couldn't help but enjoy the look on his face. 'Sorry, I thought you were one of the boys.'

'Mascal, maybe?' Claine offered innocently.

Galion chewed his lip. 'Sorry about that. If you knew the bugger-'

'I met him just before, actually,' replied Claine.

Galion nodded, turning off the hologram hastily.

'You can leave that on, it's OK,' she assured him, but he shrugged.

'It's Glaminda Galimantas versus Hurnbelad Hiledes,' he said, which did nothing to enlighten her. 'My team, the

Hiledes- we were winning by about sixty points anyway.'

He sounded extremely confident in Hurnbelad's ability to beat Glaminda, but Claine knew practically nothing about the game, so perhaps it was an obvious win on the Hiledes' part.

She looked around the place, noting how small it was. A bed stood to one side, a couch to the other. A small desk was wedged between them, and that was where the holoTV sat. The walls next to the bed were covered with posters of bands; *Nera Locon, Excess Phlegm, Spacewalk*...he had good taste in music, thought Claine.

'So, what are you doing here, anyway?' he asked her.

'I was just wanting to see if you'd got very far in looking at those articles Melchior assigned you...?'

Galion's mouth formed an O. 'Ah, yeah. Well, no. Not very far. Most of the stuff is just info we already have, or don't need. Just Tenzebah and Chasterleigh, mostly, though it does mention Tenzebah's dad- but that doesn't really help.'

He crossed back over to the hologram and reactivated it, this time selecting *resume viewing* and causing an old *Gazette* article to appear. It was titled *Aikenald Tenzebah Dies Age 83*, and pictured an old man with a shock of white hair and such a wrinkled face he resembled a Nascapalupa mummy. The article was dated 2360, which put Dunwall Tenzebah at 30 years of age, and the heir to his father's fortune- a fortune now owned by Fersilt

Tenzebah. Claine scanned the article in the hope of finding something useful, but Galion shook his head. 'There's nothing there. I can't find anything useful at all, and I don't think I will, either.'

Claine sat down on the couch, stumped. 'Well, if that's the case, what on Earth does Melchior *think* you'll find?'

Galion shrugged, and they lapsed into silence while Claine continued to futilely scan the article.

'You're from Earth,' he said eventually, and Claine looked at him, surprised.

'Yes- why?'

Galion grinned at her. 'Well, you did use the expression *what on Earth,* which nobody in the galaxy uses, save those born on Earth.'

Claine returned the smile. 'Well, you're right. I was born on Earth, but I wanted to leave, *really* badly. See the universe. But I haven't got round to much of that yet. It costs a fortune just to travel from Earth to Mars, let alone here.'

'Have you ever wanted to...go back?' asked Galion. 'To Earth, I mean.'

Claine sighed. 'Well, sometimes, yeah. As soon as I'd broken through the atmosphere, and looked out the window of my shuttle and saw the planet in all its beauty...I did feel a little regret. That I hadn't realised before how stunning my own planet was. That I hadn't known that I could just explore my own planet and get just as much of a thrill.'

She looked at Galion, who was listening intently and understandingly. 'But, that said, I have got a kick out of the interplanetary life. Just not as much of one as I'd hoped when I left Earth.'

'I've never met someone from Earth before,' Galion revealed. 'I was born on Siliphid, but my great grandmother apparently left Earth at the start of last century. Humans are so spread out now that hardly any are actually from their planet of origin.'

Claine nodded in agreement, now wanting to know more about Galion's past, like he had done when she was talking about her Earth roots. 'What was Siliphid like? I can't really imagine growing up on another planet.'

'Well, Siliphid wasn't the best planet to grow up on,' he admitted. 'My family was poor, and living in bad conditions. My parents sent me offworld to make myself a better life than they had. And that's what I *have* done...only I still feel guilty that I've got a higher paying job, and much better living conditions.'

He left out the fact that he no longer had said job, and looking around the small, slightly dingy employee's accommodation, Claine would not have described it as excellent living conditions. And it made her feel all the more sorry for Galion's family, whose conditions were, no doubt, worse.

She said so, but Galion waved her comment off. 'I've

heard they're much better off now. Siliphid has had a change of ruler, and apparently she's been slowly making things better for the poor. My mother's most recent letter said that they've been able to sell the house and buy a more hospitable one, and that my father has finally found a job in the district administrations office.'

'Well, I hope you find work under Fersilt Tenzebah,' Claine said, 'provided he isn't arrested for illegal redirection of goods.'

'Oh, yeah,' Galion remembered. 'Melchior's...escapade. The Shipyards are just next door, actually. Sometimes we have to work on some of the ships. They're top quality.'

Claine looked at him suddenly. 'You have access to the Shipyards?' she asked.

Galion frowned. 'I did, but not any more, since I've been fired. But Hellin does, and Shullsey, and a couple of others.'

Claine's mind was racing faster than ever. 'Did you ever do work on the *Shinderinnian*?'

'Yeah...actually, I did, as a matter of fact,' Galion replied. 'But I don't see how that helps. Melchior already knows that Fersilt's up to something sneaky.'

'No, but he can't pin anything on him, can he? Not without proof.'

Galion frowned again, not quite following. 'And what proof are you thinking of?'

'Well, the *Shinderinnian* did spring to mind,' Claine

said. 'That's the ship Fersilt wants to use to transport Dunwall's goods to Glaminda, isn't it? And provided he hasn't already...'

'Someone could "accidentally" discover its contents?' Galion offered, and Claine nodded.

'Wait a mo, though, Claine,' Galion went on. 'The *Shinderinnian* is a private shuttle. We're under orders from the Shipmaster that we're not to touch it.'

'Ah, but you'd have to, wouldn't you, if it were to develop a problem...' Claine said, letting the sentence hang in the air.

As soon as Galion realised what she was hinting at, he shook his head vigorously. 'You can't just sabotage a private shuttle!'

'Sabotage is a strong word, Galion,' Claine replied in a mock-hurt tone. 'I won't...render it unusable or anything. Nothing you can't fix easily. But when the mechanics *do* get round to fixing it, they'll notice that it's full of goods that shouldn't be there.'

Galion considered this for a few seconds, weighing it up in his mind. Then he reluctantly gave in. 'Hellin might be able to give you access to the Shipyards. But if you get caught-'

'I won't,' Claine interrupted firmly. 'Trust me. But somebody will, starting with *Fersilt* and ending in *Tenzebah*.'

Hellin answered without looking away from her task of microfusing the underside of a suspended car, in doing so showing admirable multitasking skills.

'The *Shinderinnian*?' she asked. 'No, that's not left yet, but it's due to go tomorrow, bound for Glaminda of all places.'

'That's where Nebula's HQ is located, isn't it?' Claine asked innocently.

'Yes, that it is,' Hellin replied. 'But why are you so interested in the *Shinderinnian*, anyway?'

'No reason,' she asked. 'I'd just...heard a rumour that it was leaving Eluxure for the first time in twenty years.'

Hellin nodded, apparently satisfied, and busied herself removing one of the tyres from the precariously suspended hover vehicle.

'And...damn!...speaking of the Shipyards, I'd nearly forgotten! A friend of mine put one of his miniature shuttles in for service, and he asked me to collect it for him.'

'Oh yeah?' asked Hellin. 'What's his name?'

'Cablios Gargaflit,' Claine told her, rehearsing the name of the client Galion had told her.

'Ah, yes, we know old Cablios,' Hellin replied. 'A troublemaker, he is. Likes doing all these atrocious stunts in his miniature shuttles, that's why they're always in for service.'

'Tell me about it,' Claine replied. 'He tried to take me

up once, but I refused.'

'Wise girl,' Hellin laughed. 'Now which particular shuttle did he ask you to collect?'

Claine racked her brains for the name that Galion had given her, that she'd thought she'd memorised. 'I think it was...the *Helli-Woll-Jetta.*'

Hellin nodded. 'Well, we're all flat out at the moment. Redn Termal would certainly not allow this if he was on today, but I'll give you my electronic pass...hang on a minute.'

She stopped what she was doing and fished around in her shirt pocket until she produced a blue holo-card, and passed it to Claine.

'There you go. Don't tell anyone. When you're in, get one of the Shipyardsmen to help you prepare the *Helli-Woll-Jetta* for removal.'

'Thanks, Hellin,' Claine told her, but the mechanic had activated a tool that emitted a loud buzzing noise, so she didn't hear her.

Then, grinning, the journalist made her way in the direction of the Shipyards.

2.

'Rastis! Hoy, Rastis!'

Melchior turned, halfway down Kenderye's elegant garden path, lined with topiary and marble faucets, at the sound of Corwin's voice, surprised that his old friend might have something important to tell him.

'What is it, Corwin?' he asked, as the policeman caught up to him, looking both delighted and very pleased with himself.

The Inspector turned a wide grin on his old friend. 'We've made yet another discovery,' he said, somewhat smugly, but did not elaborate, instead choosing to let the announcement hang in the air and annoy the Reptid, who had to prompt him to reveal more.

'Which is?' Melchior asked.

'Something else we found in Tenzebah's personal files,' Corwin told him. 'Young Cadez found it, actually, when he accessed Dunwall's accounts.'

'Accounts as in...?'

'Money, Rastis!' Corwin cried, grinning even wider, though this did nothing to detract from the Reptid's confusion. 'As Miss Glamure said, his personal accounts needed to be sorted out in order for Fersilt to receive his fortune, and for the late Mr Tenzebah's debts to be resolved.'

Melchior nodded. 'Yes, they would indeed need this. But what-?'

'And, anyway,' Corwin continued, interrupting Melchior and receiving one of the Reptid's infamous looks in retaliation, 'I got Cadez to sort it out, seeing as he did such a good job of his holomail accounts the other day...and guess what he found.'

Melchior sighed, in no mood to play twenty questions. 'I'm afraid that I don't see the point, considering you know the correct answer and I do not.'

'Well, I think it'll interest you, Rastis,' Corwin said, letting the dry humour of his old friend's remark slide. 'In the past two days alone, four thousand has been removed from Tenzebah's personal account.'

Melchior did indeed find that exceedingly interesting, for his head snapped up and stared at Corwin's. 'Four thousand...' he said. 'Astertii?'

'No, biscuits,' Corwin replied in a commendable impression of Melchior himself.

The Reptid gripped Inspector Tirranar's shoulders, looking at him intensely. 'And put where?'

'That's the thing, Rastis,' replied the Inspector, slightly unnerved, 'I have no idea. It's just gone.'

Melchior frowned, and relaxed his grip slightly, much to Corwin's relief. 'Well, it has not been removed by Tenzebah, that's for certain. Unless, of course, it was his ghost.'

Corwin looked at him sceptically, but the Reptid continued anyway. 'So somebody managed to hack his account and take money from it...'

'Yes,' replied Inspector Tirranar. 'But we can rule out Fersilt. He's inherited his father's full fortune now that he's dead. Tenzebah Jr. has no need to take more.'

'And yet,' Melchior countered, 'this reflects exactly what he has been doing with Dunwall's line of business. Redirecting it and transferring it from his father's cash stash into his own.'

Corwin shrugged. 'Well, at any rate, it's too early to say. Perhaps once we've examined the accounts of all our suspects-'

'That, Corwin, might tell us absolutely nothing,' Melchior interrupted. 'Fersilt has a constant flow of money coming in from Nebula. If indeed he is behind this, it will be impossible to tell if a percentage of that money is that taken from a dead man's account. No, you are correct when you say it's too early to tell. I daresay everything will be revealed, in time.'

Corwin shrugged again, apparently making a habit of the gesture. 'If you say so, Melchior. You've probably uncovered more information than the police already, anyway- as usual.'

Melchior smiled at him. 'Ah, yes. The old days, when you were just a police constable and I was just starting out as a detective. I seem to recall Inspector Jaffuse found me a constant source of annoyance.'

'Oh, and it's so different, now, isn't it, Rastis, because you *never* annoy police Inspectors in any way,' replied the other with a touch of sarcasm.

'Of course I don't annoy them,' replied Melchior. '*They* let themselves get annoyed by me. I assure you it isn't deliberate.'

'Oh yes? What about Rodarth?'

'Rodarth is a special case.'

'Yes,' murmured Corwin. 'That he is...'

Melchior glanced at him sharply, though he didn't notice. There was something in his voice, Melchior found, that brought to mind the strange, overheard conversation between Corwin and Rodarth, during which both Inspectors acted as though the latter were the former's superior...

'Anyway, I'd better get back to the house, eh, Rastis,' Tirranar said now. 'We'll be returning to the station soon and I think we'll remain away from Kenderye until further developments- thank goodness.'

'You have found nothing else, then?' Melchior asked. 'Besides, of course, the case of Dunwall's missing money.'

Corwin shook his head. 'No, I'm afraid not. But it means we won't have to keep going to Kenderye every day and finding nothing. I don't know why Rodarth thought we'd solve the case by doing the same thing over and over.'

'It seems to me, Corwin, that you and Rodarth don't get along well enough to function properly as co-Inspectors...' Melchior said cautiously. 'Surely one of you would have said something? I should think that, seeing as you disagree so much, one of you should have been transferred by now.'

Corwin paused, tight-lipped, as if unsure how to reply to that. 'It's...complicated, Rastis.'

Melchior was concerned at his old friend's tone, which sounded considerably more tired than before. 'How so, Corwin?'

But the Inspector shook his head. 'Nothing you need worry yourself about, old friend. Simply...circumstances of post.'

And then he bid Melchior goodbye and walked back down the garden towards Kenderye.

Circumstances of post, the Reptid mused. *What was that supposed to mean?*

Chapter Thirteen

1.

'All right, boys, let's get this fixed. We're on a heavy schedule!'

'Oi, and lass!' Durith corrected Hellin, wiping her hands on her overalls.

'Is that the *Shinderinnian,* Hellin?' asked Dendern Shulligan, observing the ship in awe.

'No, Shulls, she's Mr Gargaflit's miniature shuttle,' was the dry reply. 'Of course she's the bloomin' *Shinderinnian,* that's why *Shinderinnian* is engraved on her bloody hull! Now hop to it, she's bound for Glaminda this arvo.'

Shulls did indeed "hop to it", muttering a hasty 'yes, ma'am,' to avoid a walk on her bad side. From the outside, the ship looked fine, as though there was nothing wrong with it. Its smooth hull gleamed in the bright workplace floodlights, and it looked ready for takeoff.

'What's 'er problem, Hellin?' called Durith from over near the cargo compartment, which Balfoota was opening with exaggerated care, clearly as in awe of the shuttle as Shulls was.

'Something to do with her cargo retainers,' Hellin replied. 'Put it this way- if she tried to break through the atmosphere, the hold would open up and eject her cargo into space.'

'So, it's serious, then,' grinned Adeagre, always in good humour, as he jumped onto the still-opening ramp that led into the cargo hold and clung onto the retractable chains that were slowly lowering it to the ground like a drawbridge.

'That's one word for it,' Hellin said. 'But it's easily fixed. Balfoota, hurry up with the ramp. The ship ain't made of glass, so trust me, it won't break if you speed things up a little.'

Eventually the ramp touched the floor, creating an entrance into the cargo compartment. Shulls, Durith and Balfoota joined Adeagre in the hold, and busied themselves shifting crates away from the faulty cargo retainers.

'These don't half weigh a ton, Hellin,' groaned Shulls, hefting one of the metal crates.

'Yeah, what've they got in them, weights?' Adeagre

agreed, setting another down and rubbing his arm. 'I didn't think Glaminda had a high demand for gym equipment.'

Hellin rolled her eyes. 'You're all wusses, y'know? Out of shape. And you'd better get into shape if you can't even lift boxes full of nazcauca wool.'

Durith raised her eyebrows. 'Uh, sorry to prove you wrong, Hellin, but this stuff ain't no wool. Wool don't weigh ten tons.'

Hellin frowned and jumped into the cargo compartment herself. She looked at the four mechanics suspiciously, then bent down and tried lifting one of the crates.

BANG! She dropped it back down onto the floor of the hold and swore. 'You're right. That certainly ain't nazcauca wool.'

They all gathered around the crate, looking at it with some apprehension.

'Well, if it isn't nazcauca wool,' wondered Balfoota, scratching his beard, 'then what is it?'

'Only one way to find out,' Adeagre squatted, producing a cratebreaker from his jeans pocket. He looked up at Hellin. 'That is, with your permission, your majesty-'

'Just get on with it,' Hellin snapped at him.

Adeagre grinned and began running the cratebreaker along the edges of the crate lid, the tool making a whirring noise as it unlocked the box. Then he prised off the top of the crate and they all peered inside it.

'What the hell?' Shulls asked, frowning at the heavy-looking glass cylinders, each filled to the brim with a strange, bubbling amber-hued liquid. He reached out to touch it, but Hellin swatted his hand away.

She waggled her fingers in his face. 'See? I'm wearing gloves. I can handle stuff like this.'

She reached into the box and pulled out one of the cylinders, holding it up to the light.

'What *is* that?' asked Durith, looking at the hypnotic substance in captivation. 'It's kinda pretty.'

'I can honestly say I've got no clue,' Hellin announced, placing the cylinder back into its crate. 'But it's not supposed to be there.'

'Wait a mo,' said Adeagre suddenly, pointing at the tops of the cylinders, which were made of some kind of metal rather than the strong glass, and which sported a flamboyant logo.

'What is it?' asked Balfoota.

'That logo,' said Adeagre. 'The D.T surrounded by a circle with a line through it. That looks familiar, but I can't place where I've seen it.'

'I can,' said Hellin. Something about her voice had changed. She squatted down to peer at the cylinders closely then looked up at the others. 'That there is the symbol of Dunwall Tenzebah's trade.'

The reaction was as she'd expected.

'Dunny? No way,' said Shulls.

'What?' asked Balfoota incredulously. 'Like, *the* Dunwall Tenzebah?'

'What are Dunwall's goods doing in a cargo ship bound for Glaminda?' asked Durith.

'Well,' replied Hellin, glancing once again at the contents of the crate. 'I have a sneaking suspicion his son might be able to tell us.'

∞

'You did *what?* asked Melchior, unable to think of anything else to say.

'Well, it wasn't all me, in my own defence,' Claine replied, somewhat sulkily. 'Galion obviously helped, seeing as I can't tell the difference between a cargo retainer and a hyperspatial drive.'

Melchior sighed. 'Of course he did. You two really need to be supervised, you know. Otherwise you'll end up sabotaging expensive space shuttles and framing businessmen.'

Claine crossed her arms and glared at him. 'Sabotage is hardly the right word. I only tweaked something slightly.'

Melchior rubbed his face with his hands. 'Oh, of course. That makes it okay, then.'

'It does, actually. Galion assured me that it would be easily fixed. Besides, don't you *want* Fersilt caught? He's doing something that I'm fairly sure is illegal on every planet between here and Sildrone. So I haven't "framed" a businessman, I've brought him to justice.'

Melchior waited until her tirade was over, then asked politely, 'Have you finished, by any chance, Miss Soliss?'

Claine took a breath for the first time in a minute or so. 'I...think so.'

'Take a seat, please.'

'Thank you,' she replied, sitting down in one of the comfortable hotel chairs.

'Well done, by the way,' added Melchior. 'That was a very ingenious idea of yours, and I daresay it probably worked perfectly.'

Claine blinked a few times. 'Wait...you're praising me...for something that you just...told me off for doing?'

Melchior smiled at her. 'Personally, I probably would have done the same- if, of course, I was a sneaking sort of person. I just grilled you to see how you'd react.'

'I hate you,' Claine told him.

'Thank you,' said Melchior.

'You're welcome,' muttered Claine. 'Has the businessman been brought into the station yet?'

'I believe so,' Melchior replied. 'I also believe that he's not very happy about it.'

'Can't think why,' Claine said. 'Seeing as he's just been sprung redirecting goods.'

Melchior steepled his fingers underneath his chin in a thoughtful pose. 'I wonder if we will discover anything else...particularly interesting during his interrogation.'

'You think we might?'

Melchior shrugged. 'It's a possibility. But I find it hard to believe that Dunwall's murder, the disappearance of his account money, and now the redirection of his trade aren't all related somehow...'

'That puts Fersilt in the role of prime suspect,' Claine observed.

Melchior nodded. 'But that's just the thing. In my experience, the prime suspect is rarely the culprit.'

'Why not?'

Melchior stood and took his flowing red robe from the coat hook. 'Miss Soliss, take it from me. No murderer makes themselves too obvious.'

2.

Rodarth sighed deeply and rubbed his face vigorously with his hands when he looked out of the interrogation room window and saw not just Melchior, but Miss Soliss as well, entering the police station. Corwin had very wisely forewarned him that the Reptid would be sitting in on the interrogation again, but he had not been expecting the infuriating, irrepressible reporter as well.

Rodarth stood and walked out the door into the waiting room, in order to glare at the two arrivals.

'Ah, Inspector. I hope we're not late?' Melchior asked. It

was almost as though he was being annoying deliberately. In fact, Rodarth was fairly sure he was.

'Miss Soliss has no authorisation to-'

'Oh, I know all *that*,' Claine interrupted. 'I didn't expect to sit in. Strictly confidential, I know. I'll just sit out here, in the waiting room.'

Rodarth stared at her. 'What for?'

Claine shrugged and migrated to a seat just in front of the main desk, then smiled up at him. 'Do go on. Don't mind me.'

'I trust Corwin is present?' asked Melchior, brushing past Rodarth and (on seeing that yes, Corwin was), taking a seat on the other side of Inspector Tirranar.

'Morning, Rastis,' Corwin greeted him.

Rodarth entered and closed the door behind him. 'So you think this somehow has something to do with the murder, eh?'

'That is correct. I don't see how it would not, especially considering the fact that it involves one of our suspects and the dead man's cargo.'

The recently-closed door opened again and Cadez stuck his head in. 'Should I send in Mr Tenzebah?'

'Yes, Cadez, send him in,' Rodarth replied.

'Err, and, sir- may I ask what Miss Soliss is doing in the waiting room?'

'I don't think she needs a specific reason to be anywhere,' Corwin said, a sentence that was actually remarkably accurate. 'Just...entertain her if you can.'

Cadez nodded and retracted his head, not looking very put out at all.

Fersilt Tenzebah was not in a good mood. He glared at the Inspectors and Melchior in turn over his glasses, wringing his hands in an agitated way.

'There's no denying it, Mr Tenzebah,' said Rodarth. 'You've been discovered, and I doubt there's anything you can say to convince me otherwise.'

'You found a ship bound for the planet I use as an HQ, that just so happened to contain goods marked with my father's logo, and so you think you can arrest me?' Fersilt scoffed.

'Good, I'm glad you're beginning to catch on,' said Corwin. 'Very suspicious, I'm sure you'll agree.'

Fersilt sneered again. He did a lot of sneering, thought Corwin.

'Oh, come on,' he said. 'Of course I redirected the old fool's goods to Glaminda. What use to me was my father's business when I couldn't benefit from it?'

Corwin sat back, surprised.

'What I *said,*' Fersilt went on, 'was "so you think you can arrest me?"'

Melchior frowned. 'You mean that we cannot...as in we are unable to.'

Fersilt smirked. 'Of course you can't. What's the charge,

again?'

'Your charge, Mr Tenzebah, is illegal appropriation of goods,' said Rodarth. 'I thought that much was clear.'

'Yes, yes. But what category does that fall under?' asked Fersilt rhetorically. 'It falls under *business*. And I'm afraid you can't interfere with business, however illegal it is. It's just not your area.'

'I don't think you see, Mr Tenzebah, that whilst we cannot arrest you, once we pass you on to the business authorities, they *can* arrest you, seeing as your charge *is* their area,' growled Corwin.

'If word gets out of this, I'm ruined,' said Fersilt helpfully.

'Not our problem,' sneered Rodarth.

'It is, though,' Fersilt said. 'Because I'm still one of your suspects. In fact, I'm still your *prime* suspect. And for all you know, *I* have certain information which you might find useful. But, if word gets out of this, I won't tell you.'

'You can't bribe us,' said Corwin.

'You won't solve the case unless you rip up that charge form there,' Fersilt replied, nodding towards the form before Rodarth, which certified his guilt in redirecting cargo.

There was a tense silence, each of them unsure whether or not to believe Fersilt. It was quite likely that he knew something about the case, in which case they would benefit greatly from doing what he wanted.

'We could just...extract the truth out of you,' said Rodarth, but Melchior and Corwin vetoed the idea with a strong 'NO!'

'You're not torturing anyone, Rodarth,' Melchior said. 'It goes against all morals.'

'All of yours, perhaps,' said Rodarth. 'But this man has to learn to play by the law.'

'Even if you do not?' Melchior asked innocently.

Rodarth made as if to strike him, but Corwin stopped him. 'Rodarth! Enough!' here he glanced at Melchior and Fersilt, before saying, 'that's an order!'

Surprisingly, Rodarth retracted his hand, and Melchior found himself dumbfounded. Up until now, it had been Rodarth acting as though he were Corwin's superior. But now here was Corwin, giving Rodarth an order, even though he had no more power to do so than the latter.

'You choose,' said Fersilt, as though nothing had happened. 'Either you get the satisfaction of arresting me, or the satisfaction of solving your case. I promise I'll tell the complete truth.'

Corwin and Melchior glanced at each other, then Corwin opened his mouth to say, *'In that case, you will be handed over to business authorities to be arrested and locked up for however many years they deem necessary,'* but before he could, there was an audible rip.

Rodarth was sitting back in his chair, a smug smile on his face, one half of Fersilt's charge form in each hand. 'I'll tell Cadez to delete the digital copy immediately,' he said.

But Fersilt shook his head. 'That's not all you need to do, Inspector.'

'Oh?' asked Rodarth, ignoring the expressions on Melchior's and Corwin's faces.

'If I'm truly to walk free,' said Tenzebah Jr, 'you'll have to dispose of the evidence.'

Corwin started to say something but again Rodarth ignored him and pressed the "talk" button on his earpiece. 'Thaligger- get rid of the evidence against Fersilt Tenzebah.'

'Rodarth!' Corwin exclaimed. 'That's hundreds- no, thousands...'

'The family trust will survive,' Fersilt said dismissively. 'It's not as though my father's business is short on money.'

Rodarth disconnected his earpiece and smiled slyly at Fersilt. 'The evidence has been destroyed.'

Fersilt smiled too. 'There. See? Inspector Rodarth has acted wisely.'

Corwin glared at Rodarth.

'This case has to be solved,' the other Inspector told him, with a *for-the-greater-good* expression nobody was buying.

'Even if it means letting a guilty man walk free?' Corwin growled.

Melchior bit his lip and addressed Fersilt. 'Now, I hope that you are happy, Mr Tenzebah. Your precious reputation remains intact.'

'Oh, I am happy,' was the reply.

'In that case, there is nothing else that we can do but do it your way. I must ask you to honour your side of the bargain.'

Fersilt smiled. 'Of course.'

He did not elaborate, and Melchior realised he wished them to ask him questions. Melchior gritted his teeth at his impertinence, but did as Fersilt wanted, hoping very much that he'd be able to tell them something useful.

'All right then,' he said. 'Did you kill Dunwall Tenzebah?'

The two Inspectors looked at Fersilt closely, knowing that he would have no choice but to reply truthfully.

But Tenzebah Jr. just smirked at Melchior smugly and uttered one, agonising word.

'No.'

∞

Claine jumped up out of her seat as Melchior emerged from the interrogation room, a deep frown on his face.

'How did it go?' she asked eagerly. 'Has he been arrested?'

'No,' was the flat reply. 'He has not.'

The smile melted from Claine's face. 'Then...what happened?'

'The interrogation was exceedingly...unsatisfactory,' said Melchior, and proceeded to relate to her what happened inside the interrogation room as they exited the police station.

After he had finished, Claine's usually sunny disposition was much gloomier. 'So I had to sneak into the Shipyards and risk my neck tampering with the cargo retainers for nothing?'

Melchior wished he could say, 'No, not nothing! Fersilt revealed to us the murderer!' but he could not. All Fersilt had said was that he hadn't killed his father, and it was debatable that he had told the truth.

No, the brutal fact was that Fersilt had tricked his way out of arrest by luring them with information he didn't have. He wouldn't have got away with it, either, if Rodarth had not been so easily deceived.

Melchior wondered how the man had ever gravitated to the role of Inspector. He could hardly do the job properly.

He was so caught up in thinking that he did not answer Claine's question, and they lapsed into a gloomy silence that did not match the weather in the slightest, all the way back to the hotel.

Claine had successfully managed to catch the man, and when they had gone to interrogate him all he'd done was tell them nothing they didn't know already, trick a police officer into letting him walk free with his reputation unscathed, and deliver a single word in the place of the information he had promised.

And they were no closer to knowing who did it.

Chapter Fourteen

1.

'You'd better watch out for Red today,' warned Shulls as Galion passed him on his way to the employees' quarters.

'Why's that?' asked Galion, stopping and frowning at this piece of advice.

Shulls shrugged, hammering a piece of metal a couple of times and not really achieving anything at all by it. 'Well, you know he doesn't like you stayin' here even after 'e's fired you. I think that reporter lady visiting you the other day really p'ed him off.'

'But why would that...?'

Shulls shrugged, clenching the hammer between his teeth and screwing the metal to the side of a car by hand.

Galion waited patiently while he did this until the hammer was out of Shulls' mouth and he could speak.

'You'd better mind your step, in any case,' he said. 'Or you might not have somewhere to sleep tonight, you get my meaning?'

Galion nodded, storing this knowledge in his mind for when he ran into Redn Termal next. 'Thanks, Shullsey. I'll bear that in mind.'

'Don't mention it, kid. Now get lost.'

Galion went to "get lost", but he was stopped again, this time by Hellin.

'Hey, Vasail.'

'Yes, ma'am?' Galion asked.

'Shulls has probably told you that Redn's in a foul mood,' Hellin said.

Galion nodded. 'That he has.'

Hellin nodded back, but continued to look at him, concerned. 'Steer clear of him, OK?'

'I'll do that,' said Galion, wondering how bad Redn's temper would have to be on this particular day for two people to warn him about it. *Termal must be out for my blood.*

'And, Galion...you sussed out a new job yet?'

'Not yet, Hellin,' Galion replied truthfully. 'But I'm on it.'

'You better be,' Hellin said threateningly, and Galion found himself grinning at her mock severity- though to be honest she could be genuinely severe at times, and that was not something to grin about.

He began to make his way through the workplace to the stairs leading up to his temporary lodgings, occasionally receiving comments like, 'best stay in your room today, Gally,' and 'It's a nice day for sightseeing, if you get my drift,' and, from Mascal, 'you still here?'

And, using his common sense, Galion decided to heed their warnings and stay confined to his room until Termal knocked off work. May as well get some *Gazette* articles sorted out, he thought gloomily.

He still hadn't got very far. No further, in fact, than he had been when Claine had visited.

Once upstairs, he sat down heavily on the couch in his room and switched on the holo-viewer. At once the article about Aikenald Tenzebah's death popped up on the screen. He didn't bother examining it further- instead he clicked a button and it flicked to the next article.

This one was immediately more interesting. Galion sat up from his slumped position on the couch and peered closely at the article.

An End to Adventures for Chasterleigh and Tenzebah?

The title, Galion found, needed a little work, but the article topic itself was very interesting indeed...

Famous young adventurers Dunwall Tenzebah and Sadrien Chasterleigh have both proposed to their long-time sweethearts, who remained behind whilst their brave partners went gallivanting around the galaxy. "Neither of us knew," said Sadrien in an exclusive interview. "I'd just planned to propose to Larillian, and [Dunwall] had just planned to propose to Marsine. It's not like we deliberately synchronised or anything." On his decision to propose, Dunwall told Eluxure Gazette *associate newspaper* Galaxy Gazette: *"I felt as though the time was right, and no doubt Sadrien felt that about [Larillian] too. We'd been adventuring for nearly as long as I'd been with Marsine, so it was about time she and I were engaged!" When asked if this meant that they would put an end to their adventures now that they had other commitments, both men gave essentially the same answer. "I certainly hope not!" Sadrien laughed, whilst Dunwall's response was a little more serious. "I don't think one should get in the way of the other, actually. Before we were engaged, my gallivanting didn't come between Marsine and I in any way. We still saw each other a lot- it was just like going to work, really. But now that we're engaged, neither of us thinks that that should mean Sadrien and I's [sic] adventures are over."*

Galion peered at the accompanying photographs. The first showed Dunwall and Marsine, both looking very young and very happy. Now, as Galion knew and found slightly sad, Dunwall was dead and Marsine bitter and neglected. He looked at the other photograph and had to double-take.

It was much the same as the first, except it showed Sadrien and his fiancee, holding hands and looking just as happy. Larillian was stunningly pretty- beautiful, in fact. Galion found himself entranced by her photograph, and could easily see how Sadrien had been attracted to her. He dimly remembered Melchior saying something about her having passed away not too long ago, and Sadrien having suffered her loss keenly.

But what was really interesting about the photograph was that Galion *recognised* Larillian. His eyes darted back to the main article, caught by a sudden theory that he was desperate to prove. He skipped the section that focused on Dunwall and Marsine (though that might come in handy later), and found the paragraph on the other couple.

Sadrien Chasterleigh, 26, met his true love on his own planet of Palpoutha, when she was studying as an exchange student. Despite the women of Pristile being famed for using their almost eerie charm to seduce men, there was nothing about the development of their relationship to suggest it was not genuine. Larillian Lessete is a woman of great beauty, independence and intelligence, and needed no added Pristilian charm to win the heart of handsome young Sadrien Chasterleigh, who immediately fell in love with her, and she with him.

He looked back to the photograph of Chasterleigh and

Lessete, suddenly filled with a certain amount of excitement at this breakthrough. At least, he was fairly certain it was a breakthrough, and if his hunch was correct...

He pulled out his mobile and dialled Melchior's hotel room number. He let it ring a few times, but didn't have the patience to try again when it rang out, so instead left a message.

'Hey, Melchior,' he said, 'You'll be very interested to hear this, so I'm coming round to tell you what I've found, even if you're busy.'

He grinned, though he knew Melchior couldn't see him, and began pulling on his jacket. 'See you in a couple of minutes.'

∞

Melchior opened the door to his room, and was immediately greeted by a robotic voice, that claimed that he had "One new voice message. Would you like to open it?"

He frowned, trying to think who would be messaging him, as he hung his over-robe on the coathook and strolled over to the hotel room phone, which sat on a table in the middle of the lounge area.

'Yes, go ahead,' he instructed the robot, and it proceeded to play the message.

Melchior immediately recognised Galion's voice.

'Hey, Melchior. You'll be very interested to hear this, so I'm coming round to tell you what I've found, even if you're busy. See you in a couple of minutes.'

Melchior raised his equivalent of eyebrows. This could very well be much more productive than his recent interrogation session with Fersilt.

Knock-knock-knock!

He opened the door, only to find Galion standing there, slightly out of breath.

The young mechanic grinned at him, brandishing something that Melchior recognised as the record Claine had burgled from the *Gazette* HQ. 'There's something on here you might find interesting,' he said. 'Oh, and a certain theory of mine, which I think you might want to hear.'

Melchior blinked. 'You'd better come in, then.'

'Thanks,' replied the mechanic, approaching the central table and inserting the archive into the hotel's holographic projector.

The article he'd found sprung up in full colour, and Melchior immediately began reading, wondering what it was about it that Galion found so interesting.

'*An End to Adventures for Chasterleigh and Tenzebah,*' he read aloud. 'What's this about?'

'Keep reading,' urged Galion eagerly, and Melchior did as instructed.

'I can't say I see what makes this article so...'

'Read the third paragraph,' said the mechanic. 'The one about Sadrien and Larillian.'

Melchior skimmed to the third paragraph and read it with an increasing frown. Then his eyes widened and his eyes performed the same flick to the photograph that Galion had done when he'd first made the connection.

'I think I know what you're talking about,' he said slowly. 'Your earlier theory, about...'

'Exactly,' said Galion. 'You see the resemblance? And she's Pristilian.'

'I think, Galion,' said Melchior. 'That your hunch is absolutely correct.'

'Yes?' he replied with a little more surprise than he'd intended.

Melchior tapped the photograph, or more specifically the caption, which read, *Sadrien Chasterleigh and Larillian Lessete.*

'My Pristilese may be a little rusty, but if I remember correctly...' here he glanced at Galion with a smile on his face. 'Lessete, I believe, means "glamour" in Larillain's tongue.'

Galion replied to the smile with a grin of his own. 'Or maybe,' he said, 'Glamure...'

2.

215

Trissilan Glamure was in the middle of re-organising Dunwall's cheque folders when Galion, that other reporter woman, Inspector Tirranar and the lizard man entered the study.

She looked up in surprise, and met Galion's eyes, hoping he might enlighten her as to these unexpected visitors, but he just looked somewhat indecisive, and shrugged unhelpfully.

'Well,' she said, smiling disarmingly. 'This is an...unexpected surprise.'

'Generally, Miss Glamure, most surprises are,' said the detective- Melchior, she remembered. Rastis Melchior.

'I'm a little busy at the moment- *actually* busy, not that unusual pacing thing that Fersilt thinks is being busy...' she said, with a slight roll of her eyes, 'but I'm sure I can afford to spend a little time helping you out with whatever you need,' she directed a flashing smile in Galion's direction, and he smiled back, distracted by her Pristilian charm until the journalist woman- Claire something?- kicked him in the shin.

'So, how can I help you?' Trissilan asked them. 'Need more of Dunwall's files?'

'No, actually,' said Corwin. 'We've come to see you about a more...personal matter, in fact, Miss Glamure...' here she raised her eyebrows in polite interest, '...or should I say...Miss Lessete?'

For the first time, Melchior saw Trissilan's constant

smile flicker. She turned her head sharply to look directly at Corwin.

'I'm sorry?' she asked, with a half-laugh.

'Inspector Tirranar,' Melchior put in, clearing his throat, 'is referring to your mother, Larillian Lessete.'

Trissilan swallowed nervously, all traces of happy-go-lucky charm gone. 'I...I don't...'

'You are part Pristilian, are you not, Miss Glamure?'

Trissilan clenched her jaw and looked down. 'Yes,' she said. 'I am. How did you guess?'

Galion made a hand sign behind her back, signalling for Melchior to refrain from mentioning his involvement in her discovery, for reasons that the Reptid were fairly sure had something to do with Trissilan's enchantments. They had worked on the young mechanic, at any rate.

'We found an article,' Melchior explained gently. 'In the archives of the *Eluxure Gazette*. It focused partially on your parents- Sadrien Chasterleigh and his then-fiancee, Larillian Lessete.'

Trissilan looked up, glancing from Corwin to Melchior to Galion.

'There was a photograph in the article,' Corwin continued, taking over from the detective, 'of Sadrien and Larillian, and there was a strong family resemblance, particularly with your mother. And this was only confirmed when we were able to translate your mother's maiden name, Lessete, from Pristilese to standard Galactic, to *glamour.'*

Trissilan remained silent, but now made no eye contact with anyone.

'Can you tell us, perhaps, why you have deceived everyone by using the standard galactic translation of your mother's maiden name, rather than your real one- that is, Chasterleigh?'

There was a silence for several long counts. Then Trissilan said, 'You're right, of course. My name is Trissilan Chasterleigh, and I'm the daughter of Larillian Lessete and Sadrien Chasterleigh. And, yes, I lied to everyone about who I really am, but if I hadn't, I'd never have got the job.'

Melchior put his head on one side. 'As Tenzebah's PA?'

Trissilan nodded. 'I only wanted it to get back at my father. When he first learnt about Elixir, he consumed himself with it. All he did was research Elixir, and he had no time for his own daughter. Oh, he was a great dad when I was younger, but as I grew up I barely saw him as much as I should've. Can you imagine what that's like? I wanted to get back at him *so* badly, and the only way to do that was to get employment under his own arch enemy. It was no trouble, really, and I was Dunwall's personal assistant like that,' she snapped her fingers.

'So your...infatuation with Tenzebah was just a deception, in order to get back at Sadrien?' Corwin asked, but Trissilan shook her head violently and glared up at him. Melchior was surprised to notice tears in her eyes.

'No, you don't understand. I *did* love Dunwall,' she said. 'I don't care what Marsine thinks, or what the world thinks. I loved him, and that probably just hurt my father even more. I would *never* have killed him, and if you think I did, then you'd better think again, because you're *wrong*.'

Corwin took an involuntary step back, palms turned upwards.

'My apologies, Miss Glamure,' he said. 'I spoke hastily.'

'Now, please,' said Trissilan, 'if you're happy knowing what you came here to confirm, can you leave me to work?'

Melchior bowed slightly. 'As you wish, Miss Gla-'

Suddenly, Trissilan let out a gasping noise and leaned against her desk for support, clutching her chest. Galion and Corwin rushed to her side, alarmed.

'Trissilan?' asked Galion. 'What's wrong?'

Trissilan winced. 'I'm...I'm fine...'

'You are not,' Melchior told her. 'What is the matter?'

Trissilan shook her head.

'She must be tired,' Corwin said. 'She's been run off her feet with Tenzebah's files. And our accusation on top of that, poor girl.'

'I'll...go and have a lie down,' Trissilan said, her hand migrating to her head. 'I've got a splitting headache, and-' she broke off and swayed slightly.

'Are you sure you don't need a hand, Trissilan?' asked

Galion, concerned.

She waved him off weakly, heading for the door. 'I'll be fine,' she assured Corwin as he too tried to support her. 'Yes...a lie down. I'll be fine.'

Melchior and Claine remained in the study.

'Do you think she's alright?' asked Claine, in a strange tone, as though she was concerned for Miss Glamure's health but didn't particularly want to be.

'We shall see, I expect,' replied Melchior. 'Trissilan would have been better to accept the help of Galion or Corwin. But she seemed...adamant that she was all right.'

'Even though she's clearly not,' Claine scoffed. 'You don't honestly think that she's just *tired*, do you? And if she's got a headache, I'll eat my holo-camera. She clutched her chest, not her head, didn't you see?'

Melchior nodded. 'It is clear that something else ails her, though I am uncertain as to what.'

Claine's face lit up with an idea. 'You don't think...?'

'What?'

'You don't think she's been *poisoned*, do you?'

Melchior, who had considered this, nodded gravely. 'That is the most likely answer.'

'Then, she's in danger!'

'She may have been in danger for quite some time now. We have no idea how long the poison has been inside her.'

'Then, isn't there something we can do?'

Melchior shook his head. 'Trissilan has made it clear she

won't accept assistance. She's obviously used to being independent, and even if she did allow us to check on her, there may not be time enough to diagnose the poison and conjure up an antidote.'

Claine fell silent, and Melchior glanced at her.

'We shouldn't suspect the worst,' Melchior assured her. 'But we shall see.'

'Hey, Melchior!'

They turned, surprised, to see Constable Cadez, slightly out of breath, approach the study.

'What's wrong with Triss?' he asked. 'I mean- Miss Glamure, of course.'

'We know not as yet,' Melchior replied, truthfully. 'Fatigue, it appears, is all.'

Cadez nodded, not entirely convinced. 'I passed her just then. She didn't reply when I called out to her.'

Claine glanced at Melchior, and he at her.

'She was in as much of a state when she left the study,' Melchior told the anxious Constable. 'But I'm sure she'll be fine in the morning.'

Cadez nodded, not looking convinced that Melchior's statement was true, and, to be fair, it wasn't. Then the Constable bade the two goodbye and left again.

'Curiouser and curiouser, said Alice,' muttered Claine.

'What?' was Melchior's response.

'It's an old quote from Earth history,' she explained. 'What I meant was, Cadez seems awfully worried for

Trissilan, even though we know she didn't return his affections.'

Melchior nodded. He recalled Corwin telling him about Cadez's flirtatious tendencies, and that his advances towards the beautiful Miss Glamure were received with an air of impatience. Needless to say, Trissilan hadn't attempted to seduce Cadez as she had Galion, which Melchior found somewhat out of character. It seemed, once again, Melchior thought, that in solving mysteries, he had uncovered yet more.

Chapter Fifteen

1.

The next day Miss Glamure was perfectly fine, and in fact seemed full of life, much to the false relief of Marsine, who still possessed a strong dislike for the source of her husband's infidelity. Trissilan came downstairs to breakfast with all traces of her previous discomfort gone.

'I trust you are better, Miss Glamure?' asked Marsine, smiling as she poured a spot of lavender milk into her morning coffee.

'Vital, Mrs T,' was the reply, as Trissilan took a seat at the elegant breakfast table and helped herself to a breakfast brastry. 'Just a spot of fatigue, that's all.'

A spot of fatigue, thought Mrs Tenzebah, was an

understatement. The girl had, from what she had heard from the police Inspector, Corwin Tirranar, been close to collapsing last night, due to reasons they did not know but were almost certainly not simply fatigue.

'Will the policemen be back again today?' Trissilan asked casually.

'I'm glad to say they will not. But that reporter, apparently, wishes to pay another visit,' replied Marsine, clearly not entirely happy with this arrangement. 'I could refuse, of course- it's very tiring having journalists and police officers flocking around the house.'

'Well, there's not much you can do about it at the moment,' said Trissilan. 'Not if you want your husband's murder solved.'

Marsine looked up at her sharply. 'Of course I want Dunwall's killer caught, girl! Why wouldn't I? I loved him!'

Trissilan looked down at her brastry and muttered under her breath, 'It's a shame he didn't return the affection...'

'What was that?' barked Marsine, and Trissilan remembered that the old woman's hearing had not deteriorated in the slightest. She smiled up at her innocently.

'Nothing, Mrs T,' she said. 'Just talking to myself. I've still got a lot to do, what with sorting out Dunwall's files.'

Marsine snorted to herself. *Dunwall's files were not in*

enough of a mess that they needed to be sorted out so much following his death, she thought. *Miss Glamure has no reason to be experiencing fatigue- not when there's been practically nothing for her to do. She must have been faking fatigue for some reason- or else she was poisoned!* She took a sip of coffee, and found it far too bitter. *Personally I hope it was the latter, though she seems to have recovered.*

'Oh, I'm sure Dunwall's files can wait,' she said aloud. 'You've been run off your feet. You should rest for a day, relax.'

Trissilan smiled back. *She doesn't actually care whether I've been run off my feet or not, the old witch,* she thought. *No doubt she doesn't believe all I say. Too clever for her own good, especially at the age she is. She knows as well as I do that my dizzy spell wasn't fatigue, but as for what it really was...* She shrugged and took another bite of brastry. *But why would she pretend to be sympathetic? She hasn't in the past.*

'Well, I'll take your advice, Mrs T,' she said. 'It won't hurt to take a break from working, at any rate.'

Marsine raised her eyebrows as Miss Glamure took another of the fairly large brastries and began to tear it apart.

'Hungry, my dear?' she asked lightly.

Trissilan nodded. 'Yes, I've got a rather large appetite this morning. Being sick will do that, I suppose. I do hope you don't mind if I devour several more of these delicious brastries?'

'Oh, do go ahead,' was Marsine's dry, barely-audible reply. '*I* certainly wasn't going to eat any more.'

∞

'Here, let me help you with that,' said Claine, as T'chisa came round the corner with an armful of cleaning equipment. The maid looked as though she would drop something at any second, and was glad of some assistance, which Claine was all too happy to offer.

'Thank you, miss,' T'chisa said, and Claine lifted some of the load from her arms. '*K'lish Tri'tk'ona.*'

Claine looked at her, surprised. 'That's N'choth'nian?'

T'chisa let out a little laugh, the first time Claine had seen her do so. It was a sign, she thought, that the maid was beginning to feel more comfortable, more relaxed, in her presence.

'The word is wrong,' she told the journalist. 'My language is simply *N'choth'ni,* like my race. Just in here,' she added, as they entered what was obviously T'chisa's storeroom and, from the looks of it, quarters. The living conditions were no better than Galion's, but the maid was lucky nonetheless. Claine knew a lot of N'choth'ni maids had terrible lodgings.

'Do you miss your planet, T'chisa?' she asked. 'Err,

what's it called? N'choth? N'choth'nia?'

T'chisa laughed again, setting down her load of cleaning supplies. 'No. It is called-' here she let out a string of clicks and other strange noises that denied the shape of the average human tongue, but that evidently rolled smoothly off hers.

'Oh,' said Claine. 'Of course. Silly me.'

'And, to answer your question,' T'chisa went on. 'Yes, I do miss it sometimes. Though I did not know it in its height of society, when we were a free race and a successful people.'

Claine frowned. She didn't know much about the history of the maid's race- the extent of her knowledge of N'choth'ni were just useless bits of trivia she had picked up here and there. 'What happened?' she asked.

T'chisa looked suddenly sad. 'We were enslaved,' she said. 'By humanoids called Rozan Imperials. They took advantage of the simple appearance and the obedience of my people, and turned them into slaves, to labour and mine for lunar quartz that would fund their empire. At the end of their reign, we were liberated, but only a fragment of what we once were. My planet is now the ruins of a thriving population, as though we have...regressed from what we once were. So my childhood was not as it might have been if I had lived two hundred years ago, but still I miss my home, and my family.'

Claine looked around the storeroom. 'You live here?'

'Yes, miss,' replied T'chisa, as though such conditions were an honour. 'It is good of Mrs Tenzebah to keep me on after my master has died.'

That was the first time Claine had heard "good" and "Tenzebah" in the one sentence, especially from T'chisa's mouth. She held up a pitcher of clear green liquid. 'Where does this go?'

'Up in that store cupboard, miss,' was the reply. 'You don't have to keep helping. I can manage.'

'It's no problem, T'chisa,' Claine assured her, opening the indicated cupboard and placing the pitcher on the top shelf, which she assumed was the correct place for it.

'Watch out, miss,' T'chisa warned. 'The shelves are...precarious.'

'I'm fine!' she said, brightly, but that was before she accidentally knocked over a jar of what looked like bath salts.

She made a spectacular catch and saved the jar from smashing into pieces on the ground and creating another mess for the poor maid to clean up, but she was too late to stop the lid, which had shaken loose, and which, alongside half the contents of the container, now fell to the ground.

'Sorry!' she cried, placing the jar back on the shelf then crouching to clean up the mess she'd made (though T'chisa, raised to be a good maid, was already scooping the bath salts from the floor).

'It's no problem, miss,' T'chisa assured her. 'It was an

easy accident to have.'

In Claine's experience, there was no such thing as an "easy accident". Accidents generally had a tendency to be difficult for at least someone.

She began picking up individual bath salts and placing them in her cupped palm, still apologising to T'chisa, then stopped suddenly as she caught a whiff of them.

'T'chisa?' she asked with a frown. 'What sort of bath salts are these?'

'Just the ordinary kind,' replied the maid, confused. 'What is the brand? Ah, yes- *Crisse-Talin.*'

Claine frowned again, and sniffed the collection of bath salts in her hand. *Crisse-Talin* was a popular brand of self-care products. She herself had used their bath salts back on Earth. And the smell was very different from how she remembered.

'These aren't *Crisse-Talin,*' she told the maid, who looked over at her, confused. 'And I very much doubt they're bath salts.'

'Well,' said the police pharmacist, examining the bath salts under a strong microscope, before looking up at Claine approvingly. 'You're right, miss. These certainly aren't bath salts.'

Claine beamed, pleased with herself for noticing such a potential clue.

Melchior stopped in his routine pacing at the

pharmacist's words, obviously intrigued by them, and turned to face Dr Elpaine. 'Then what are they?'

Elpaine stuck his hands in the pockets of his white lab coat. 'Well, they appear to be pure millovernin crystals.'

Claine looked at him, none the wiser. 'Which are?'

'They're a drug, are they not?' interjected Corwin suddenly.

Elpaine nodded. 'They are, Inspector. They won't have an effect on you in small doses, short term *or* long term, except for a vague feeling of light-headedness. But taken in large doses, consumed or otherwise, it's enough to send you into a deep sleep.'

'How deep, exactly?' asked Melchior.

'Up to twenty-four hours,' was Elpaine's reply. 'But it's hard to say without knowing the exact amount administered.'

'And how, may I ask,' drawled Rodarth, clearly uninterested, 'does this help in any way with the investigation?'

'Well, for starters, it could be what was used to poison Miss Glamure,' said Claine. 'Doctor, can enough of an amount kill someone?'

Elpaine took off his holo-powered glasses. 'Well, I daresay it could, but if it's a deliberate poisoning you're talking about, I can safely say the difference in taste would be most definitely noticeable.'

Rodarth smiled. 'There you go. See? The millovernin is

no doubt an unhealthy habit of one of the family members, who is addicted to such a drug. Even the maid, of course, seeing as it was found in her storeroom cupboard.'

Claine shook her head. 'Millovernin doesn't have to be ingested. Dr Elpaine said so. Seeing as the drug was disguised as bath salts, I think it's obvious that it was absorbed, after being dissolved in a bath. Except, of course, the fact that Trissilan did not put into the bath a sufficient amount to kill her.'

'May I interject, Miss Soliss,' Melchior winced. 'Though your ideas are, of course, brilliant, a murderer would not replace bath salts with millovernin unless they were absolutely sure they would reach the intended target.'

Claine crossed her arms. 'So what do you suggest the drug was used for?'

'Who was T'chisa's immediate master?' Melchior asked.

Claine blinked. 'Well, Dunwall Tenzebah, I suppose.'

Melchior nodded. 'Ah,' he said. 'So, it seems only natural that any self-care products found in Mr Tenzebah's servant's quarters would be used mainly by Mr Tenzebah himself, does it not?'

Nobody replied, no doubt wondering where he was going with this.

'So therefore, whoever swapped the bath salts with millovernin intended to poison not Miss Glamure, but...'

He looked around at the other four with a small smile.

'Dunwall Tenzebah,' finished Corwin, astonished. 'But he wasn't killed by an overdose of millovernin, he was killed by the theft of Elixir.'

'And,' added Rodarth, for possibly the first time ever agreeing with his co-Inspector, 'his skeleton wasn't found in his bathtub, either.'

Melchior was silent for several seconds, while he turned these points over in his head with his eyes closed.

'On the other hand,' said Claine, breaking the silence, 'The skeleton wasn't wearing any clothes, now, was it?'

Melchior's eyes snapped open.

'By the time a human is reduced to a skeleton, the clothes have mostly decomposed,' Dr Elpaine said, confused. 'That's not unusual.'

'Except,' said Melchior, 'Dunwall Tenzebah became a skeleton in the space of a few minutes.'

'Excuse me?' asked Elpaine, taken aback, though nobody bothered to enlighten him.

'I think,' the Reptid went on, 'that our murderer has been very clever indeed. We have been puzzling our heads over how someone managed to steal Elixir from Dunwall's very person, but it's been staring us in the face!'

'What has?' asked Claine.

'Something one of the retirees said. That Tenzebah had Elixir on him at all times...*except for when he was in the bath.*'

Corwin's eyes widened. 'So somebody replaced his bath

salts with millovernin, waited until he was out cold...'

'Then snuck into his private quarters and stole Elixir!' Claine finished, eyes wide and excited.

'And,' Melchior added, 'dragged Tenzebah's unconscious body from the bath, from the crime scene, and into the armchair by the fire.'

Rodarth snorted. 'Without spilling a drop?'

Melchior shrugged. 'Millovernin can send someone into a semi-coma for up to twenty-four hours. Plus, we don't know the precise time Tenzebah died, due to the body being a skeleton. That, I think, is plenty enough time for him, the armchair, and the drag-marks from the bathroom to the hearth, to dry.'

Claine grinned. 'That's brilliant.'

'It is,' Melchior agreed. 'But I'm afraid our murderer may continue to be brilliant. I might remind you that this case is far from being solved.'

Rodarth raised his eyebrows. 'Really? I would have thought it was quite obvious that the maid was the culprit.'

'We have no proof of that!' Claine growled.

'Oh, is it we now?' Rodarth asked. 'I thought you were just out for a good scoop.'

'It might help, of course,' interrupted Corwin before he was given reason to arrest the journalist for minor assault on a policeman, 'to know where one can acquire millovernin.'

Elpaine coughed. 'That one is easy. Millovernin deposits

can be found on several uninhabited worlds, but the most likely source of this particular lot is the planet Kilmorim.'

Melchior smiled widely. 'Kilmorim! Of course! What else?'

Claine paused in the act of giving Rodarth a particularly vicious greaze and looked at the Reptid with one eyebrow raised. 'Are you OK, Melchior?'

'Oh, fine,' he assured her, which wasn't very reassuring at all. 'Claine, can you tell me- who do we know who's been to Kilmorim?'

2.

Sadrien Chasterleigh was surprised, not to mention unamused, to find two police inspectors and a lizard standing at his front door.

'I'm sorry, can I help you?' he asked, frowning at this rude interruption.

Rodarth smiled his thin smile. 'I rather think you can, as a matter of fact,' he told the confused retiree.

Sadrien stuck his hands in the pockets of his crisp white suit (Honestly, thought Melchior, who wears a suit for casual use?) and returned Rodarth's piercing gaze with an unwavering, level one.

'I might ask you to quit playing games, Inspector, and tell me the reason for this.'

'And I might ask you to invite us inside, seeing as we

are policemen, on police business,' Rodarth replied. Sadrien, after a few seconds of holding the Inspector's gaze, reluctantly gave in and gestured for them to enter.

Mr Chasterleigh's hallway was very different from Tenzebah's. Everything about this one was crisp, white and modern, whereas Dunwall's seemed older and more traditional. The house, inside and out, reflected Sadrien's character well, thought Melchior, though he wondered if the contrast between his abode and his arch enemy's was more out of spite than personal preference.

'I hope you'll find this a suitable interrogation room,' said Sadrien, ushering them inside a sitting room politely.

'A suitable interrogation room,' Corwin told him, 'is the one that extracts answers from suspects. I, too, hope that this room satisfies our expectations.'

'You want answers again, eh?' asked Sadrien, sitting down and producing a large cigar filled with what smelled like cinnuric, an exotic spice with tobacco-like qualities. 'You already questioned me, if I remember correctly. All you managed to extract from me was my past with Tenzebah. I assumed I'd been ruled out as a suspect.'

'Rule one of investigating a murder,' said Rodarth. 'Never rule out a suspect.'

Sadrien sighed and took a long drag from his cigar. 'Well, get on with it.'

Melchior smiled indulgently and produced a brown paper bag from his coat.

'I presume you aren't about to offer me a boiled sweet,' muttered Sadrien, before Melchior emptied the contents of the packet onto the table. Mr Chasterleigh gave a slight but unmistakeble jolt of surprise, which he covered up by adopting a disinterested expression.

'Bath salts?' he asked. 'What in the world would I want bath salts for?'

'Well, primarily to have a bath,' Melchior answered truthfully. 'But they aren't bath salts. And you never intended to have a bath with them.'

'Excuse me?' scoffed Sadrien.

Rodarth sat forwards. 'Let's not pretend you don't know, shall we? We've run tests on these...*bath salts,* and we discovered that they are actually pure millovernin crystals.'

Sadrien gave a telltale cough as he choked on his cigar.

'Now, Mr Chasterleigh, can you tell us how you murdered Dunwall Tenzebah- because the why is rather obvious,' Corwin said.

Sadrien closed his eyes and sighed deeply, but did not reply.

'I think I can answer that question,' Melchior offered. 'You used your daughter, didn't you?'

Mr Chasterleigh looked up at him. 'Please, she didn't agree to it. I just told her to steal Elixir- she didn't know it would kill him. I gave her the millovernin and told her to replace the bath salts with it.'

'She agreed to this?' asked Rodarth.

Sadrien nodded. 'Like I said, she didn't know. The whole thing was just too easy. I confess I'd been setting up this trap for a while, though I'm not sure I had any murderous intentions back then, when I sold Kenderye to Marsine.'

'It was you who sold Marsine her retirement house?' asked Corwin.

'It was. Kenderye used to be mine- my intended retirement, when I was obsessed with Elixir, and immortality and all that stupid stuff. You noticed the symbols, the statues of Astelpine? I needed to be rid of anything that linked me to Elixir, and therefore Tenzebah, if I was going to kill him, and my house was something that did tie me to my old friend. So I had to sell it, and who better to sell it to than the wife of Dunwall Tenzebah? I thought it fitting. But all of that, only to have my daughter fall in love with the fool. I know what you're thinking- she's part Pristilian, so she must have used her charm to get a well-paid job. But no. She did love him, silly girl. I couldn't get her to do it if she knew it would kill him, so I just told her to steal Elixir. Trissilan thought that if she took away his immortality, they could have a mortal life together. Marsine would pass away in due course, but she and Tenzebah would still have had a long enough life together.'

Melchior put his head on one side, assessing Sadrien

critically. 'You lied to your daughter so you could have revenge on your old enemy. No wonder she hates you.'

Sadrien nodded, looking for the first time surprisingly regretful. 'Yes. I am aware. But,' he added as Rodarth made to say something, 'there's something else you should know before you lock me up.'

Rodarth raised an eyebrow skeptically. 'Do tell.'

'I didn't kill Dunwall Tenzebah.'

Corwin made a strange noise in his throat and Rodarth's skeptical expression melted into one of mixed bewilderment and exasperation. 'Excuse me? Of course you did, man, you just admitted to the crime!'

Sadrien shook his head. 'No. I tried to kill Tenzebah, yes. Of course I did. Thieving bastard deserved what he got. And Trissilan did everything I told her to do, right down to drugging Dunwall into a deep sleep so she could steal Elixir from the bathroom ledge.'

Corwin frowned. 'Then what...?'

'When Trissilan tried to steal Elixir...it had gone. Someone had already beaten her to it. She came back to me distraught, and I must say I was partially relieved that Elixir had been taken from Tenzebah. But I didn't get the full satisfaction of taking it myself.'

Corwin sighed, rubbing his face. 'So another red herring. You didn't do it.'

'Did you try to poison your daughter?' asked Rodarth, seemingly desperate to convict Sadrien for something other than the attempted murder of his old friend.

Sadrien looked shocked. 'Trissilan...is she dead?'

Melchior shook his head reassuringly. 'She is not. But she may have had a near miss, I suspect. We can't confirm if she was poisoned, but there was certainly something wrong with her.'

'Well, I didn't poison her, if that's what you mean,' replied Sadrien. 'I'm only guilty of one attempted murder, thank you, not two.'

'And,' continued Melchior, as Rodarth opened his mouth to speak, 'may I ask you one more question, since you're headed to prison anyway?'

Sadrien nodded. 'If it will help, I suppose, though trust me, I don't particularly want that fool's killer caught.'

'That holo-mail. Signed with your initials, threatening to take Elixir. Did you send that?'

'With complete and utter honesty,' Sadrien told him, 'I can safely say I did not.'

Melchior frowned, and dissolved once more into a state of rapid-fire thinking as Rodarth stood up and activated holo-handcuffs around Sadrien's wrists.

'Sadrien Chasterleigh,' he announced, 'I'm arresting you for the attempted murder of Dunwall Tenzebah.'

But, Melchior thought to himself as he glanced metaphorically towards Sadrien's unfinished cigar, lying on the table without hope of ever *being* finished, *no cigar.*

'It was the maid, of course,' Rodarth declared, matter-of-fact-ly, as they walked back to the police car, Corwin and Melchior with a certain air of anticlimax, Rodarth convinced of T'chisa's guilt.

'We have no proof,' said Corwin, 'we can't jump to conclusions.'

'But I can!' replied Rodarth. 'It makes perfect sense. The maid has access to every room in the house. Tenzebah was out cold from the overdose of millovernin absorbed through his skin, and when the little chitterer came in to do some cleaning, she saw her master lying there unconscious in the bathtub, she did what her kind do and pinched Elixir from the bathroom ledge. She obviously had no idea it would kill him, but she knew it was valuable.'

The other two made no reply. Melchior was thinking, regrettably, that Rodarth's reasoning actually made perfect sense. He wished he had not, but he had indeed considered the possibility. He had discarded it, however, when he decided that T'chisa was not one to steal anything, despite the millovernin being found in her storeroom when naturally it should have been kept in the bathroom...

Melchior let out a long sigh. All evidence pointed to T'chisa, but the Reptid was convinced she wouldn't hurt a fly on purpose.

But if she had hurt Tenzebah, or killed him rather, that wouldn't have been on purpose. Merely the consequences of her act of theft, which Melchior was reluctant to believe happened. *No,* he thought, *the killer, or the thief, whichever it was, is someone else. And that leaves Marsine and Fersilt Tenzebah.* It always came back to family, Melchior found, though which member was still a mystery.

'Right,' said Rodarth, shoving the handcuffed Sadrien into one of the police cars. 'Get in.'

He tipped his hat mockingly towards Corwin and Melchior. 'Trust me, the killer- whether she intended to kill or not- will be brought to justice before the end of the day.'

And with that, he hopped into the passenger seat and the robotically-programmed driver started the engine and drove off down Mr Chasterleigh's driveway, leaving Melchior and Corwin standing by the second police car.

'He's going to arrest that poor maid,' sighed Corwin. 'And I'm convinced she didn't do it.'

'There isn't, however, anything *I* can do to stop it,' Melchior replied with a meaningful glance at his old friend.

But Inspector Tirranar shook his head. 'I don't like to admit it,' he said, 'but the same goes for me, too.'

Chapter Sixteen

1.

Galion had been hoping to make it at least one more day without hearing what he was dreading, but when he heard the unmistakable yell of Redn Termal calling what was unmistakably his name, Calmooth suddenly seemed a great deal nearer.

'Vasail!' was the yell. 'You still here, kid?'

Galion sighed, got up from his bed, on which he had been lying, and picked up his already-packed bag before beginning the tentative descent down the stairs to the main workplace. There he saw Hellin, Durith, Mascal and Adeagre, all doing their best to ignore what they all knew was coming. Hellin shot a brief, sympathetic look over her shoulder but wisely said nothing.

Redn Termal stood in the middle of the garage space, red face glaring at him. 'There you are. I thought I told you to get lost?'

'You told me I was fired,' Galion corrected. 'In my experience, that's a bit of a different thing.'

'Don't get clever with me, kid-' started Termal viciously, but Galion interrupted him.

'I can get as clever as I like with you, actually Redn,' the mechanic told his ex-employer lightly. 'As we've already established, I no longer work for you. Which makes you no more my superior than I am the President of Eluxure's.'

Termal looked taken aback, and rightly so. This was the first time *ever* that anyone had spoken to him like that, and he wasn't used to it in the slightest. Adeagre made a snorting noise like he was containing laughter, and luckily for him Termal ignored it.

'Listen here,' he snarled. 'Sure, you don't work for me no more. But you're still living in the rooms set aside for employees. Kid, you ain't an employee.'

Galion shrugged. 'Well, everyone here has their own lodgings, don't they? So nobody's missing out.'

Redn lowered his voice so that it grated harsher than his previous snarl, but he did not lower the volume, as it was something he was physically incapable of doing.

'When I say get out,' he said, 'I expect the moron who I'm talkin' to, to get out.'

Galion nodded. 'OK. Well, I'll be off then.'

Termal scowled deeply. 'Yeah. That's right,' he said, as Galion turned and left, holding his battered, shapeless old suitcase in one hand.

Then the mechanic turned and looked at Redn Termal once more, almost as an afterthought. 'Oh, but just one more thing.'

The workers, by this stage, had completely forgotten they were supposed to be ignoring this, and were looking at Galion as though wondering what he'd do next. Termal just looked angry- one of the only things he'd excelled at at school, if you don't count yelling and injuring people.

'You, Redn Termal, are possibly the biggest *flamp* I know,' he said as though he was complimenting Termal on his new haircut. Hellin's eyebrows shot up as though they were attempting to hide in her hair.

'I'm really sorry to burst your bubble if you actually think you run this business well,' he went on, 'but you probably flunked mechanics as well as every other subject you took. And if you ask me, Hellin would make a much better boss.'

He glanced at Hellin, who was grinning widely, then at all the other mechanics, who seemed to be enjoying this equally as much.

'Consider it, Hellin,' he told her. 'And all of you, as well. Just a suggestion: let the right people know how fantastic Hellin'd be at managing this trade, and how terrible Termal is at attempting it.'

'Will do, Gally!' called Adeagre.

Then Galion turned and left for real, leaving the workers in a good mood and Termal so red you could practically see the steam pouring out of his ears.

Melchior was not entirely surprised to find Galion at the door to his hotel room, looking slightly unsure of himself and clutching a suitcase so battered it would hardly be recognisable as one if the mechanic had not been holding it as though it were.

'Ah, Galion,' he said, smiling and ushering him inside. 'What can I do for you?'

'Well...' he started, then chewed his lip and began again. 'Termal finally kicked me out. I'm not pleased, exactly, but...it took him long enough, I guess.'

Melchior said, 'Ah.'

'I didn't actually want to leave for Calmooth until the case was solved,' Galion admitted. 'I was enjoying myself, believe it or not. And...yours and Claine's company.'

Melchior didn't say anything, just looked slightly gratified and at the same time somehow slightly concerned.

'So...' Galion went on, slightly perturbed by his friend's silence, for Melchior seemed to always say something when there was something to be said, and always said something wise when he did say something. 'I just wanted to say goodbye, I guess. There's nowhere for me to stay, and I've only got enough money for a one-way trip to Calmooth.'

'Except,' said Melchior, chidingly, 'you aren't going to say goodbye yet.'

Galion looked confused. 'I'm not?'

'You're not.'

'*Why* not?'

Melchior smiled. 'Well, you may have noticed that I tend to do some things outside the law when necessary,' he said. 'And for you not to see the case solved wouldn't be...proper. So provided I'm not caught for this and fined, which would be regrettable and most unfortunate, I'm willing to risk it and offer you someone else's lodgings until the case is over.'

Galion moved his head slowly in something that was neither a nod nor a shake, but something in between that more likely signified the fact that he still had no idea what Melchior was getting at.

'Namely the hotel's,' said the Reptid, and Galion finally got it.

'You mean-'

'Yes,' agreed Melchior. 'I mean-.'

He looked at Galion, expecting a response, and the response he got was, 'That's illegal.'

'Yes, yes, I thought we'd covered that bit. Do keep up, Mr Vasail,' the Reptid said. 'I wouldn't be doing this, but

I've made an...unofficial vow.'

'Which is?'

'To solve this case by tomorrow night.'

Galion raised his eyebrows. 'It's that close to being solved?'

Melchior sighed and sat down. 'No.'

'And you're going to solve it by tomorrow? When you're not even close?'

'That's the plan,' admitted Melchior. 'I'm sure I'll have a revelation. It's happened before. If I was looking at all the evidence at the right angle, I'm sure it would be obvious. Problem is- I'm not.'

Galion let out a laugh despite himself. 'Lucky it's an unofficial vow, then.'

Melchior looked up at him with a somewhat dry expression on his face. 'There is an old saying on Earth,' he said, and Galion replied with a raised eyebrow. 'It goes "oh ye of little faith" and it was used by people when they wished to inform a skeptic that their doubt would prove unfounded.'

'Why an Earth saying?' Galion asked.

Melchior shrugged. 'I don't know. I could have used the Malkrazi saying "ellephit melpethite", which translates literally into "You're wrong and I'm right", but...I suppose I chose an *Earth* saying because Miss Soliss is from that planet.'

'How do you know that?'

'Well, I thought it might have been because of her frequent use of Earth-originated sayings that nobody else understands...' was the reply, and Galion grinned.

'Just for that,' he announced, 'you've restored my faith in your detective prowess.'

'I'd like to think you never lost it,' muttered Melchior.

Galion ignored that statement, instead taking a seat and saying, '*Now*,' he said, 'I think that you might well crack this case by tomorrow.'

2.

'What the hell is going on?' asked Claine, accosting Corwin and causing him to jump out of his skin as he exited the police station.

'What are you doing here?' he asked.

Claine smiled, though the expression did not extend to her eyes. 'Please, Inspector, we aren't in an interrogation room, so could you please answer my question first.'

Corwin scratched his head. 'Well, I can't say I understand it.'

'The maid, T'chisa, has been arrested, I hear,' Claine elaborated. 'And I'd like to know why, and on what charge. The poor innocent girl hasn't done *anything*.'

'How do you know about this?' Corwin asked.

'I'm a reporter,' was the reply. 'It's my job to snoop.'

Corwin sighed. 'If it makes you feel any better, I was as

against it as you are.'

Claine relaxed slightly. 'And what was "it"?'

'Melchior hasn't filled you in on the results of our interrogation with Sadrien Chasterleigh?'

Claine shrugged. 'I haven't seen him since Dr Elpaine tested the bath salts.'

'Well, I'll tell you, then. He confessed to the attempted murder of Dunwall Tenzebah, said he instructed Miss Glamure to swap the bath salts with millovernin.'

'She's in on it too?' Claine asked.

'Let me finish. Apparently, Trissilan had no idea stealing Elixir would kill the one she loved. But that doesn't really matter, because somebody beat her to it.'

Claine sighed bitterly. 'And Rodarth suspects the maid.'

'I don't think the poor thing would steal anything,' Corwin agreed. 'But all evidence points to her being the culprit. She had access to Dunwall's personal chambers, so if she went to do some cleaning and found Dunwall unconscious in the bath, with Elixir on the shelf...' he shook his head. 'Rodarth arrested her this morning. She looks in a right state, and I'm worried he'll make her crack, even if she didn't do it. Which I'm certain she didn't.'

Claine felt a flare of anger and hatred of Inspector Rodarth, but managed to keep it in check without marching into the interrogation room and knocking his lights out.

'Can I tell Rodarth what I think of him?' she asked politely.

Corwin shook his head and responded, equally politely, 'Not unless you want to be arrested for verbal assault on an officer of the law.'

'In that case, I'll be off,' said the journalist. 'But if you could injure him for me, that would be great.'

∞

'Now, T'chisa,' said Inspector Rodarth slowly, as though the N'choth'ni was a small child. 'You stole Elixir, didn't you?'

T'chisa nodded furiously.

Rodarth smiled cruelly. 'Is that a yes, T'chisa?'

T'chisa nodded all the more vigorously, seemingly unwilling to speak.

'Is this a confession?'

'No!' blurted the N'choth'ni. 'I did not steal.'

'Then what's the meaning of this head-nodding business?' scoffed Rodarth. 'If you can't give a straight answer I'll have no choice but to charge you nonetheless.'

'No,' insisted T'chisa. 'I did not!'

'From what I remember,' Rodarth said, 'you have no alibi.'

Cadez, who was standing just inside the door, had been watching this unfold very uncomfortably. The poor girl evidently hadn't done it, but the Inspector seemed adamant that she had. There was nothing Corwin had been able to do to dissuade his colleague, and he had eventually stormed out of the police station in protest. And the N'choth'ni had just sat there in the interrogation chair, completely terrified, and Cadez was convinced that she'd crack. He wished he could do something about it. Technically, he could if he wanted to...but Rodarth controlled everyone at the station, even though he was-

...Cadez shook his head. It was something he shouldn't even think about. So he just continued to stand there whilst Rodarth worked away at T'chisa's resolve.

The N'choth'ni had begun to tremble.

'The bath salts found in *your* supply cupboard,' Rodarth was saying, 'were not bath salts, but a drug called millovernin. Do you know what that is, T'chisa?'

Cadez had to stop himself from interfering. He couldn't believe his ears. Sadrien had confessed, he'd said that he'd got Trissilan to swap the bath salts with millovernin! The maid had nothing to do with them, and Rodarth knew it! He was using lies to crack the poor N'choth'ni.

T'chisa nodded her head again.

'Don't be stupid, of course you don't know what it is,' sneered Rodarth. 'You're race can't possibly be intelligent enough to be aware of such a drug.'

'Sir!' Cadez said. 'If it helps, sir, when N'choth'ni nod their heads, they mean *no*.'

Rodarth turned at him and smiled, that smile that Cadez always wanted to wipe off the Inspector's face, but couldn't, because Rodarth controlled the police station entirely.

'Thank you, Cadez,' he said, 'but I'll take it from here. I have been managing, you know, without you spouting nonsense.'

He turned back to the maid. 'I'm going to ask you...*one more time*. Did you steal Elixir?'

And very slowly, T'chisa shook her head.

'Speak up, please,' smiled Rodarth, pleased with himself. 'I can't hear you.'

'Yes,' said the maid. 'Yes. I am guilty.'

'There we go,' beamed Rodarth, turning round to look jeeringly at Cadez. 'I think that's plain enough, don't you, Constable?'

Chapter Seventeen

'Look,' sighed Claine, 'if you're planning on solving this case by tomorrow-'

'Which,' said Melchior from his position at the table, where he was sitting with his eyes closed and his fingers steepled, 'I will.'

Claine rolled her eyes. 'Point is, you've been sitting there for about a quarter of an hour-'

'You don't have to stay and watch, you know.'

'-and you don't seem to be getting anywhere,' Claine finished. 'So...do you need any help?'

Melchior shook his head slightly. 'The clues are all there,' he said, 'we know everything we need to know about the case...I just need to assemble it so that it forms a picture that does *not* involve the maid stealing Elixir.'

Galion swung his legs off the couch. 'Then we'll brainstorm.'

'I do not brainstorm, Mr Vasail,' Melchior said. 'I am a solitary thinker...'

'Who,' interrupted Claine, 'isn't getting much thinking done solitarily.'

Melchior made a sort of *harrumphing* noise, but did not open his eyes.

'Right,' grinned Claine, 'so- first we need to establish what we don't know. Let's make a list.'

She cleared the table and slammed a piece of paper onto it. 'Anyone got a pen?'

Galion pulled one from Melchior's coat pocket, which finally got him to open his eyes, and passed it to Claine. 'Trust Melchior to have such a primitive device in his pocket.'

'Oi,' said Claine. 'Careful what you say to the girl who just put a piece of paper on the table.'

She looked up at Melchior, who was looking somewhat annoyed, but as though he knew there was no point resisting. 'Right!' she said. 'What don't we know?'

'How Trissilan was poisoned, what she was poisoned with, and why she was poisoned,' said Galion immediately, and Claine wrote it down.

'Who sent the holo-mail,' Galion continued.

'What's going on with the police,' Melchior muttered reluctantly. Claine grinned at him and wrote it down.

'Bonus points for participation,' she said.

'Who did it,' said Galion.

Claine rolled her eyes. 'Wow, what an insightful observation. I didn't realise we needed to work out who did it!'

'That's all we don't know,' said Melchior suddenly. Claine looked at him, surprised.

'You're sure?'

'Absolutely. Trust me, I'm a detective.'

'Okay,' said Claine, drawing a line beneath their list. 'What next?'

'A method I saw used once,' Melchior offered, 'by a police inspector on the jungle planet Jumujan, was to go through each suspect and establish how they did it- if they did it.'

'So, like theoretically?' Claine asked, and Melchior replied with a nod. 'Okay. Umm...Marsine Tenzebah.'

'She was jealous,' Galion said, 'and spiteful. She hated her husband for carrying on with his assistant, so she...murdered him? That doesn't make sense, shouldn't she have killed Trissilan?'

'That wasn't her only motive, mind,' said Claine. 'She hated him for abandoning her for Elixir. When he became immortal, he kind of...gave up on her.'

'So,' said Melchior, 'she killed him in revenge. She would have known that taking Elixir would kill him, if he'd told her- and if he hadn't, she stole Elixir to get back at him.'

'And,' said Galion, 'she tried to poison Trissilan, because we all know they hated each other.'

Claine wrote this down, then nodded. 'Right. That's one suspect sorted. What about Fersilt?'

'Inheritance,' said Galion. 'He wanted the family fortune, plus Dunwall's business.'

'He wouldn't have known what stealing Elixir would do,' Claine pointed out. 'But that hardly would have stopped him from taking it for himself and using it to become immortal, I guess.'

'And,' grinned Galion, 'there's always one of us, of course.'

Claine blinked. 'Excuse me?'

'We've all got a motive,' Galion insisted. 'You needed a scoop. And what's better publicity than the murder of an immortal?'

'But the *Gazette* beat you to it,' Melchior added, 'so you tried to poison Miss Glamure to get the story you'd murdered Dunwall Tenzebah for. You were the first person, outside of police, to hear of the murder. Is that a coincidence?'

'Lock her up!' Galion declared. 'She's awful!'

Claine raised her eyebrows. 'It could've been you, mind,' she said.

Galion laughed. 'How?'

'You were the only person who went to Kenderye for

reasons other than the knowledge of the murder. You could have been there for any amount of time before we showed up. Also, you've got the motive.'

Melchior nodded. 'Indeed. You need a new job, do you not? But you knew Fersilt Tenzebah wasn't coping particularly well financially, and you knew that if his father died he'd inherit enough money to support Nebula Co. So you killed Dunwall Tenzebah to ensure your employment.'

'But that's forgetting the innocent detective,' Galion retorted, snatching the pen from Claine and adding to the list. 'Who suspects the famous sleuth? The one who's trying so hard to solve a murder he committed just to get another dose of spotlight.'

He and Claine high-fived, and Melchior sighed. 'Well, this is all very well, but "brainstorming" is getting us nowhere.'

'Umm...I actually think it is,' Claine pointed out, brandishing the piece of paper on which they had been writing ideas. 'We've got a list of how our remaining suspects did it, now all we need to do is work out which solution fits the clues.'

Melchior shrugged. 'Neither,' he said. 'How was Trissilan Glamure poisoned anyway, if Marsine did it? What poison was it? How was it administered? This is pointless.'

Galion shrugged. 'If she *was* poisoned,' he said.

'Mm,' agreed Melchior absentmindedly. Then he looked

up again. 'What?'

'I said, "if she *was* poisoned",' he repeated, bewildered. 'I don't know what I meant- just that it could be something else that happened to Trissilan.'

Melchior stood up and began to pace.

'Uh-oh,' said Claine, grinning. 'I think that we've just sent the cogs into motion.'

'What if-' began Melchior, then stopped. 'No. That's not right.'

'Still a bit stuck?' asked Claine. 'Need a push?'

'No,' replied Melchior. 'Thank you. I think I'm gaining momentum well enough on my own...wait! Wait! Wait! No!'

Galion raised an eyebrow. 'OK there? Sure you aren't stuck?'

'They hated each other,' Melchior mumbled.

'Who did?' asked Claine. 'Fersilt and Dunwall? Marsine and Dunwall? Marsine and Trissilan? Or Trissilan and Sadrien?'

Melchior stared at her, wide-eyed. 'Yes! You're right!'

'About...which one?'

Melchior ignored her, but continued to pace, more frantically even than before. 'But then, why the maid? Unless, of course, he knew. Oh!'

Galion gave a jump at that. 'Oh?'

'Oh, yes!' Melchior said. 'But not close enough. I need...something else! Run me through the things we don't know?'

Claine looked at the list. 'Umm...who sent the holo-mail...'

'Yes! Ah, now, let's see...Unknown...S.C...'

Claine and Galion glanced at each other, bewildered and left far behind in the dust cloud left by Melchior's mind.

'And then who would be *able* to...?' Melchior asked himself. Then he stopped pacing and breathed slightly heavily, an enormous smile on his turquoise face.

'Are you...all right?' asked Claine tentatively.

'Y'know...in the head?' added Galion, and got an elbow from the journalist.

'Fine!' declared Melchior. 'In fact, I've never felt better!'

'I'm sure you have,' remarked Galion, but instead of dignifying that with a response, Melchior chose to ignore him.

'Call Corwin,' he said. 'Tell him to gather everyone at Kenderye tomorrow morning, as early as he can. And that includes Cadez, Rodarth, T'chisa and Sadrien as well.'

'Why?' asked Claine, bewildered.

'Because,' announced Melchior, 'I know who did it, and how they did it, and *why* they did it.'

'You're certain?' asked Galion.

Melchior nodded, smiling as he began pacing again, though this was not because he was thinking furiously any longer, but because the knowledge of the solution to the case made him want to *do* something, even though there was nothing to be done until the next day.

'Oh, by the way,' he said suddenly, pausing and turning to the two, who were still slightly confused, 'neither of you own a shock-gun, do you?'

'What do *you* think?' Galion remarked incredulously. 'If you need to shoot someone that desperately, I'm sure Corwin's got access to one.'

Melchior nodded. 'Yes, of course.'

'Well, can you tell us who did it, at least?' asked Claine, almost desperately, and so anxious to know she was certain it would keep her up all night in frustration.

But Melchior, showing her the door, just winked and said, 'Spoilers!'

Chapter Eighteen

1.

When Melchior's lift pulled up at Kenderye, he was pleased to see two police cars parked outside, signifying that both Corwin and Rodarth were there, as he had requested.

Everyone had to be there, and hopefully everyone was, if Rodarth had been decent enough to release Sadrien and T'chisa from prison, just temporarily. Seeing as Rodarth had never done anything to classify him as even a little bit decent, Melchior thought the chances were very slim indeed- unless Corwin had twisted his arm. Although, as Melchior knew, nobody *could* twist Rodarth's arm, as it stayed firmly in place unless it was twisting someone else's.

'Good morning, Inspectors,' he greeted them as he got out of the hover-car. Corwin nodded to him in greeting, but Rodarth just sort of sneered.

'I do hope you haven't called us here for something that will waste my time,' he said.

'Rest assured, Inspector,' replied the Reptid, 'I haven't.'

Corwin cleared his throat. 'Everyone involved is gathered in the lounge room,' he informed Melchior. 'Like you requested, Sadrien and T'chisa are there as well.'

'Thank you, Corwin,' said Melchior. 'We'd better join them before they all murder each other.'

The Inspectors followed him inside, Corwin looking interested as to what might happen, Rodarth looking doubtful that anyone other than the maid had committed the crime.

When they entered the room, Melchior took a quick visual sweep of the assembled suspects.

Fersilt, predictably, looked impatient, standing at his mother's elbow, his foot tapping in the tell-tale sign of irritation. He also appeared as though the accusation of either himself or his mother would be protested against forcefully. Unfortunately, they were both prime suspects.

Fersilt looked up when the three entered and proclaimed, 'Good! Now we can get this over with. I'm very busy at the moment, you know.'

Marsine, in contrast to her impatient son, appeared calm, cool even, and held herself with the usual regal dignity. This was a proud woman, and a strong one too, as Melchior had previously noticed. She surveyed the other occupants in the room with the same assessing expression, though the Reptid knew her opinions of them all differed greatly.

Trissilan looked uncharacteristically quiet, though even while silent, she still radiated her usual air of carelessness, vast amounts of energy and twice as much Pristilian charm. This meeting, she knew, would solve the murder of her lover, though whether this made her satisfied, upset or something else entirely, Melchior couldn't tell. She was dressed as distractingly as always, and unless the Reptid's eyes deceived him, she was the first person Corwin's eyes found.

He wasn't the only one. On either side of Miss Glamure were Cadez, standing apparently as impassively as he was supposed to (though his eyes kept flicking towards Trissilan), and Sadrien, also standing but a lot more frustrated-looking than the Constable.

He kept trying to get Trissilan's attention, but she was having none of it. It was clear she'd just discovered what he'd tried to get her to do- kill Dunwall without even realising she was doing it. It might have been some consolation to her that her attempt had failed, but she still acted exceedingly cold towards her father. Sadrien himself was looking at Trissilan with an expression of regret, and possibly even some sympathy, making up for his negligence of her when she was young.

The maid sat not far off, looking as though she had given up. Rodarth, apparently, had forced a confession out of her, but Melchior was now absolutely certain she didn't do it. For he knew who did. He caught T'chisa's eye and smiled, and the corners of her mouth may have twitched in response, but she could not manage a full smile.

And by the door stood Claine and Galion, both of whom grinned and waved as they saw the Reptid enter the room.

'Everyone's here,' reported the reporter, as though Melchior hadn't already noticed. 'Just like you requested.'

Everyone looked up as they noticed the sudden presence of two Inspectors and a Reptid in the lounge room, and the murmured, subdued chatter between Claine and Galion, Marsine and Fersilt, and Sadrien's one-sided conversation with his daughter, all came to an abrupt stop.

'I think,' said Melchior, addressing the expectant room, 'that you are aware as to why I have gathered you all here this morning, so I will not...' he glanced briefly at Claine, '*beat around the bush.*'

Claine smiled at him.

'I will begin,' continued the Reptid, 'at the place where most things are usually begun, by which, of course, I mean the beginning. More specifically, the first adventure of Sadrien Chasterleigh and Dunwall Tenzebah.'

Everyone automatically turned to glance at Sadrien, who

remained impassive.

'In the year 2355,' said Melchior, 'two young, brave friends set off for the abandoned planet Namaddas. Their names, I think you're all aware, were Sadrien Chasterleigh and Dunwall Tenzebah. The expedition was a joint effort- the planning, navigating and route organised by Sadrien, the costs covered by Dunwall's father Aikenall Tenzebah. Their goal was nothing in particular- just the thrill of adventure. But it gained them both interplanetary fame and a fair amount of riches- enough riches, in fact, to fund yet another expedition a couple of years later, to the planet Malzyme. After a handful more adventures, followed closely by many galaxy-wide, the two parted ways on cheerful terms, in order to marry their respective partners; Marsine Tenzebah, then Pelgeur,' he nodded at Marsine, who nodded back, 'and Larillian Chasterleigh, then Lessete,' he gave a quick look at Trissilan, who smiled ever-so-slightly.

'Later, each would sire one child, a fact which we will cover later. But for now, let us return to the men themselves. After a hiatus from adventuring, Sadrien became obsessed with a fabled icon known as Elixir, and studied it closely until he was certain he had chanced upon the miracle drink's location- a planet called Kilmorim. So, another expedition was launched, in the year 2380, for this planet, both members intending to split the prize both ways. But they soon discovered that Elixir did not work that way, and once they had procured it, a fight broke out over who should keep it. Both men wanted immortality, a prize Elixir was fabled to give, all thought of sharing gone, and eventually Dunwall won, by abandoning Sadrien on a desolate planet and claiming that he perished on Kilmorim. And thus, the name Tenzebah became famous as that belonging to an immortal and a billionaire, while the other half of the famous partnership was forgotten and, if I may say so, most definitely mortal.

'And now, back to the children. The son of Marsine and Dunwall, as we know, was Fersilt Tenzebah, who has grown up, now, to be a very successful businessman at the head of mechanics organisation Nebula Co. And it must be said, no matter how much he denies it, that Nebula is currently suffering from regrettable financial problems. Or, they were, I might specify, until Fersilt inherited both his father's fortune, and his father's trade business, something he never expected to receive. Because, remember, his father was widely considered immortal by everyone who knew his name. Fersilt and his father, I believe, had a heated argument some years back, which led to Fersilt's unofficial estrangement from the family. Consequently, Tenzebah would probably not have left his son his fortune, had he been as mortal as any of us. But Dunwall was, of course, under the impression that he was incapable of death, so naturally he had not bothered to write a will. And since the absence of a will could not keep the fortune from

Fersilt's grasp, it fell, by family line, into his possession.'

Fersilt stirred indignantly, but his beloved mother put a hand on his elbow, and he let Melchior proceed.

'Now,' said the Reptid, 'we come to the other child. Trissilan, after the Pristilian fashion, and Chasterleigh, after her father, she grew to resent her father for neglecting her for his in-depth obsession with Elixir even after it had been taken from him, and eventually became Dunwall Tenzebah's personal assistant in order to get back at Sadrien. She had not intended to become romantically involved, but soon she fell in love with her father's sworn enemy, much to the understandable fury of Mrs Tenzebah. Marsine hated her husband's PA with a passion, for it was no secret that they were having an affair. She already resented her husband for abandoning their retirement plans in favour of Elixir's life-extending properties, and his romantic involvement with his personal assistant was quite possibly the final straw.'

Melchior surveyed them all again, then continued.

'A few months ago, Dunwall Tenzebah received an anonymous holo-mail threatening to take Elixir from him, a holo-mail that was signed with the initials of his friend-turned-enemy- S.C. Sadrien Chasterleigh. This scared Dunwall, and was enough to send him hiding on Eluxure, the retirement planet, his location, of course, now unknown by the media and the galaxy. He was convinced that Sadrien Chasterleigh could not find him there, but unbeknownst to him, Sadrien was already living on Eluxure, and it was not, in fact, Sadrien who sent the anonymous holo-mail.

'Some months later, some days ago, Dunwall Tenzebah was discovered murdered, nothing but a skeleton in his armchair by the fire. The cause of death was not poison, or any other typical murder weapon. The cause of death was the absence of the item he had come to completely rely on- the source of his immortality, Elixir. When Elixir was stolen, Dunwall's life followed soon after, though it was at first unclear whether it was deliberate murder *by* theft of Elixir, or accidental murder *by* the deliberate theft of Elixir. A few interesting points, however, were as follows- the room was untouched, with no sign of a struggle; the skeleton was not fresh, the flesh just recently dissolved off the bone; and said skeleton was not wearing any clothes. This may not be unusual behaviour for a skeleton, I grant you, except for the fact that Dunwall Tenzebah became a skeleton in a matter of minutes. This was the result of Elixir deprivation. The more specific points of the murder will be covered later.

'After many red herrings, many investigations and many interrogations, I eventually chanced upon what I presumed was the solution, but was in fact only a portion of the answer. On discovering a jar of bath salts that actually turned out to be millovernin crystals, the moving finger pointed, not for the first time, at Sadrien Chasterleigh. For millovernin is a drug found on the planet Kilmorim, which is the very planet where he and Dunwall found Elixir. Sadrien Chasterleigh is the only one present who has visited this planet, so only he could be in possession of the illegal millovernin. The third interrogation of Sadrien Chasterleigh yielded a confession- of a sort. Sadrien admitted to the attempted murder of Dunwall Tenzebah, but this attempt, he told us, failed. Mr Chasterleigh here used his daughter to replace Tenzebah's bath salts with millovernin, which sent him into a deep sleep when taking a bath. Trissilan was told that taking Elixir would not kill her lover, that his lack of immortality would enable them to live a proper life together. But before she could steal Elixir, it was stolen by someone else. The Inspector, that is Inspector Rodarth, was adamant that the culprit was the maid, T'chisa, simply because of her race. But I suspected otherwise. One thing that did stand out for me was the fact that Sadrien did not send the holo-mail message signed with his initials that caused Dunwall Tenzebah to hide on Eluxure.'

He looked dramatically at his audience. 'The answer, I think, lies *here*,' and with that, he pulled a shock-gun from the folds of his robes, startling several of the people in the room. Rodarth raised his eyebrows, and looked accusingly at Corwin, who looked as innocent as he could.

'So,' said Melchior, 'there were still many unanswered questions after Sadrien's confession, chiefly the question of who sent the holo-mail message?'

He flipped the gun and caught it. 'What was always odd about it was that the message was *anonymous*. From an anonymous account, and an anonymous person. The reason I found *this* odd is because *nobody* could have sent that message. If Fersilt had, it would have come up as *Nebula Co-operations*. Marsine, I presume, Dunwall had on contacts, so therefore it would have come up as *Marsine* had she sent it. The same goes for Trissilan. And the maid doesn't have an account, so therefore none of our suspects could have sent that holo-mail. Sadrien!'

Sadrien jumped slightly. 'Yes?'

'You know more about Elixir than anyone here. Can you tell me the effects of Elixir deprivation?'

Sadrien frowned. 'Well, in the long-term, death, but until then my best estimation is...dizziness, nausea...a stomach or headache.'

'And once the user had dosed up on Elixir again?' Melchior asked.

'Ah...an increased appetite,' said Sadrien. 'That would be my best guess, bearing in mind I never got to use Elixir.'

'Thank you,' said Melchior. 'Which moves us onto the next...clue, I suppose. Everyone in this room hates somebody else, not necessarily Dunwall Tenzebah. Marsine loathes Trissilan, Trissilan hates her father, Sadrien hated Dunwall, as did the maid and Fersilt. But one of these doesn't quite add up with the information we've been given.'

By this stage the audience was thoroughly perplexed, and exchanged glances with one another.

'The final unanswered thing,' said Melchior, 'was *who poisoned Trissilan Glamure.* Because Trissilan was poisoned, and had to lie down, but was much better in the morning, thanks to a miscalculation in the amount of poison administered. So: who stole Elixir? Who sent the holo-mail? Who poisoned Trissilan Glamure? The answer is the same for each question.'

'So who did it?' asked Fersilt impatiently. 'Tell us, please!'

Melchior smiled at him. 'That is precisely what I am about to do.'

Then, in what could only be explained as a fit of madness, the Reptid spun around and fired the shock-gun directly at Trissilan's head.

Chapter Nineteen

1.

'Melchior!' cried Galion, starting forward. Corwin did the same, advancing with a cry of 'Rastis!'

Claine's expression was one of shock, and the other occupants of the room all stared at the Reptid in horror, as though he had taken leave of his senses- which, of course, it appeared he had.

But then Galion and Corwin stopped in their tracks, and the rest of the room frowned in confusion and surprise, as they noticed Trissilan sitting in her chair calmly, in completely one piece and having not so much as flinched when Melchior pulled the trigger that would have killed her. That *should* have killed her.

'What's the meaning of this?' demanded Sadrien, rising to his feet in indignation.

Marsine said, 'The shock-gun wasn't loaded!'

'Indeed it was, madam,' Melchior corrected, before firing a couple of rounds out the open window. One tore a hole in one of the hedges, and the other glanced off a statue. Marsine adopted a look of surprise and curiosity.

'I did fire a shock at Miss Glamure, yes,' Melchior told the room. 'But she did not die, unless the fact had escaped your notice. This was due to the fact that she is immortal.'

'She's *what*?' asked Fersilt.

'Impossible!' declared Marsine.

'Immortal, eh?' smiled Rodarth skeptically.

Melchior nodded. 'Immortal. At least, unless she forgets to take her next dose of Elixir. In that case she would die, just like Dunwall...or perhaps that will not affect her, seeing as she has not been taking the miracle-drink for very long. I certainly hope that is the case, because I will ensure that she will never drink Elixir again.'

'What are you talking about?' asked Trissilan.

Melchior beamed at her. 'I'm afraid you did it, Miss Glamure. You killed Dunwall Tenzebah.'

'Excuse me?' Trissilan responded incredulously. 'How? And why?'

'Well, if you insist,' said Melchior, 'I'll explain.'

The others looked at him expectantly.

'You might recall,' said the Reptid, 'that I mentioned the

fact that Trissilan despised her father for neglecting her all those years ago. So much, in fact, that she took up employment under his sworn enemy. Why, then, may I ask, would she assist Sadrien in any way? When Mr Chasterleigh admitted to Dunwall's attempted murder, he said that he had used Miss Glamure to plant the millovernin, and to steal Elixir. Why would she agree to such terms? The answer is simple. Trissilan was never on anyone's *side.* It is understandable that Tenzebah would be attracted to her, but her to him is a bit far-fetched, especially seeing as the maid told us Dunwall was a horrible man. All *you* ever wanted, Trissilan, was Elixir, so you seduced Dunwall Tenzebah with your Pristilian charm, then pretended to forgive your father, therefore resulting in him using you to steal what you wanted. He gave you the millovernin, yes. And you replaced the bath salts with it, yes. But nobody beat you to Elixir. You stole it, then told Sadrien that someone else had taken it first.'

Trissilan swallowed, aware of everyone's eyes on her. 'And how can you prove I did it?'

'Well, I cannot,' said Melchior. 'You left no clues. But I believe I can produce evidence. For starters, the holo-mail message. Nobody could possibly have sent it, because it was *never sent.* You, Miss Glamure, were Dunwall's PA. you had access to all of his files, including his holo-mail account, so you knew how to hack the system and plant the message in Dunwall's inbox.'

'Why would I do that?' protested Trissilan.

'Because,' said Melchior, 'you needed him to move to Eluxure because you knew your father was there, and you knew he could supply you with millovernin. So you scared Dunwall into retirement by threatening to steal Elixir, and signing the message S.C- your father's initials, that Dunwall knew only too well.'

Trissilan laughed, looking from face to face. 'You can't prove that I did it,' she said.

'I have more evidence,' Melchior continued. 'Sadrien, can you please remind me of the symptoms of Elixir deprivation?'

Sadrien looked at him, his face unreadable. 'Nausea, headaches, stomach-aches...'

'A feeling of fatigue,' Melchior said, looking back at Trissilan, who was beginning to look extremely uncomfortable.

'And the effects of taking Elixir after an amount of time without it,' Marsine spoke up, surprising everyone. 'Like you said, Sadrien- an increased appetite. You should have seen Trissilan the morning after her "poisoning". She was stuffing her face in a most undignified manner!'

Melchior nodded. 'Indeed. Trissilan was never "poisoned". She merely went too long without Elixir- which explains her speedy recovery, when she *did* dose up! And, of course, we can't forget her involvement with Constable Cadez! He was definitely attracted to Miss

Glamure, and Miss Glamure saw this as an opportunity to incapacitate the police slightly. In fact, Cadez had been attracted to Trissilan since before the crime was even committed- he knew of T'chisa, and her characteristics, before he could possibly have met her, which means he'd been to Kenderye before, with some police-related excuse or another to see her.'

Cadez shifted from foot to foot slightly uncomfortably, avoiding the gaze of both Inspectors.

'But she didn't return his affections,' Claine pointed out.

'The only person who ever said that,' Melchior replied, 'was Trissilan. She made us believe she was just another one of Cadez's...obsessions, when she was in fact playing along with him- despite her lack of attraction towards him. This is exactly what she did with Dunwall Tenzebah. In fact, she made almost everybody believe she really did love him.'

There was a silence for several seconds. Then Trissilan said, 'Well, I don't suppose there's any point in telling you I didn't do it, now that you've shot me and I've survived.'

Nobody looked surprised except for Sadrien. 'Triss!'

'Oh, shut up, Dad!' snapped Miss Glamure. 'I lied about forgiving you, okay? You were a terrible father- obsessed with getting revenge on Dunwall! Do you think that I'd *help* you get that revenge? No. I was getting revenge on *you* when I took Elixir for myself.'

'Cadez, can you search Trissilan's quarters?' asked

Corwin. 'You know what Elixir looks like, don't you?'

'Yes, sir,' replied Cadez, and went to obey.

Rodarth, very reluctantly, walked up to Miss Glamure and activated holo-handcuffs around her wrists.

'Trissilan Glamure,' he said, 'I'm arresting you for the murder of Dunwall Tenzebah. You don't have to say anything but it may harm your defence...'

It was then that Melchior noticed the unreadable look Trissilan was giving Inspector Rodarth as he activated the cuffs, and the suspicion he'd had for some time doubled to an almost certainty.

'Excuse me, Inspector,' he said politely. 'Could you, perhaps, stop for just a moment?'

Rodarth glared at him. 'And why, Mr Clever Shedskin, would you want me to do that?'

'Because,' replied Melchior, 'I'm not quite finished yet.'

2.

Everyone looked at Melchior again, caught by surprise at the sudden announcement.

'I thought the case was over?' Fersilt sighed.

'It is,' Melchior replied. 'But there is still one more mystery that remains unanswered.'

His eyes were still trained unwaveringly on the thin Inspector, unnervingly so, causing Rodarth to raise his eyebrows and return the stare.

'Go on, then,' he said.

'I will,' replied the Reptid with a slight bow of the head.

He gazed once more at those assembled, more specifically Corwin and Trissilan. The latter's face was impassive, no doubt having accepted the fact that she'd been caught, the former's suddenly and oddly nervous. He looked away when Melchior met his eyes.

'A vast sum of money,' said the Reptid, 'was transferred from the late Dunwall Tenzebah's account, after his death. We have answered the question of who killed the immortal, who sent the mysterious holo-mail message, and who..."poisoned" Miss Glamure. But as to who transferred the money...?'

'Trissilan,' said Marsine immediately. 'Who else?'

Melchior nodded. 'Well, yes, Trissilan. Perhaps I misphrased the question. A more accurate way of putting it would be...to whose account was the money transferred? The answer to this question, I think you'll find, is someone else entirely. Now, ask yourselves this. Why would Trissilan be paying someone off, out of her victim's savings account?'

'Because...she owed them money?' suggested Claine.

'Because they knew she killed Tenzebah,' said Galion, and Melchior smiled at him in response.

'So, someone discovered you, Trissilan,' said the Reptid. 'And you paid them with Dunwall's money to keep quiet. But who would you *need* to pay to keep quiet? Certainly, none of our suspects.'

'Then who?' asked Claine.

'The answer is Mr Rodarth,' replied Melchior.

'Excuse me?' asked Rodarth, deadly quiet. 'How dare you accuse a police officer! And it's Inspector to you, may I remind you.'

Melchior shook his head. 'No, I'm afraid it isn't.'

'You're what?' asked Rodarth, smiling thinly, eyes glinting dangerously.

'See, I suspected something when I first met you, Rodarth. You never treated Corwin as your equal, despite him being no more inferior than you were to him. You acted as though you were his superior, a fact which I initially put down to selfishness and ego. But as the investigation went on, I overheard you talking to Inspector Tirranar, and to my surprise I found that he too acted as though you were his superior. I entertained the possibility that you *were* superior, but I eventually found it much more likely that you were quite the opposite.'

'Are you accusing me,' said Rodarth, a little bit louder, 'of posing as a higher rank than my own? Let me tell you, you stupid shedskin, that I am much more experienced than Tirranar! I was posted on Everlifalta! I was behind the solving of the famous Mortenhead case, and found the solution to many more without the help of an inexperienced Inspector or a lizard in a cloak!'

'Ah,' said Claine, nodding understandingly. 'I presume

that's why they sent you to a retirement planet.'

Galion let out a bark of laughter, and even Marsine allowed herself a brief smile.

Rodarth's head snapped towards Claine, glaring venomously.

'You, Mangery Rodarth, did nothing of the sort. Constable Cadez is more experienced than you in solving a crime, seeing as you are not a police officer!' said the Reptid.

Corwin was looking very pale, in contrast to Rodarth's vivid red skin tone (a rival to Termal's).

'I don't know who you are,' Melchior continued, when the "Inspector" didn't reply, 'but you managed to get hold of material that you could use to blackmail your way to the position of Inspector. No wonder Cadez and Corwin are scared of you, and why they won't stand up to your iron grip over the police station. You could bring anyone there down no problem. Is this correct, Corwin? For goodness' sake, there's no crime in being blackmailed by a crook.'

Corwin looked up, swallowing hard. 'Yes. Everything you say is completely true. Mangery Rodarth is actually a crook known as Falmir Almatoose. He had contacts in the police force, and managed to get hold of blackmailing material. He's been in charge of Leisopolis Police for quite some time now.'

Rodarth, aka Almatoose, sneered at his colleague. 'You complete fool, Tirranar. You're the only policeman in the room, the only one who has the authority to expose me- and if you tried, what's to stop me from bringing down the police force?'

Melchior smiled at him. 'I should think a number of *bars* should do the trick.'

'Haven't you been listening?' scoffed Rodarth. 'I knew Reptids were primitive, but...' he shrugged. 'I overestimated you.'

'I'm afraid that incriminating evidence of corruptness would enable Corwin to put you behind bars,' replied Melchior. 'For instance- if your bank account has increased by the exact number taken from Tenzebah's account, at the same time that it was taken from Tenzebah's account.'

'And what makes you think you'd find anything like that?' Rodarth asked.

'Because,' explained Melchior, 'you knew that Trissilan was the culprit for much longer than I, but by accident. You accidentally stumbled upon Miss Glamure when she was taking her dose of Elixir, and at once knew that she was the murderer. You may have arrested her, of course, but she bribed you with Tenzebah's money, and what Inspector but a corrupt one or a posing one would take that offer? Ever since you took the bribe, you've been trying to lead the case in the direction of T'chisa's arrest, knowing that it would clear Trissilan's name and earn you the final payment.'

'You're lying,' Almatoose said disdainfully.

But Trissilan most definitely thought otherwise, rolling her eyes and saying, suddenly and surprisingly, 'Oh, shut your trap, Almatoose. There's no point in covering for you since you failed to cover for me. I can tell you all now, the detective's right.'

Melchior smiled again at the fake Inspector, who now seemed rather deflated. 'There we go,' he said, cheerily. 'I think that's proof enough, don't you?'

Chapter Twenty

1.

Marsine looked up as Melchior sat down next to her on the garden bench. It was a beautiful day, as per usual, and whilst on any other planet such weather conditions would be a blessing, Melchior felt that the complete lack of such normal occurrences as partly cloudy days with a slight chance of rain in the afternoon, was unnatural, and he would be glad to be back on Sildrone, with its ever-changing weather patterns.

They sat there together for a little while, before Marsine Tenzebah glanced at the detective, who was sitting enjoying the tranquility, and said something she had been meaning to say ever since he had revealed Trissilan's guilt:

'Thank you, Melchior.'

The Reptid shook his head, waving her remark off as though it were nothing. 'As they say on Earth: do not mention it, for it was nothing.'

Marsine smiled at him. 'No, but actually. I know you would have solved it even if I hadn't asked you, but I really am grateful that you have brought my husband's killer to justice.'

Melchior acknowledged this with a nod. 'And how do you feel, madam?'

Marsine looked at her feet. 'Well, strangely enough- guilty.'

'Oh? Why is that?'

'Well, I had considered repaying my husband for being so unfaithful. I hated him for carrying on with Trissilan, and I might well have killed him if I knew how. But now that I know who the killer was, and what their motive for killing him was...' she sighed. 'I am well aware that I was angry at Dunwall for nothing. The affair between him and Trissilan was not real- just a lie spun by that witch, in order to steal his immortality.'

Melchior considered these words, and found that Marsine Tenzebah was not so cruel a woman as he had originally judged her to be. She was capable, indeed, of remorse, and that was what defined her as, deep down, a good person, if somewhat curt.

'You can't blame yourself,' he assured her, 'Not for your

husband's death, nor for failing to realise Trissilan's true intentions. Neither were your fault, and both were Miss Glamure's. If it's any consolation, you were right in being suspicious of her, even if you didn't realise the full extent of her plans.'

Marsine nodded. 'It is, thank you, Melchior. May I, also, compliment you on solving the case. I think you should be told, even if you know so already, that you are a fine detective.'

Melchior smiled modestly. 'Thank you, madam.'

Marsine stood, sighing. 'Well, there is still much to be done before the day ends,' she said. 'I do hope you will not consider it rude if I attended to these matters?'

'Of course not, madam,' replied Melchior, and with that Mrs Tenzebah, the widow of an immortal and completely innocent of murder, left him sitting on the sun-bathed garden bench.

∞

'Enter,' said Fersilt Tenzebah with his usual air of impatience, and the door of his temporary study opened to admit Rastis Melchior.

The study was not nearly as cluttered now as it had been when the Reptid had previously paid a brief visit. Then, it had been to subtly accuse Fersilt of illegal redirection of goods without actually saying so outright.

This time, his reason for entry was not for the purpose of investigation- though it did relate to Fersilt's illegal activity.

Where the study had previously been filled with papers of all sorts, (half of which were ornamental and whose real purpose had been to make the busy air of Fersilt seem much busier,) the room now resembled what it was- a guest room- and all that remained inside it of Fersilt's belongings were a couple of heavy suitcases, no doubt filled with the papers Melchior had seen previously.

'Ah,' he said. 'I see you have been packing.'

'Now that I am no longer needed to complete the case, I'm off to Glaminda,' said Fersilt. Then he looked at Melchior somewhat cautiously, and said, looking away again, 'I...noticed that you failed to mention my...uh...activities outside the law when you revealed the murderer.'

Melchior nodded. 'You noticed correctly.'

'Why is that?' Fersilt asked.

'Well,' Melchior said, choosing his words carefully. 'Seeing as you blackmailed us when we interrogated you about your..."activities outside the law"- or rather blackmailed *Rodarth* into destroying the charges against you, I figured that I couldn't exactly expose you.'

Fersilt looked vaguely surprised. 'So...you're just going to let me go then?'

Melchior smiled. 'I did not say that.'

Fersilt watched in apprehension as Melchior produced a small, portable holographic projector, on which appeared an image of a formal-looking sheet.

'What's this?'

'I'm going to ask you to sign it,' Melchior said. 'I am, technically, unable to expose you due to the absence of charges, but I will do my very best unless you agree to sign here.'

Fersilt looked at it as though it were something disgusting. 'And...can you tell me what it entails?'

'This,' announced Melchior, as though it were something Fersilt would find pleasing (which he knew it wasn't), 'is an unofficial form that renders you unable to redirect your father's business, or indeed do anything at all with it. If you supply a handprint, you will no longer be able to partake in such illegal activities. Nobody needs to see this, but if you decide to benefit illegally from Dunwall's trading business again, I can produce this form and it will be sufficient enough to send you to prison.'

'And if I don't sign?'

'If you don't sign,' answered the Reptid, 'I'm sure I can find some more incriminating evidence at the Shipyards.'

Fersilt glared at him, then looked down at the hologram and glared at it, too, then, after a moment's hesitation, reluctantly pressed the palm of his hand to the projection, which lit up with a glowing green tick.

'There we go,' smiled Melchior. 'That is processed and

saved *forever*. I hope this discourages you from straying outside the law again.'

'Trust me, it will,' Fersilt said, in the sort of impatient tone that was his trademark, but that was not often used when one was just blackmailed by a reptilian detective brandishing a holographic projector. It was clear that Tenzebah Jr. wished to forget about the whole thing and keep his spotless record just that- spotless.

'What will?' asked Melchior in mock-confusion, tapping the side of his nose with a finger. Then he bid Fersilt good day and left the study.

∞

Claine knocked tentatively on the door of T'chisa's quarters, and was pleasantly surprised to be greeted by a wide smile on the maid's vaguely insectoid features.

'Come in, come in,' insisted the N'choth'ni, looking happier than Claine had seen her in her entire time knowing her. The quarters themselves, the reporter noticed as she entered, were vastly tidier than she had last seen them, and she noticed several new items that greatly improved the liveability of the room.

'Done some renovations, have you?' Claine remarked.

T'chisa shook her head, which, of course, meant yes. 'Mistress Marsine has been good to me since your detective solved the case.'

Claine, personally, was pleased and a little satisfied to hear this. Marsine had not, perhaps, treated T'chisa much better than Dunwall had, and the journalist was heartened by the fact that even Mrs Tenzebah could have such a profound change of heart.

'Well, that's fantastic!' she said. 'So, she's decided to keep you on rather than fire you?'

The maid looked down modestly, though she was still smiling broadly. 'Yes. She said I was an...excellent maid, and she was sorry that she had mistreated me. It is more than Dunwall ever praised me for.'

Claine nodded. 'And are you okay yourself, T'chisa, after your arrest? I know they forced a confession out of you.'

'I am fine, now,' T'chisa assured her. 'And Constable Cadez was very nice to me after Trissilan's arrest.'

'Was he now?' asked Claine, with her eyebrows raised. *For his sake,* she thought to herself, *I hope he isn't as false as, say, Trissilan.* But Cadez was not Pristilian, (that she knew of) and she had seen him comforting the maid afterwards. He'd certainly looked genuine, and Claine was very happy on T'chisa's behalf.

'I've come to say goodbye, T'chisa,' she said.

'I see, you are going now,' said the maid.

'Yes, I am,' replied Claine. 'Goodness knows *where* I'm going, but I honestly hope it's somewhere that isn't so damn sunny!'

T'chisa laughed. 'I know what you mean. N'choth'ni live in hollows, mostly, so I did not experience so much sunlight until my arrival on Eluxure,' she giggled. 'I had to wear sunglasses.'

Claine found that she was constantly learning something new about the maid, and she was pleased to know that the very person who Almatoose had classed as below him actually had much more depth and sensitivity than he ever would.

'Anyway, goodbye, T'chisa,' she said. 'I hope we meet again.'

To her surprise, the maid hugged her. 'I hope so to, Claine. And I hope your next article sells well.'

Claine smiled at the thought of her next article, which she was almost certain would sell well. The *Gazette,* she thought, would be very jealous indeed...

∞

'You're off tomorrow, aren't you, Rastis?' asked Corwin. They were outside Melchior's hotel, having caught a lift into Leisopolis together.

Melchior nodded. 'I can't say I'm disappointed to leave Eluxure, but I'm certainly disappointed to leave you, old friend.'

Corwin grinned at him, but then his grin faded-something was evidently on his mind.

'Listen, about Rodarth...'

Melchior held up his palm. 'I understand completely, Corwin. There was nothing you could do but play along with him.'

'Yeah, well...' replied the Inspector. 'I'm glad he's behind bars now, at any rate.'

Melchior nodded. 'I presume you've taken over as sole Inspector?'

'Yes,' said Corwin. 'I have, though I'm not sure what I'm getting into. Inspector is a lot of work.'

Melchior smiled. 'Not on Eluxure.'

His friend laughed. 'Well, no, you're right there. Unless another immortal gets murdered, I shouldn't think my work will be too hard.'

'Don't say that- I actually mean to leave for Sildrone this time,' said the Reptid. 'But I can safely say there are no more immortals on Eluxure. The effects of Elixir wore off Trissilan without much more than another bout of dizziness- she hadn't been taking it for as long as Dunwall, so she didn't die as soon as it was removed and stored somewhere safe.'

'That's good,' was Corwin's reply. 'Anyway, the police station has recovered well from Rodarth's influence. His arrest lifted a weight from the place, and improved the atmosphere a great deal. At least *now* the police aren't hiding anything from the public.'

Melchior nodded. 'I'm sure the public are glad of that.

Does anyone know of Rodarth's...not being Rodarth yet?'

Corwin shook his head. 'We haven't told anyone yet.'

'Well, I predict they might know sooner rather than later,' replied Melchior.

'What's that supposed to mean?'

'You'll see,' said the Reptid cryptically. 'But anyway- I've been wanting to ask you, old friend...how, exactly, did Rodarth- Almatoose- manage to blackmail you?'

Corwin didn't reply, and Melchior, seeing the expression on his face, didn't press him for more information. There were, after all, some things even friends found they could not share with one another. 'I'll say goodbye properly tomorrow, but for now you'd probably better get back to the station.'

'You're right,' admitted Corwin. 'Well, I'll see you.'

Melchior gave his usual miniature bow, then headed into the hotel, now able to safely say the night would be his last on Eluxure.

Chapter Twenty-One

For the third time since the case had begun, Claine interrupted Melchior's breakfast, and for the second time it was to show him a newspaper article.

The first time she had thrown a newspaper onto his table; however, it had been a copy of *Eluxure Gazette,* and the word that had best described her mood was *furious.* This time, on the other hand, the newspaper she used to disturb the most important meal of the day was a copy of her own magazine, *The Galaxy Roamer,* and the word- or phrase, rather- that best described her current mood was *pleased with herself.*

Melchior tore himself away from the food, which wasn't actually so hard as to require much tearing, seeing as said food was somewhat substandard, and looked at the front-page article, which was titled, *Corrupt Inspector Revealed as Known Fugitive,* and showed a picture of Rodarth, looking furious and being led out of Kenderye by Cadez. Melchior recalled the presence of Claine's holo-camera at the arrest, and should've known that she'd use it to take sneaky photographs. She was a reporter, after all.

Yesterday saw the arrest of two criminals, and the end of the impossible Tenzebah murder investigation (see pages 3-4 for details on the case), solved excellently by famous Reptid detective Rastis Melchior, whose quick and efficient mind caught not one, but two crooks. One of these crooks was criminal Falmir Almatoose, who had been masquerading as police Inspector Mangery Rodarth through blackmail of fellow police officers. It was revealed that Almatoose discovered the murderer, Trissilan Glamure, when he caught her drinking Elixir, the prized item of Dunwall Tenzebah, the theft of which killed its owner. Almatoose, then known to everyone as Rodarth, would have arrested Trissilan had she not offered him vast amounts of Dunwall's money, which she transferred directly from Tenzebah's account into Rodarth's. It was revealed that the criminal had had a hold over the police station for quite some time, and...

Melchior read the rest of the article, then praised Claine on its use of language and wording, which, he had to admit, far surpassed the *Gazette's* previous lie-filled edition.

'Already 10,000 copies sold on Eluxure,' she boasted, and Melchior looked at her, surprised at the figure, which was much higher than he'd anticipated.

'It must be popular,' he said.

'It most definitely is,' Claine replied smugly. 'I believe it's even more popular than the *Gazette's* scoop, which, of course, they stole from me anyway. Everyone wanted to know about an immortal's murder, but even more wanted to know who did it. And the feature on Rodarth was popular as well- especially seeing as Rodarth himself wasn't. Apparently old Professor Quaddle had some choice words to say about his method of policing.'

'And what,' Melchior wanted to know, not entirely surprised by this revelation about Almatoose, 'did the *Gazette* have to say about your hit scoop?'

'Well, it's funny you should ask that,' replied Claine, grinning in a satisfied way, 'because I bumped into Garro Tagg just before- you know, that complete *philger* from the *Gazette* who wrote that terrible article about the case- and he appeared very subdued and rather bitter. It was hilarious. I smiled at him sweetly and waved, and he just sort of glared and ordered something alcoholic from the hotel bar.'

Melchior returned his attention to his as yet unfinished breakfast, smiling at the thought of Claine's personal nemesis bested by the independent journalist's superior article.

'And what are you going to do now?' he asked. 'After that bestseller, you probably have enough money for a flight to Sembarsimon or somewhere equally as...' he searched for the word Claine had used a few days ago to describe the ideal scoop, '...juicy.'

Claine shrugged in response. 'Sembarsimon is an enticing prospect,' she grinned. 'But I've always wanted to visit the salt caverns of Hapsduit- I hear they're stunning, and, you know, the readers love travel.'

Melchior smiled. 'Well, good luck.'

'But enough about me,' she said. 'You're back to Sildrone today yourself, aren't you?'

Melchior nodded. 'Thank Castor,' he confirmed, to a laugh from Claine. 'Eluxure was beginning to become unbearable.'

'And Galion?' she asked him. 'Did Fersilt...?'

But Melchior shook his head. 'No luck there. I think Fersilt is anxious to get away from Eluxure as soon as possible and...short answer: he isn't looking for employees.'

Claine's heart sank. She couldn't bear the thought of Galion having to go to Calmooth, but in the end it seemed as though he would have to.

'Well,' said the Reptid, standing up. 'I had better see if Mr Vasail needs any assistance in the packing of his belongings.'

Claine nodded. 'Not that he has much in the way of belongings.'

'I had better anyway,' was Melchior's response, though it was accompanied by a meaningful look that Claine tried- in vain- to read before the Reptid disappeared up the hotel stairs.

Galion looked up as Melchior entered the room.

'Melchior,' he said in greeting. 'There's no need helping me pack. I barely *un*packed, actually.'

Melchior did not reply, so Galion just smiled- as a mask, albeit a transparent one, for what he was actually feeling about his fate on Calmooth- and extended a hand to shake Melchior's.

'Well, I'd better be going,' said the mechanic, 'if I'm going to catch the next flight to Calmooth.'

Melchior took the offered hand and shook it vigorously, noticing the brave facade begin to crumble.

'I will most definitely shake your hand, Galion,' he said gently, 'but you are *not* going to catch the next flight to Calmooth, whether you want to or not. Nor are you going to catch any flight at all bound for that forsaken planet while I am still able to prevent you from doing so.'

Galion furrowed his brow, confused and not entirely certain he knew what the detective was going on about. 'What?'

Melchior smiled, enjoying his young friend's momentary confusion. 'What I mean, Galion, is that I believe there is a job opportunity on Sildrone- one that requires somebody like you, no less!'

Galion stared at him, dumbfounded, then, slowly, a smile crept across his face before morphing completely into a wide, delighted grin.

'So I'm pleased to say,' continued Melchior, pretending to ignore the mechanic's expression, 'that I've made a formal recommendation to Corlail Mechanics on Sildrone, and the owner, a Chankistrii man by the name of Orlunce, with whom I am well acquainted, assured me that you would be highly considered for the position. Thus, I am also pleased to say that you will therefore *not* be bound for Calmooth next time you board an interplanetary shuttle, but rather bound for Sildrone with me.'

Galion looked as though he intended to hug the Reptid, but seemed to decide against it. Melchior's reaction was a very unpredictable thing.

'Well, I'd better...oh wait, yes, I've already packed...erm...' He gave a strange little laugh here, then cleared his throat and tried to look serious and mature. 'Well, thank you, Melchior. Erm... I suppose Claine is going her own separate way?'

Melchior nodded. 'I do believe she's headed for Hapsduit, although she has promised to keep in touch. I doubt we've seen the last of that reporter.'

Galion laughed. 'Neither has the rest of the galaxy. After her massive success with her latest article-'

'So she told you about that, too?'

'Not so much told as accosted,' Galion admitted. 'But it's great, really. The success and all that. I have a feeling the *Roamer* will only gain popularity.'

Claine cleared her throat from behind them, surprising both with her serva-Coff skills of sneaking. 'Why, thank you,' she said. 'I'm glad you've got so much confidence in me.'

'Oh, no, not you,' he assured her, though he was grinning. 'Your newspaper, yes. But I find it hard to picture you popular.'

She gave him a punch on the shoulder. 'Thanks a lot.'

Then she looked somewhat questioningly at Melchior, having noticed Galion's dramatic change in mood from when she had seen him last.

'A friend of mine offered Vasail here a job on Sildrone,' Melchior explained, obviously pleased with himself. 'Well, I say offered, but realistically I hassled him a great deal...'

Claine's face lit up like Galion's had. 'Well, that's fantastic! You're not headed for that bog of a planet after all! I thus propose a toast,' she announced.

Melchior frowned. 'I'm afraid that may be slightly difficult during our lack of alcoholic beverages and, more importantly, vessels with which to toast.'

Claine rolled her eyes. 'What's wrong with an invisible

toast?' She raised her hand as though she was holding up a glass, which the Reptid found slightly ridiculous and overly theatrical. Ridiculous or not, however, Galion copied her action and Melchior reluctantly found himself doing the same, though he still thought of it as an exceedingly corny thing to do.

'To where we're all headed next,' Claine said. 'To Sildrone...'

'To Hapsduit,' Galion put in, nodding at the journalist.

'And,' said Melchior. 'To the next case.'

Claine and Galion clinked imaginary glasses, but the Reptid swiftly retracted his own hand and said, as he headed for the door, 'may she be considerably less impossible than the last...'

Glossary

Acasatt - a breakfast food similar to porridge

Ackeracki - an untrustworthy, vertically-challenged race

anchora - a species of ornamental tree, genus *optithestin*

astertii - a galactic unit of currency. There are 125 *feristii* (see below) in an *astertii*, and fifty astertii in a *draudr*

bucklesythe - a pungent flower that attacks your nasal passages if you get too close

bvq - an abbreviation of bovaq, the basic unit of measurement regarding distance

Calmooth - a last-resort planet to which those with limited options go to seek employment

catrassi - a sweet ingredient used commonly in baking, trendy in the 25th Century

cetrice - the ground up roots of the cetrintinian plant, used for smoking

chadris - a sophisticated alcoholic drink

Chankistrii - a clever and good-natured, but money-loving species

Earth - a planet in the Solar System, on which Claine grew up

Elapamp - a planet in the Kandaruan System

Eluxure - a retirement planet

feristii - (see *astertii*)

Fiskerbab - a planet in the Naurunet System. Translated literally into galactic standard, its name means "that planet nobody ever visits, for good reason"

gaffleut - an exotic fruit with an inedible outer layer but a vitamin-enriched interior, said to be delicious (although the fact is disputed due to differences in taste bud formation between those species game enough to try the fruit)

Glaminda - a planet in the Galmarora System

gordnu - a non-alcoholic drink enjoyed by Reptids, made from fermented springwater and elemeris extract

Gridney - a planet in the Narunet System

Hapsduit, *the salt caverns of* - a visually spectacular planet said to be haunted by "salt wraiths"

holomail - a way of sending messages through hologram

Hurnbelad - a planet in the Mellitorn System

inchery - an ingredient used in old photograph development processes at the end of the 24th Century, before holo-photos were invented

inciner-whiskey - a highly alcoholic, flammable beverage banned on most planets due to several people's heads exploding after they drank too much

Kelxaragg - a starless planet

Kilmorim - the dwarf planet on which Elixir was discovered

Kerra'lai - a naturally bad-tempered, red-skinned species

maglothian succuli - a type of succulent, desert-dwelling plant covered in spines. Untamed, they have been known to change position while desert dwellers aren't looking

Malzyme - a starless planet

millovernin - a sleep-inducing drug, deadly in large amounts

Mishtiik - a desert world

mondanythus - an ornate, intricate plant

Morborgue - a funeral planet

Myne - a planet of the Callose System

Namaddas - an uninhabited planet

nazcauca - an animal with such an absurd amount of wool nobody knows what it looks like underneath

N'choth'ni - an obedient but intelligent insectoid race

Noctival - a night planet, on which there is one brief day per year

Odar's Brew - a beverage involving a substantial amount of chemically-generated froth, popular among the Barbarousins of Klemm

orgite - an expensive, rare mineral

owalk - fierce animals native to Mishtiik

Packerawl - a popular competitive team sport, involving a holographic pitch

Palloupai, the King of - nobody knows where Palloupai is, but the King of it claims it used to be "right there, between that planet and the other small misshapen one. Could've sworn it was there a moment ago". The King has since undergone psychiatric treatment.

Palpoutha - a planet in the Kandaruan system

piloto - an alcoholic drink

pitchon - an alcohol serving size. Also comes in a stuth, a widdle or a chugg

Plota - a planet of the Adranozadi system

Pristile - a planet on which has evolved a race entirely of females, who seduce men of other races using their telepathic abilities. Due to their genetical makeup, the children of such seductions are always pure Pristilian

raspins - a species of marsupial, and a common pest. Can be dealt with using "RaspinAway" or goskedott vinegar

Regalder Major - a planet of royalty and nobility

Reptis - Melchior's birthplace, a seclusive planet on which the dominant species dislikes contact with any other race

sabril - ferocious predators that have eaten pretty much everything on Scorpid's main continent

saspilia - a flower used in herbal remedies

Scorpid - a wild, untamed world where the most intelligent species has been eaten by the local wildlife

Sembarsimon - a vibrant, exciting planet

Serva-Cof - a warrior species known for their stealth and reflexes

Silder Sau - a gambling game involving a four-dimensional board and a large amount of skill. Melchior is particularly good at it, having taken a course in the Fourth Dimension

Sildrone - the city planet on which Melchior now resides

Silliphid - an overpopulated planet on which Galion was born

Tildive - a planet that is apparently uninhabited, but rumoured to be haunted by the ghosts of the particularly stupid crew of a passing spaceship that took a wrong turn and smashed into it

Acknowledgements

In order to make a book happen, there's a lot of *stuff*. I wrote the book, yes, but a lot of the other *stuff* was done by certain people who need to be thanked.

First, there's my family, of course, who have always supported my writing. Mum and her expert proofreading, my sister, Alex, pointing out any (minor) plot-holes that may have opened up, and Dad being an extremely captive audience, all contributed to *Live a Little* being what it is.

Then, of course, a massive thanks to Andrew Tesoriero, who's been not just a fantastic publisher, but a writing mentor. Andy has been really enthusiastic about this book, and has given me feedback, designed the cover, edited the novel and published it, among other things.

Acknowledgements

And finally, I can't forget to thank my various English teachers, without whom this book would have been filled with "and"s instead of commas and lots of "it's" where "its" is supposed to be.